Q: The Very First Gospel

Kurt J. Peterson

Publisher: Kurt J. Peterson, Mandan, ND 58554

Publisher's Note: This is a work of fiction. Names, characters, places, and incidents are a product of the author's imagination. Locales and public names are sometimes used for atmospheric purposes. Any resemblance to actual people, living or dead, or to businesses, companies, events, institutions, or locales is completely coincidental.

Book Layout ©2017 BookDesignTemplates.com

Q: The Very First Gospel/Kurt J. Peterson -- 1st ed.
ISBN: 978-0-578-60287-5

Contents

Introduction v

PART I

Fortunate Shipwreck 1
The Dawn of Freedom 6
Accessorize! Accessorize!! Accessorize!!! 9
Object Lesson 15
A Brutal Attack 20
Two Roman Soldiers Pass By 24
Brick, Mortar and the Victim of a Brutal Attack 27
Sanctimon & Viktorius 31
The Ministrations of Brick and Mortar 38
Tongue UnTied 44
Call of the First Para-Apostles 49
Your Story 54

PART II

Annunciation 62
Be Not Afraid 65
Something Out of the Ordinary 70
Gypsy Boy 74
Tooth and Yoke 75
Grilled Cheese Jesus 78
Parting the Jordan River 81
Night Terror 90

The Burning Bush 92
Secrets Aborning 94
Throwing Stones (Jesus at 12) 97
Roll Away the Stone................................ 102
Identity Crisis 104

PART III

Seven Times Seventy/
The Call of James, Son of Alphaeus 110
Jesus Meets Smokey 115
The Wine at Cana: The Modest Water
Saw Its G-d and Blushed 121
Words Count.. 124
The Magdalene and the 7 Demons...................... 129
The Magdalene's Clarity............................ 136
So, You Want to Be a Rabbi 141
The Desert Gets Crowded 148
Jesus and John the Baptist..........................151
Literal or Figurative Language? 155
No-More-Sick-of-the-Palsy 159
The Waiting Father 162
Jesus Heals... Sometimes 165
Black and White.................................... 169
Naked Crazy Nate 171
I Hate That Story 174
Unbelief in Nazareth............................... 179
The Mother of All Conflicts 182
The Resolution of the Mother of All Conflicts 187
And Women?...191

PART IV

We Need to Talk 195
Mortar Employs His Prerogative 202

Slave or Free 205
Swine Before Pearls 208
Hey! Homo! 213
Jesus' First Nightmare 216
Mightier Than the Words 219
Fling Open the Gates of Mercy 221
Smokey on the Water 223
Professional Development Day 227
Unpleasantries 231
Jesus Tells of Abraham Pleading for Sodom and Gomorrah 233
The Water Test 239
Truth and S'mores 244
PART V
Letter of the Law, Spirit of the Law 248
Pan-Seared Tilapia with Citrus Vinaigrette 252
Mary's Paps 256
Curse G-d, and Die 259
Meat of Life 261
Upon This Rock 266
Peter Professes His Faith to His Wife 271
Here and Now 276
That's the Way G-d Planned It 283
The Lost Saying of Jesus 286
Up from Jericho 287
Fetch Ye the Ass 292
I Need Two Volunteers 295
Triumphal Entry into Jerusalem 300
Take Ye Back the Ass 303
Gethsemane 307
Cleansing the Temple 313

The Woman Caught in Adultery.................... 319
"I'm From the Empire and I'm Here to Help" 321
G-d Doubts 324
Long Distance Letters.............................. 329

PART VI

Fire and Sword..................................... 335
Reflections.. 341
Great Drops of Blood................................ 345
The Arrest in the Garden 347
Naked Save Sandals................................. 353
Trials.. 359
Mockery 363
Water Test Test 367
Crucifixion 369
Two Thieves Crucified with Jesus..................... 371
Sanctimon and Viktorius at the Cross 373
About Judas.. 377
James the Less at the Cross 379
Stand by Your Man 383
The Deaths of Gestas and Dysmas..................... 387
Deposition of the Body.............................. 389
Afternoon in a Garden 391

EPILOGUE

The Waiting Room................................... 397
A Garden on the Mount of Olives...................... 399
Resurrection 403
Lord of the Dance................................... 407
The Apostles' Unbelief............................... 411
The Ascension....................................... 415
The Last Word 417

Dedication

To Byron Bohrer and Denis Montplaisir. My life has been immeasurably better for your presence in my life. I wish that both of you could have seen the finished project, but you made your exits entirely too soon for my liking. It has been friends like you who have informed my faith and growth and walked with me through times both good and bad.

Introduction

Scholars have long posited the existence of a written source, which by convention has been designated Q, from the word *Quelle* in German meaning source, to which the Gospel writers of Mark and Luke had access. If accurate, then our four Gospels were preceded by an earlier document or book that is now lost. Mark and Luke share some stories in nearly the same words and biblical scholars suggest that the Q document is the original source for these stories.

Q has always been assumed to be no more than a bare list of events in Jesus' life, including aphorisms or sayings in their sparsest form. Quite the contrary, Q has been found to be a fully developed work of such creativity as to rival the most famous writings of its day. So now what we see is that rather than elaborating and fleshing out their Gospels, Matthew and Luke, and perhaps even Mark, seem to have drastically cut and trimmed Q to meet their own theological ends by removing much of Q's historical material, eliminating all references to the first two para-apostles, Jesus' dog Smokey, and any hint or cigar smoking.

We can only speculate as to why the Gospel editors/authors would feel the need to suppress knowledge or memory of the para-apostles. Perhaps like Stalin erasing traces of Leon Trotsky in photographs, these men did not want posterity to even know of the para-apostles. Perhaps they felt their own position extremely weak in that they frequently failed to comprehend the message of Jesus and failed to understand even the Man himself. The disciples in Q appear as bumbling boobs, ill-suited to the task Jesus committed to them at his Ascension. Thaddeus, if we are to single out one disciple, comes off in these pages as a mean-spirited, belligerent jerk.

What I present to the reader is a whimsically speculative and partly fictional account of the life of Jesus. Much of what I write is true to Holy Scripture and is merely an attempt to plumb the depths of the Gospels. Some of what I write is untrue and deliberately so; remember, this is a novel. Any written piece, novels included, may be said to have a twofold purpose: to entertain and to provoke thought. If my book entertains you, I will be happy. If my book provokes you to deeper thought, I will be really happy. In any event draw your own conclusions; G-d gave you a good brain. Use it, along with your heart, to better understand the great gift of life that we have been given.

Jesus wept. It's the shortest verse in the Bible. No one has a problem with it. It's easy to relate to weeping, well, not as easy for men as it is for women. But try this out: think of a verse something like, 'Jesus laughed'. You can see that at first glance the danger that such a verse might pose! The

Savior?! Laughing?! Life is too serious for laughing!! But a fully human Savior might have found much among women and men to laugh about! If that's true, why isn't it in the Gospels? Let me offer the gentle reminder that our Gospels are just four small books and John's Gospel explicitly states that if everything about Jesus were written down, all the books in the world couldn't hold it!

Some items in my book, as I said, are purely fictional; for example, Jesus and his pals are not known to have enjoyed smoking cigars, but neither is it certain that they *didn't* enjoy cigars. It is also unlikely that the wine at Cana was of modern French vintage. It likely was not French at all! Anyone who has studied the matter would certainly conclude that Jesus provided one of our superb California vintages instead of anything merely French. There I go again!

So, why even include such things in this book? First, it's my book and I'm writing it the way I want it to be, and when I asked for input about the book, only a few people had anything to say.

Second, we all live in our own times and we try to bring the life of Christ into our own milieu. Renaissance artists frequently created paintings of Biblical scenes with the subjects in Renaissance period dress. It provides a way to make Jesus' life and teaching relevant in our modern times. Do these deliberate anachronisms detract from the story or do they enhance the story? You be the judge.

What did Jesus know? When did Jesus know it? These two questions for which we can thank President Richard Nixon, reach to the very core of the mystery of Jesus' dual nature as fully man and fully G-d. For instance, did Jesus know as a teenager that he would die on a cross at the end of his public ministry? Did he know as a child that he would die on a cross? That sounds just a little more than grotesque! And yet there are his own prophecies of his passion in all the Gospels. These could have been inserted by the writers to bolster the case for Jesus as fully divine. They must have reasoned that if Jesus was fully divine, then he must have known how things were going to turn out. An additional possibility is that I could be wrong.

I prefer to think that the events of Jesus' life unfolded before him just like they do for any other person. We hardly ever know how things will turn out in advance, and I would suggest that for Jesus to be fully human, he would have to experience all aspects of human life. I suspect that Jesus may not have been fully aware of his divinity until after he was raised to life.

Given that G-d the Father, Jesus the Son, and the Holy Spirit form a Trinity, a perfect union of three personalities, it is only natural that a mere human being like me would have trouble expressing this and other mysteries about our G-d. My understanding, my knowing and my believing seem to wax and wane along a steadily rising path, and that is probably more typical of other believers than I realize.

So, we've come to several important points of agreement: I'll write my book the way I want to and you may choose to read some or all or none of it; we all can retain our own beliefs about G-d and Jesus; we will respect the individual sovereignty and dignity of all persons and their beliefs; and all of us hope that this book will be an enjoyable and, at times, an enlightening read. I wish you happy reading.

PART I

Fortunate Shipwreck

Suggested listening: *Beyond the Sea* by Bobby Darin

Jade green waves broke themselves into foam all along the tan, sandy beach where the remains of a ship washed ashore. Among the wreckage of what used to be a Roman galley, two men chained to a specially constructed raft had washed ashore in the foam with the flotsam and jetsam. These men narrowly missed the fate of their fellow shipmates, well, they weren't exactly shipmates for their status was below that of even a common sailor, for these two were the property of a Roman master, who was nowhere in sight.

The thing wasn't exactly a raft, it was more of a floatable box and it contained a very rich man's portable wealth, to which his other 'portable' items of property were chained, one tall and thin, the other short and squat, two of what the rich man referred to euphemistically as 'man servants', legally referred to as chattel, and in common parlance, slaves. The rich man had preferred the phrase 'man servant' rather than the vulgar word 'slave' to assuage his conflicted conscience for owning other human beings, and the slaves themselves, or rather 'man servants', preferred it as well, for it allowed them to think of themselves as something far more exalted than mere slaves.

The shorter, squatter man rocked gently to and fro in the foamy waves, while the slender rail of his friend floated about by the spent strength of the waves which so nearly deposited them both permanently along with their master in the deep, watery vaults of the Mediterranean Maritime Sea Bank and Trust.

Long, lean and lanky was the first to come around to his senses. Casting his eyes about, his first instinct was for his colleague, to whom he crawled through the sand and surf, and fetched him up bodily to the beach, safely away from the fickle waves. He slapped his friend's inert cheeks frantically trying to return him into consciousness – midwifing him back into existence, for unknown to them as yet - they were reborn. The sea had dissolved all the bonds of their servitude except for the chains and rendered up to them their drowned master's wealth, for what is poverty, after all, but another word for slavery.

The short, squat, stocky man vomited forth a lungful of salty seawater and coughed his way back into the land of the living. He looked round assessing their circumstances and he asked the other, "Where is the master?"

"N-N-Not h-h-h-here," said Brick, for Brick was his name.

"Well, I can see that for myself, stupid! Do you happen to have knowledge of his present whereabouts?" asked squat Mortar.

"T-T-There," said Brick pointing offshore-ward, "sw-sw-swimming".

"S-s-s-swimming, you s-say?" asked Mortar mocking Brick's stutter, stroking the air with his arms miming the dog-paddle.

Brick shot an exasperated look at Mortar. "I-I-I haven't seen h-h-him with m-m-my own e-e-e-eyes, s-so I-I-I t-t-think he's s-swimming. And s-s-swimming *f-for his v-very l-life,*" observed Brick. He let go a small chuckle of delight at his wordplay.

"I'm sure he'd be flattered by that generous characterization of his aquatic prowess, but I think a more likely conclusion might be that he's deceased swimming and he'll be lucky to even be flotating. Maybe we can get away," said Mortar.

"O-O-Okay," said Brick, "b-b-but w-w-what ab-b-bout these ch-ch-chains?"

After a moment of quiet as this new freedom made its impact on their brains, Brick stated the obvious, "F-F-Find out w-w-where w-w-we are, f-first."

"Wait a minute. Let's think this through. I propose that we determine the exact location of our fruituitous landfall and seek out the local authorities and ascertain our exact whereabouts," said Mortar laying his finger along his cheek and gently tapping to loosen the thoughts from his brain.

"N-N-No auth-th-thorities," cautioned Brick.

"I'm just thinking out loud... If our master indeed swims with the fishes, I venture to say we might be the captains of our own ships, or gastronomically speaking, chefs of our own kitchens, authors of our own destinies."

Brick listened intently planning on speaking only in disagreement, if he must speak at all.

"How about this? We take the money and do whatever we want to?" asked Mortar somewhat rhetorically, for he had already made up his mind.

Brick nodded eagerly, so appealing was this idea.

Mortar, looking up to find the ideas in the air, continued in this vein, "In a 70/30 partnership..."

Brick began to shake his head vigorously in dispute, but before he could speak, Mortar continued, "Of course we can't go back home. We'd be resold into someone else's service, whilst here we may be taken at face value – as free men."

Brick again nodded with enthusiasm, eyes shining at the words 'free men', but held up a finger to mark that he would like to speak, but Mortar continued, brooking no interruption.

"Anyway, it's going to be dark soon. So, quit your yapping and do something useful, like go find some wood for a fire while I keep guard over our belongings," commanded Mortar.

"We're going to have to elect a leader to head up our new enterprise..." Mortar's voice trailed off as he continued on this rich train of thought.

The Dawn of Freedom

Suggested listening: *Me and Bobby McGee* by Janis Joplin

The fire lit by our heroes the previous evening was a cold pile of black and gray ash by morning's first light. Brick and Mortar lay sleeping on the beach cuddling together like spoons for warmth. Both men had slept deeply that night with the knowledge that they were on the threshold of a new existence as free men.

Mortar, short and squat, awoke to find himself in the intimate embrace of the lengthier Brick, and being embarrassed about their intimate posture, jumped to his feet, using his friend's head as a support and pushing it deep into the soft sand. Mortar stood, yawned and stretched long and satisfyingly. He beat his chest with his fist as if to jump-start his heart, and he said.

"Brick, how does it feel to be a free man?"

Mortar's employment of Brick's noggin to support his rise had effected the latter's return to consciousness.

In the village near their 'fruituitous' landfall, the two men found what appeared to be a blacksmith's/ironmonger's forge with a burly man preparing a fire.

"Let me do the talking," said Mortar, shoving Brick back a step.

"Ahem, ah, we, ah, would like to, ah, ah, have our chains, ah, ah, *rearranged,*" said Mortar haltingly, for he wasn't yet familiar with the air of command that derives from monetary wealth.

"Rearranged?" puzzled the burly man.

"Yes, re-ar... re-ar... removed, actually," replied Mortar uncertain in the choice of his words.

"Slaves don't usually come round 'requesting' that their chains be 'rearranged'," said the burly man suspiciously eying both men.

"Rich men, if you please, not slaves," said Mortar with a tone displaying displeasure at the word 'slaves', "but rich men with gold might make such a request. These chains were oh, so chic in Rome, but they do restrict movement, to say the least."

"Gold, you say?" asked the man.

"Gold," affirmed Mortar.

"I could turn you in," challenged the burly man.

"Then you wouldn't receive payment for removing our chains... and a generous gratuity, as well..."

"Gold, you say," mused the burly man rubbing his chin.

"Generous gratuity, as well," coaxed Mortar.

"How generous?" asked the man.

"Very generous," assured Mortar. Brick added his nodding assent.

"He don't talk much," observed the burly man pointing to Brick.

"Silence becomes a fool," quipped Mortar, to Brick's frown of disapproval.

"Let's see about these chains of yours," said the burly man, "for I am a practical man, a businessman and not a politician, and your gold holds more interest for me than strict interpretations of social and legal codes."

Accessorize! Accessorize!! Accessorize!!!

Chink, chink! Ping! Chink, chink! Ping! A few seconds sufficed to remove the physical bonds of slavery. Brick and Mortar parted with a generous portion of their gold for having their chains 'rearranged'.

"If I might be so bold as to suggest that your beggared appearance could stand a little improvement," offered the burly man, "my cousin, just down the street, is a purveyor of fine goods of all kinds. You go to his shop; he can help you fulfill your needs, for he, too, is a businessman with little passion for the letter of Roman law. He looks just like me; just down there." The burly man pointed to a sumptuous looking establishment farther along the market street.

Brick and Mortar stood outside the shop gazing at the fine product lines on display in front of the shop. Another burly man with the kindest of greetings ushered them inside. "I can see for myself that you gentlemen are strangers and, without wishing to give offense, I can see for myself that you are in need of improved habiliments."

"Ah, a civilized man, I see," said Mortar, "but, no, we are in need of new clothing, clothing as befits, no pun intended, free and wealthy gentlemen." He gave Brick a smug smile.

"T-T-That's ww-w-hat he s-s-said," whispered Brick to his partner.

"Keep your trap shut, stupid," said Mortar sharply out of the corner of his mouth.

"H-Habiliments. T-That m-means c-cloth..." stammered Brick.

"Shut! It!" cried Mortar vehemently.

In a tone of resignation Brick said, "I-I-I j-j-ust w-want t-t-two n-n-new t-t-tunics."

Brick chose a simple, wine colored tunic that would suffice for everyday wear, but he chose a fine-woven, seamless tunic of white with blue stripes for occasions that he perceived would require kicking it up a notch. (He did, additionally, pick out a travel bag, new sandals and a brown leather belt.) Without much haggling, to the chagrin of the proprietor, they settled on a price much more suited to the seller than to the buyer, something like a surcharge for failing to observe the local customs required when striking a bargain.

Mortar gave a short snort of contempt as Brick left the shop and went to wait in the street. He waited for what seemed like hours. Waiting in unfamiliar surroundings, with strange foreign people, trying to look like a free man instead of a slave, this was no easy task. Brick fidgeted frequently, uncertain about his stance, uncertain about looking at people or not looking at people, anxious to get going to... to the G-ds knew where. He eventually found a place to sit, out of the way of people, but within sight of the well, where the women and slaves of the place came and went.

He was just getting interested in the pageant of daily village life when Mortar stepped forth from the merchant's shop. The merchant was inspecting the customer and his assistant, Abdul, was fussing about Mortar, adjusting his clothing, picking at lint, and generally insuring that his master's fine wares were being properly worn by this new client of his.

Mortar struck a majestic pose, arms akimbo with a commanding air, freshly coiffed, oiled and perfumed, manicured, pedicured and polished. In all the splendid and sordid annals of history, the greasiest comb-over of his bald pate completed this make-over of epic proportions.

Dressed to impress, Mortar stood resplendent in a bright orange tunic with golden fringe along the bottom hem, fancy beadwork done in blues, greens and aquas across the chest in a wave pattern. A wide, crimson leather belt gathered what it could of Mortar's belly, but slipped badly below the equator highlighting rather than understating the roundness of his corpulent corpus. A yellow, hooded, fur-trimmed cape with silver tassels for ties carefully thrown casually over his shoulders would have reminded a latter-day observer to think of a superhero rummage sale of left-over costume items.

"Abdul! Abdul!!" The proprietor clapped his hands sharply to summon his assistant. "Bring Hosannah!"

"Not Hosannah?!" cried Abdul in disbelief, clapping his hand to his cheek.

"Yes, yes, Hosannah and Sweetness! Quickly!!"

"Not Sweetness!!" said the doubly dismayed Abdul, clapping his other hand to his other cheek.

"Yes, Hosannah *and* Sweetness!! Now!!" said the proprietor in a voice that admitted no argument.

Mortar stood by and waited imperiously, nose in the air.

Abdul returned leading a fine-looking and placid she-ass and a kicking, fighting, struggling, biting, unbroken fireball of a young woman. Her hands and feet were shackled and tied around her neck was a leather thong, used as a leash.

Taking the thong in his hand, Mortar suffered only a few, recalcitrant tugs from the girl before he suddenly reached out and slapped her face, as he had been slapped himself many a time. The girl, Sweetness, caught by surprise, stared at her new master; stared with eyes aflame and then to the shock and awe of everyone, she reached right up, quick as lightning, and backhanded Mortar hard across the kisser, splitting his lip.

"She's a spitfire, this cunning, little bitch!" cried the proprietor. "You will have many pleasurable hours taming her!!"

"She doesn't talk is only problem, but she listens, but that is virtue in woman and dogs," said the burly man. "She listens especially well after I beat her. But the gods have seen fit to allow bandits to steal my camels. And I must put business before pleasure. The will of G-d has reduced me to humble penury. Nothing is spared. I lose a daughter, and my ass, too."

A look of horror passed across Mortar's face.

The burly man, thinking that Mortar didn't understand his joke, began to explain.

"I lose my ass," he said as he patted the flank of the animal, and then he said again, "I lose my ass," as he patted his own backside.

"Ass," he repeated with rising intonation and patted Hosannah. "Ass," he repeated with falling intonation and patted his backside. "Ass means two things."

"No, no, no! You sold your own daughter to me?!" cried Mortar in astonishment.

"Yes, my own daughter!" said the man, taken aback and clearly offended by this comment. "I cannot sell what does not belong to me. I bought her for a great price. She is more sweeter than honey. That's why I call her Sweetness. She do everything I tell her!"

At that point the Sweetness made a lunging feint in the direction of the proprietor who fell for the ruse and pulled up his hands to protect his face and pulled his hips back and spun a half turn to fend off any potential blow to the crotch. It was clear that someone, indeed, had learned something from the Sweetness's 'internship' with this proprietor.

Meanwhile, Brick had witnessed all of this with eyes wide and mouth open and his stutter was the worse for all the wonderment.

"W-W-Where d-d-did you g-g-g-get that t-t-tunic? T-T-That f-f-fine a-a-ass? A-A-And w-w-who's t-t-that?" stammered Brick in astonishment.

I don't want you wearing my clothes, taking my ride, or borrowing my slave', and for added emphasis he added, "Don't even think about it!!"

"W-W-Wow! Y-Y-You really k-n-n-now h-h-how to acc-acc-access-ss-ssorize!"

Object Lesson

As Brick and Mortar were taking their leave from the burly man's cousin and Abdul, shouts were heard coming up the street. Soldiers were escorting condemned men to the outskirts of the town.

"What's going on here?" asked Mortar.

The burly man explained, "Crucifixion! Runaway slaves! The whole town is turning out for the festivities."

Now it was Mortar's turn to stutter, "R-r-run away s-s-slaves?" He gulped hard. "Are you talking to me?"

"Yes, of course. You just asked and I just told you: runaway slaves," said the burly man.

Brick pulled Mortar aside and speaking into his ear, he said, "R-R-Runaway, n-n-not r-r-run aw-w-wway s-slaves. (Runaway slaves, not Run away, slaves.) N-Not us."

So great was Mortar's relief from his sudden fright that he nearly peed himself.

"Yes," said the burly man, "they stole their master's gold!"

"G-g-gold?" said Brick.

"An outrage!" cried the burly man. "Is nothing sacred?! Damn thieves!!"

"Yes! An outrage!!" agreed Mortar.

"O-o-o-outrage!" said Brick weakly.

"At least those damn thieves will get what's coming to them," said the burly man, his fine sense of justice and proportion being satisfied. After a short pause, he mused, "What would become of society without strict interpretations of social and legal codes?"

Brick and Mortar with their newly acquired property Hosannahand Sweetness, fell in with the crowd that was making its way out of the town, eager to witness the administration of justice.

When they came to the place outside town, the Roman soldiers set about their task with workmanlike efficiency for this was not an infrequent task. The slaves were stripped of their clothing. They reached down to cover themselves but the soldiers grabbed them by the arms, laid them down onto the upright beam and 'affixed' their hands and feet to the wood. Screams of pain punctuated the piercing of hands and feet as they were nailed to the wood. The crosses, now complete with bodies-soon-to-be-corpses, were erected into the earth. Both slaves broke out in a sweat as their bodies worked vainly and involuntarily to escape the pain. They breathed as if they had just finished running a marathon; every part of their bodies had joined the effort to seek relief from the pain. In their pain and indignity, they felt utterly alone.

This theater of the macabre with its cruelty and death drew a large audience. Spectators couldn't look away. The victims groaned in their pain, pain that was theirs alone to bear. The guards sat down and waited. As it was still morning the guards speculated that it was going to be a long, hot day. They had strict instructions that they were not to break the men's legs; that they must be made to suffer as long as it pleased the Emperor.

Gradually overcoming their initial silence, the crowd began to express its opinions and to offer commentary. Even muted laughter was heard mixed in with other comments. But after all, this was not justice, this was a public display of the empire's power and will. The main message conveyed was that if you defied the state, the state would hurt you. Badly.

Two well-dressed men standing in front of our Brick, Mortar and Sweetness talked among themselves and our trio couldn't help but overhear.

"Pity the poor man!" cried the one named Sanctimon.

"Yes," purred Viktorius in agreement, "'tis a shame; 'tis a damn shame!"

"Imagine! Losing two slaves in one day!"

"Yes, losing the value of their work, not to mention depreciation on a capital investment!"

"At least he won't have to go to the expense of feeding them any longer."

At last our party was able to tear themselves away and head down the road. Talk about miserable! They had been feeling quite good about themselves but this display of Roman might reminded them of their former status and what would likely happen to them if they were found out to be runaway slaves. Sullen, sulky and sour were the moods. Sweetness was anything but; she trudged along on her leash that Mortar held tightly in his hand. She didn't resist for the object lesson had its effect on her as well. Only Hosannah seemed to be satisfied with the situation, but even she would have preferred lying in the shade and munching some oats rather than carrying the short, fat passenger along the dusty road.

A Brutal Attack

Gestas and Dysmas. Do the names ring a bell? Even the most illiterate persons in Western societies have seen them rendered in the graphic arts hundreds of times. When I tell you who they are, you're going to slap your head and say, "Uff da!! What are their names again?" Gestas and Dysmas.

What should have been a scenic byway was turned into a treacherous track by those two archfiends of the road, Gestas and Dysmas. They robbed and plundered travelers on the road and so far, had foiled all the attempts by the Romans to put a stop to their nefarious misdeeds. Gestas and Dysmas had their pictures posted in Roman post offices on their X Most-Wanted List all across the province.

Huge rocks, behind which many men could hide, stood close along the road between Nazareth to Capernaum. A lone traveler, lost in contemplation, was suddenly stopped by two men, the shorter of them calling out in a voice pretending good will.

"Ho, pilgrim! This is your lucky day! Opportunity knocks. Knock, knock and your purse shall be opened," cried Gestas. Dysmas repeated the "Knock, knock," of his partner and sharply rapped the man on his shoulder twice with his stout walking stick, and laughed a patronizing laugh with a malignant grin, revealing such rotten teeth that at least one need not fear his bite.

Dysmas stepped sideways and moved to the man's flank, gaining a more advantageous position.

"Let's get down to business." Gestas turned back to the man and asked solicitously, "Whatcha got in the bags, pilgrim?"

"Tools and stuff," replied the man humbly.

"Tools and stuff?" asked Gestas, opening his eyes wide in mock surprise. "'That is an inadequate response to this great opportunity, Friend!"

"Tools," said the man simply with a slight shrug, "and stuff." He shook his head and grew wary.

"What *kind* of tools? What kind of stuff, pilgrim?" spat Gestas evilly. And he nodded to his partner.

Dysmas, on the flank of the man, reached out and smote him viciously on the cheek, sending the man reeling backward, but he didn't fall down. Although he lived in a violent age, he was shocked by this personal act. He couldn't imagine why anyone would want to hurt another person.

"Now, I asked you, pilgrim, 'what *kind* of stuff'. If you can't be polite and answer a simple question when you're asked, my friend here would be delighted to teach you some manners," said Gestas.

"Don't hit me, please, I have only a little money..." said the man.

"It seems," said Gestas to Dysmas, "that he would like to enroll in your 'crash' course."

Dysmas, having circled behind the man to the other side, lashed out quickly, smashing him on the other cheek and knocking him to the ground. Dysmas stood straddling over him and with his walking stick punched the man in the stomach, doubling him up on the ground.

"There is a small fee to be paid; no such thing as a free lunch, you know, unless, of course, you can turn these stones into bread," laughed Gestas. "It won't take long and satisfaction is guaranteed. Educate him, Dysmas." And Dysmas struck the man another crunching blow.

"Now, I can tell what you are thinking: we're *common thieves,*" suggested Gestas as the man writhed in pain upon the ground. "You would be in error, Pilgrim. We are not *common thieves* at all. We are *innovative educators*! Dysmas, try to knock some sense into his head." Dysmas delivered another blow, this time to the back of the man's head.

"But enough of this delightful intercourse. Be a polite pilgrim and pay up," said Gestas. The man tried to remove the bags that were slung over his shoulder and give them to these miscreants, but the pain in his stomach prevented him from reaching over his head and so Dysmas dealt him another blow with the stick, this time to his back, just above the kidneys.

Gestas reached down and separated the man from his bags using a small knife and turned the bags upside down, shaking their contents out on the ground. Carpenter's tools, a cloak, a clean tunic, clean underwear, sandals, and a book with writing materials, nothing really of any great value, except one silver denarius.

"One stinking denarius," said Dysmas, rifling through the man's belongings.

"It would seem he was telling us the truth. Let him have the bonus for being so honest," said Gestas and Dysmas struck another unimpeded blow against the man's back.

Gestas clucked his tongue to get Dysmas' attention, and pointed with his chin back to the west, to two soldiers on horse approaching in the distance. "Dysmas, I believe and our work here has come to an end. Let's leave this honest and wiser pilgrim to his studies. C'mon, let's go."

Two Roman Soldiers Pass By

The aforementioned mounted patrol of two Roman soldiers happened to pass along the road and as they gaily rode along they discoursed thusly after the manner of occupation troops the world

over:"How are we ever going to raise up this unruly and stiff-necked people, up above their present conditions," said Soldier Romulus.

"You know," said Soldier Remus, "when we first got here to this land, I was all optimistic and I think the gods favored our enterprises here, but now, it seems to have devolved into one giant cock-up. I think that we've lost our focus."

"Yes," said Romulus thoughtfully, "focus."

"To tell the truth, I find this occupation duty more stressful than plain, old battle," lamented Remus. "You never know when or if you're going to be attacked or if you'll be welcomed!"

"Yeah, I hate that!" agreed Romulus.

"Me, too! I hate that!" Remus seconded his own motion.

"Bunch of lowlife scum! You'd think they'd *want* to live in peace. You'd think they'd *want* better lives."

Remus mused, “it is so frustrating trying to civilize these sons ‘o’ bitches.” He shook his head and tsk, tsk, tsked.

“Trouble is, you can’t tell the good Jews from the bad Jews; they all look alike. Here’s an idea,” said Romulus, suddenly animated, “let’s kill them all and let their one god sort them all out!”

“Now you’re on to something,” said Remus. That’s another thing wrong with this place. They only got one god. Now that’s spiritual poverty.”

And they came around the bend, and there in the road lay the victim of the brutal attack. They reined in their horses and Remus continued their conversation saying, “for example, take this lazy bastard lyin’ around in the middle of the day. He should be working somewhere, earning money...so he can be taxed.”

“Perhaps if there were innovative educators that could help these people understand economics...” mused Romulus, but the thought ran out of steam.

Romulus slid down from his horse and gave the victim a polite kick to gain his attention without actually having to touch him with his hands, and he said, “Hey, you there. Get up and get moving. Loitering’s not allowed on the Emperor’s roads. Legitimate traffic only.”

“Hey, hold it, Romulus,” said Remus. “Look at all the blood.”

“Oh, yeah,” agreed Romulus, “so he’s not napping. This must be the handiwork of those desperadoes Gestas and Dysmas.”

“No signs of a struggle?” said Remus in puzzlement. “Same M.O.?”

"Looks like it. This is just intolerable!" said Romulus, throwing his hands in the air. "What if he had been a citizen of Rome?! There'd be all hell to pay!"

"Well, thank the gods, that it's just a Jew," said Remus.

"Yeah, c'mon. Let's go," said Romulus. "Maybe we can catch those two thieves."

Remus shouted at another traveler on the road and ordered him to take the body of the man out of the Emperor's road and lay him off to the side. In this way neither of the soldiers had to actually touch the man. (The only contact that these soldiers wanted with their enemy was at the point of their swords.) The passerby cursed because he came into contact with this bloody body.

Romulus remounted his horse and the two soldiers left the man and galloped off down the road.

The traveler, having complied with the order of the two soldiers, hurried away to avoid any further 'enmeshments.'

Brick, Mortar and the Victim of a Brutal Attack

Not much of a wait transpired before two men, one mounted and one afoot, and a woman came into sight, making their way down the road. One of the men was tall-ish and slender-ish. The other was short-ish and stout-ish and rode upon a donkey. The woman was tethered to the short, fat man and her hands and feet were shackled. Her chains chinked at every opportunity.

Remember... no, wait. This is the party we've already met, Brick on foot, and Mortar astride the ass, leading his newly acquired slave, whose hands were tied tightly with a rope the end of which Mortar was holding in his hand. Mortar was considering all of the ways that he would 'put to use' his new property.

"Look there!" said Mortar pointing to the heap by the road. He held out his hand to prevent Brick from proceeding further. Both men and the woman slave had stopped, but then continued to approach the body on the road, warily attentive and fearful of a trick. They looked all around and then came right up to the man lying by the road. They were wary because, really, you can't be too careful in a strange country. Mortar jumped down from the ass and stood over the man, who groaned in agony.

Brick had bent down to examine the man, felt for his pulse and stammered, "He-e-e-e's n-n-not d-d-dead."

"I can see that for myself, you imbecile," retorted Mortar with disdain.

"D-D-D'ya th-th-think h-h-he will l-l-l-live?" said Brick.

"Well, that would be a prognosis to be made by competent, licensed health care providers. We simply lack the proper credentials for that, least ways, I'm not trained for this. Are you trained for this? No, and I don't think you are neither. Do we want to expose ourselves to liability issues? I think not," said Mortar. "But laypersons, such as ourselves, might be permitted the observation that the breathing is a good sign. But, he is bleeding copiously, and all in all, his prospects look bleak."

Mortar looked around absently but Brick couldn't take his eyes off the injured man. Mortar shrugged. Mortar remounted the ass and struggled awkwardly, his large belly being a substantial obstacle to lithe motion. "Let's go," said Mortar as he spurred the ass. A troubled look passed over Brick's face and he kept looking back at the man as Mortar dragged him down the road by the shoulder of his tunic. Sweetness had decided to not interact with the two men. They seemed 'funny' to her. Something wasn't right.

The man groaned piteously.

"How stupid of me," said Mortar. "He had a nasty head wound and I've always been fascinated by head wounds.

Thank the gods for this chance! Let's examine it before we leave. All for the advancement of science."

"Y-Y-Yes, b-b-but you're a b-b-butcher," said Brick in mild protest. Concern for the man began to formulate an idea in Brick's mind.

"Some phenomena are interdisciplinary, imbecile!" said Mortar irritably as he dismounted the ass. His tunic didn't dismount at the same time, but bunched up in an immodest manner. Mortar pulled his tunic into proper position after looking around to see if anyone had seen. Then he squatted down, turning the man's head this way and now that to inspect the bruises and lacerations.

Mortar fell into his superior and accustomed role as enlightened sage. "Notice how the life blood spills forth in small pulses, Brick. Why so? Dunno for sure, but some say it's due to the phases of the moon and just as our moon affects the tides of the oceans, so it sings it siren's song to the sanguine sides of our physical self and makes the blood pulse, like tiny, wee tides."

He returned his attention to the body before him and pressed gingerly at the wound to the man's face. The man recoiled from the pain of his touch.

As Mortar conducted his less-than-expert examination of the man's wounds, two other men, a renowned faith promoter and a storied athlete and motivational speaker, came upon the scene.

Sanctimon & Viktorius

The men, known as Sanctimon and Viktorius, stopped and introduced themselves and graciously offered their assistance, saying, "Good day to you gentlemen and good day to you, sir (louder to the inert man). Far be it for me to idly cast words of advice to complete strangers for free, but your friend, who seems to be napping, might try to find a better location. You know, there are thieves operating in these parts of our happy Holy Land."

"And who is this lovely creature?" inquired Viktorius with a salacious leer toward Sweetness.

"What makes you think he is our friend?" asked Mortar hoping to take offense.

"N-n-n-not n-n-napping," declared Brick earnestly.

"Then why is he lying in the road in such a devil-may-care posture?" inquired Sanctimon. "And, by the by, sartorial elegance will die with you. Nice threads."

"Why, thank you. The key is accessorizing," said Mortar offhandedly.

And who is this lovely creature?" asked Viktorius, still staring at Sweetness.

"He's been robbed, beaten and left for dead, is what I think," said Mortar. "Lovely, ain't she? Got all her teeth, too."

"You don't say," said Sanctimon aghast. "That would explain all the blood. I'm sensing that G-d wants to communicate with me. But first, does he have any money?" Receiving a negative answer, he held his hands to his head to better receive the Message of G-d as if it were a radio signal. "G-d talks to me frequently, but that only makes sense because I am a very, very humble man of great and trusting faith. G-d has richly rewarded my goodness and my faith in Him with wealth and he wants me to share some of my boundless spiritual insight with this man."

Sanctimon bent over the victim, rifled through his pockets in a definitive search for money, and then lovingly shouted at him, "Hey, you, person of the road." He looked back at Brick and Mortar and smiled, silently inviting them to watch and learn. He returned his attention to the prostrate man with the admonition, "It's dangerous for you to loiter so in the road, if I may be so bold in saying."

The victim replied nary a word, but continued to bleed.

Sanctimon again looked back at Brick and Mortar and slowly blinked his eyes, as if saying, "Don't worry. I've encumbered many situations like this before."

Turning back to the victim, he said loudly, "I'm going to share spiritual wisdoms with you, at no charge. Pay close attention."

Mortar looked to Brick and nodded approvingly and repeated, "No charge!"

Sanctimon enumerated spiritual wisdoms, expounding on them at length and in great detail, which to recount all that he had said would keep us here for rather longer than we could bear, so I'll employ shorthand here: G-d loves you, but He loves men better, attractive people more, wealthy people more, light-skinned people more, smart people more; and other incredibly loving and caring propositions.

While this spiritual diatribe was washing over him like a wave of overpowering love, Viktorius had begun a low-earth orbit around Sweetness, very much liking what he saw.

The victim of the brutal attack lay there and did not move. Not even one syllable in response was Sanctimon able to elicit. His traveling companion broke off his attentions to Sweetness and said, "Well, I don't know what more I could say that would convince him, but I don't believe his is a hopeless case. So, I'd like to echo your fine sentiments by saying," and here he turned to address the man, "No one can help you, like you can help yourself."

Still nothing.

"We might sooner squeeze blood from a stone," said Sanctimon in a snide aside to Brick and Mortar. "By the way, do you know if he has any money?"

With a dramatic flourish, the other man jumped to the center of attention with various flexes and a pose.

"I. Am. Viktorius, gold medalist in the recent Games by the grace of G-d," and here he pointed skyward in acknowledgement of said grace, "currently providing motivational training and invaluable, personal insights wrapped into a single, affordable program called 'Good-As-Gold', patent pending. All for the incredibly low price $49.95. Results guaranteed or your money back."

Sanctimon nodded with whole-hearted approval while Mortar opened his eyes and mouth wide in surprise at such an incredible bargain.

"I offer such 'Good-As-Gold' motivational sayings as, 'Give yourself a hands up!', 'Your money and your life', and 'You cannot glean what you cannot dream!'"

Sanctimon turned again to the victim of the brutal attack and said in his kindest, gentlest voice, "You can't beat a deal like that."

This time when he turned to look at Brick and Mortar, making certain that they, too, were watching attentively and not letting this rich spiritual lesson pass them by, a look of frustrated consternation passed over his face.

"You can lead a horse to water, but you can't make them drink!" pronounced Sanctimon with great love in his voice.

Viktorius said, "I'd like to resonate with those statements." Then turning again to Sweetness, he asked, "And how much for the girl?"

"She's not for sale," said Mortar, proud that others valued his property as highly as he did.

Viktorius gave a grunt of displeasure at hearing that Mortar intended to keep the girl.

Sanctimon sighed with an air of divine resignation and said apologetically, "Pearls before swine. Beware lest they turn on you and trample you to death."

"He d-d-don't l-l-look like he's g-g-going to t-t-trample anyone," observed Brick.

"Sarcasm ill becomes a moron!" said Mortar in a loving attempt at brotherly correction.

Sanctimon tilted his head in annoyance but recovered himself. "Well, I must be off for my spiritual exercises," said the happy holy man brightly. Viktorius agreed saying something about the strictness of his training regimen and diligence in adhering thereto. They made their exit posthaste, after wishing them all the goodly graciousness of G-d, et cetera, et cetera, et cetera.

"Now there go two truly devout and kindhearted persons! Spirits of the highest quality and finest sensibilities," said Mortar admiringly. "I see now why they call this the Holy Land."

Brick had been thinking hard and now the man groaned in pain again, which brought the attention of the two companions back round to the immediate problem." Yes, well, he is clearly not well and likely to expire very soon if he doesn't bind up those wounds," said Mortar with an air of authority. "Let's go."

Again, they turned to go and Mortar climbed halfway up the ass when the man with what seemed his last breath gasped out the words, "Help me."

"W-W-Wait, M-M-Mortar," said Brick. Mortar slipped back off the ass and turned back to Brick.

"Now what?" said Mortar in exasperation.

Brick stumbled and stammered to voice his thoughts which had coagulated in his mind.

"Spit it out, dumb ass! I haven't got all day."

"I-I-I was j-j-just thinking. If I-I-I were l-l-lying in the r-r-r-road l-l-like that m-m-man is, I-I-I would w-w-want someone to h-h-help me," said Brick speculatively.

"Well, you aren't lying in the road like that man, are you? No. So let's go," said Mortar.

"I-I-I w-w-want to h-h-help h-h-him," said Brick.

"Oh, all right," said Mortar peevishly. "You're such a sucker, always being taken advantage of, and mark my words, you'll regret it someday."

Brick and Mortar tended inexpertly, but adequately, to the injured man. But actually, it was Sweetness who stopped the bleeding by applying a pressure bandage to the wound.

The Ministrations of Brick and Mortar

Finally, after much discussion of the manner in which the injured man should be conveyed to the next inn, they slung him over the ass like a sack of wheat flour. To their credit, they did not drag him behind the ass, but Mortar was considerably put out that he had to walk.

And, lo, ere long, cometh they unto an inn, an international franchise outfit that offered a point-system based rewards program, where the Two took a suite of rooms and lodged the man at their own expense, thereby earning double points. Sweetness and Hosannah remained out in the stable.

The injured man lay unconscious for a day in his bed, despite Mortar's brotherly exhortations to 'stop his lollygagging', (he had paid close attention to the great efforts expended by Sanctimon and Viktorius to assist the victim of the brutal attack), while he enjoyed the amenities of the place including free high-speed wireless Internet connection, cable television, in-room mini-bar, choice of hard or soft pillows, free continental breakfast buffet, those little soaps and shower caps. Brick had spent his time caring for the man.

Out of their own coin, actually out of Brick's own coin, they fetched to the room, a local healer, to see what influence he might exercise over the unconscious victim of the brutal attack. As the healer entered the room he conducted a wary scan of the premises for lurking evil spirits or other paranormal manifestations. Results being nugatory, he set about his business.

Placing a Star Wars® lunchbox in the center of the floor, filled it with feel-good, Genuine Lou'siana MoJo, Ally Oops' Original How-Wow®, and organic, free range, gluten-free, certified herbs, the healer set alight the contents. A sweet-smelling smoke soon filled the room. (Since this was in the days before hotel rooms were managed smoking or non-smoking, this was not an issue.) The healer was just beginning his chantations, "Karo, Karo, dhark korn siruup..." when the fire alarm and sprinkler system activated, piercing ears and dousing everything. The Two hustled the healer out of the room. The man in his bed remained unmoved and unmoving, but soon was soaking wet.

Not knowing what else to do, Mortar ordered room service and waited. During this time the man babbled constantly saying such jumbled and outlandish things as "the Kingdom of G-d is within you; love your enemies; turn the other cheek; and your sins are forgiven."

Mortar's suspicious comment was, "He seems to operate on a *different* plane." He had the troubling feeling that he was being taken advantage of. He fretted over the cost of the suite even though he enjoyed every bit of it and he always returned to the happy thought that he didn't have to pay for it. He wondered when they would be able to get going again.

Finally, Sweetness came to the room and sat with the unconscious man. She spoke lowly and softly, encouraging him to return to the world and take his place again. There must be many who are waiting for him and the purpose that he must fulfill with his life.

Meanwhile, Brick was sitting with the man when he began to come around. First his eyelids began to flutter, his fingers twitched and then he began to move his hands.

Brick welcomed these developments and when the man had fully opened his eyes and seemed to become aware of his surroundings, Brick said, "B-b-b-back fr-fr-from the d-d-d-dead?"

The man winced from pain at trying to move his arms, but the pain strengthened his grasp on the here and now.

"Who? Where?" gasped the man with difficulty through a chapped and dry mouth.

"H-H-Hey, M-M-Mortar, come l-l-l-look!! G-G-Guess who's c-c-coming to?" said Brick.

"Well, I know it's not you, dumb-ass! I've given up hope that you'll ever come to your senses," said Mortar sarcastically as he came into the man's room.

Brick gave a disgusted 'hmpf', but not without stuttering, and then he turned to the man and said, "W-W-What's y-y-your n-n-name?"

The man looked around the room and said haltingly, "Water, please?"

"S-S-Sure," said Brick, helping the man to a drink.

"What happened?" asked the man.

"You were robbed and beaten, and left for dead, and in the Holy Land, no less" said Mortar.

"W-W-We t-t-took c-c-care of y-y-you," said Brick.

"Who are you?" asked the man after taking a drink.

"I-I-I a-a-axed y-y-y-you f-f-first," said Brick laughing to himself. "D-D-Did you n-n-notice I-I s-said 'a-a-axe? I-I-It's a j-j-joke."

"I can't believe the shit that comes out of your mouth. Do you ever think without speaking?! For G-d's sake!!" said a disgusted Mortar.

"I-I-I thought i-i-i-it was f-f-f-funny," said Brick defending himself.

"Just shut up, stupid," said Mortar.

"Are you two friends?" asked the man.

"Longtime associates," replied Mortar.

"From where? And what do you do?"

"Ah... ah... We're from somewhere not around here," mumbled Mortar quickly and without emphasis.

The man, who hadn't quite heard the answer, thought he heard, 'Samaritans' or 'Samaria.'

Mortar thought it best to not emphasize the first question, so he put all he had into the second question.

"We're.... ah....ah...morticians, yes, that's it, traveling morticians," said Mortar, lying through his teeth. Brick gave a disapproving look to Mortar. "We are re---searching ...... on a grant from World of Registered Morticians, WoRM. We set up trade shows around the known world, inviting vendors to display their wares, ah, ah, on a fact-finding mission on behalf of mortuary scientists belonging to an international consortium seeking out best practices for cost cutting tips and promoting good will among the national chapters, and ah, ah, ah promoting a new line of products designed to make death a more pleasant experience," dissembled Mortar.

Then to put the cherry on top, he attempted this bit of humor, "We were hoping you

might become a customer, but your recovery from your injuries has, at best, delayed that prospect, but you might consider pre-planning as an act of love to your family," laughed Mortar in the fakiest laugh you've ever heard.

"Death? Pleasant? You must be optimists," said the man.

Again, Brick asked, "W-W-who a-a-are y-y-you?"

"I-I'm a carpenter, or *was* a carpenter," said the man. "I'm Jesus of Nazareth."

"*Was* a carpenter?" asked Mortar suspiciously.

"I'm taking up a new line of work," said Jesus somewhat evasively.

"Yes," said Mortar, "so have we."

"Well, then. We've got something in common," said Jesus. He tried to sit up in the bed but he groaned with great pain and gave up the effort and laid back down. There followed an uncomfortable pause.

Brick broke the awkward silence saying, "We-we-we're g-g-going to J-J-Jerus-s-salem."

And Mortar hastened to add, "First, we have to find a lake to the east of here, then follow the river south to Jericho, then take the road up to Jerusalem. There's some grand temple or some such to see there."

"I'm on my way to the town of Cana, which is near the lake. Galilee. You could travel with me that far, crash the wedding and then continue on to Jerusalem," said Jesus.

"Whaddya mean, 'crash' the wedding?' asked Mortar.

"'C-C-Crash'," said Brick, "m-m-m-means to g-g-g-go un-un-un-uninvited."

Mortar looked to Jesus to confirm what Brick had said and Jesus nodded in accord and said, "You'd be most welcome."

"W-w-well, y-y-you can't t-t-travel in y-y-your c-c-condition; n-n-not y-y-yet, anyw-w-way."

Tongue UnTied

Later that evening Brick came into Jesus' room and found him bent over the desk in prayer. Raising his hand to his mouth, Brick coughed politely to break the silence and capture the Rabbi's attention.

Brick stammered, "I-I'd like to t-talk to y-you."

Startled, the Carpenter scrambled to cover something with his hands, and then cocked his head to the side to hear better and said, "I beg your pardon?" Jesus didn't quite understand at first, what with the Brick's foreign accent and his stuttering.

This misstep at the beginning unnerved Brick, which made his stutter gain momentum.

"C-C-C-Carpent-t-t-ter J-J-J-J-J-Jesus-s-s-s-s, I-I-I-I-I..." s-s-s-s-tutt-t-t-t-tered B-B-Brick... (Now he's got me doing it!) "Why d-d-d-did G-G-G-d d-d-do t-t-this to me?"

M-My t-t-tongue? T-T-To m-m-me?"

"For G-d to be glorified through you," answered Jesus, and before Brick could say another word Jesus posed this question to him which seemed odd. "Do you want me to heal you?"

"Y-Y-Yes, b-b-but..." said Brick without hesitation for he truly had a lot to say.

"Moses was so afflicted," remarked Jesus, "slow of speech, slow of tongue."

"W_W_Who? Who?" asked Brick.

"Moses the Lawgiver, our greatest prophet," said Jesus. Here the Carpenter Jesus commanded, "Stick out your tongue."

"W-W-W-What d-d-d-did you s-s-s-say?" spat out a confused Brick.

"I said, 'Stick out your tongue'," said the Carpenter.

"W-W-W-Why?" said Brick.

"Trust me. Just do it," countered the Carpenter, "and you will find out why."

So, Brick stuck out his tongue, and the Carpenter reached up and touched it with a quick motion. Before Brick knew what was happening, his tongue was loosed and his stutter blew away on the evening breeze.

"Thank you, sir," said Brick just as slick as you please. His eyes widened in surprise at his freedom of speech and in his wonder, Brick turned his head as if to look at his tongue freshly freed from it fetters and to admire the Carpenter's handiwork. And then he began to talk and talk and talk and talk. There poured forth from his mouth such a torrent of words, beautiful words, tongue twisters, sibilants, consonant clusters, gutturals, nasals, vowels, and everything.

"She sells seashells down by the seashore." Superb! "Greek grapes. Greek grapes. Greek grapes." Great! "Six sick slick slim sycamore saplings." Sublime! "Rubber baby buggy bumpers." Flawlessly. And he could say, "Fire truck, fire truck, fire truck" fast and furiously and without a slip, Freudian or otherwise.

But Jesus admonished Brick to not tell anyone. "What?! Are you kidding?!"

Was he serious wondered Brick. It would surely be obvious that he could speak clearly now. Was he supposed to fake a stutter? That didn't make any sense.

That night as he lay down to sleep, he talked softly under his breath, a conversation that continued after he fell asleep and only stopped when he began to dream. And in his dreaming his tongue flew out of his mouth and soared among the clouds. His tongue morphed into a sword and was lovingly sharpened by a woman whom Brick loved, but did not recognize. And as she returned the tongue/sword to his mouth she silently warned him showing him a deep, dark dungeon where of the dangers of intemperate speech, of hot words carelessly flung, of lies black and white, of sarcasm, of half-truths, of complaining and whining for which a special torture had been designed that is just too awful to commit to print even in these days when literally everything has found a lucrative market under the rubric of 'free communication'.

"Hey, stupid! Get up!"

And when Mortar as usual began to abuse him in the morning, he felt on his tongue a burning sensation much like heartburn or when a person eats too many jalapeno peppers or Chinese Red Dragons, and a deep, deep resentment began to rise within him like vomit and he opened his mouth and out came... out came... out came... a torrent of abuse, like the eruption of a long dormant volcano, an eruption so powerful that it changes the landscape for the next hundred millennia.

Now it was Mortar's turn to stutter, "Wh-wh-what?!" He had no idea of what had transpired the night before and was stunned by the words that poured from Brick's mouth, words unfettered by stuttering, but flowing fast and free.

With malice, Brick spat, "What?! Did I stutter?!" The effect was diminished when Brick inadvertently bit his tongue and he clapped his hand to his mouth and pulled a long face. Ouch! It hurt like hell!

Even though Brick's diatribe was mean and nasty in the extreme, you could almost forgive Brick his outburst because of all the abuse that he had endured over some years that he had spent with Mortar in the 'employ' of their Roman master. There could be no argument refuting the fact that Mortar deserved every bit of verbal abuse that Brick might give him.

Brick turned and walked away from Mortar whose jaw had dropped to the ground in shock at Brick's new-found freedom of speech. Momentarily he felt pleased with himself and his response. But then his painful tongue and his dream came back to him and his words to Mortar, measured against the standards in the dream given him by the woman, were found wanting in charity and he moaned softly in discomfort. He felt remorse almost immediately, but it was confused remorse because he also, if he admitted it to himself, enjoyed the feeling of cutting loose on his companion. Not only did he think that Mortar deserved what he, Brick, might dish out, it felt good to heap abuse on Mortar. But again, there was also a tinge of remorse that soured the pleasure he felt.

Brick had always imagined himself as being able to speak easily and freely, and now that he could, he wasn't so certain that it was turning out like he had thought.

Call of the First Para-Apostles

"Lemme do the talkin'," said Brick putting out his hand to restrain Mortar and he stepped up front. Mortar gave a look of exasperation. Our two heroes had conferred and decided that they wanted to lay low for a time, and join forces with this Jesus fellow, who seemed to them a fair and even person.

The two men begged the Lord to take them on as Apostles, but the Lord demurred saying, "I am come to the lost sheep of the House of Israel. Jews, yes. Gentiles, no."

"But we won't be no trouble, sir, and Brick here's got a real talent for words. He can talk circles around me!" said Mortar by way of testimonial. "Besides, him and me, we're a team."

"I thought you guys were morticians? On your way to a convention? If that's not true, what is it you *do* do?" asked Jesus.

"I'm a scribe, translator, secretary, bard, man of letters, poet, novelist, writer, playwright, essayist, dramatist, pamphleteer, brochurer, speechwriter, penman, overall Man-'O-Words, sir," said Brick.

"Formerly a man of few words, but now, a man of *manifold* words, are you?" said Jesus. "And you, Mortar?"

"Butcher and such like a chef; my father sent me to Gaul to learn the Beaux Arts de Cuisine, sir," said Mortar.

"'Butcher of Men' isn't going to work, is it? And Brick, do you happen to be familiar with Greek or Aramaic?" asked the Rabbi.

"Yes," he lied, but thought better of it immediately and hastened to add, "No, but I can learn," insisted Brick, "and right quick!"

"Everybody needs to eat and I can cook," put in Mortar earnestly.

"Man does not live by bread alone," responded Jesus.

"Man does not live without bread, neither," replied Mortar.

"I have only a limited roster and at this stage it's an entirely House of Israel operation. I don't really have room for any more Apostles... just thinking out loud here... you could possibly be *Para*-Apostles, a position that calls for a bit more personal responsibility and independence of action. You say you have a talent for words?"

"Most assuredly, my principal oeuvre is words," said Brick excitedly.

"And hors d'oeuvres is where I begin. Please find a place for us, sir. We won't cause no trouble," said Mortar.

"Please, please, please. We'll be good," pleaded Brick.

"Do you happen to have a sample of your work?" asked Jesus.

"What, d'ya want something to eat? Now?" asked Mortar incredulously.

Brick looked down his nose condescendingly and clarified, "He means a sample of my writing."

"Actually, I'd like both," said Jesus. "I'd like to hear something you've written. And if Mortar can cook as well as he says he can, then I should have a passable meal and an entertaining literary interlude within, say, an hour? I've just got to run up to Peter's house and I'll be back in an hour. I want to hear some literary wonder and eat a light, nutritious meal. See you in one hour."

And with that, the Carpenter turned and followed a path to the village of Capernaum.

Jesus returned in exactly one hour and he found Mortar, in formal attire with a four-in-hand bowtie and a white rose boutonniere, waiting for him by a small table set for one, complete with a white tablecloth, vase with a rose, the finest silverware, all under an umbrella to shield the diner from the harsh rays of the noonday sun. Jesus stared, mouth gaping in disbelief.

Mortar gave a slight bow of the head and said, "Al fresco dining for one, Monsieur? Allow me to see you to your table." He led Jesus around the table and pulled out the chair and helped his guest into the chair. Jesus felt the gentle pressure of the chair at the back of his knees and was gently and effortlessly guided into the chair. With elegant ease, Mortar dropped a spotless white napkin in Jesus' lap. With two sharp claps of the hands and a discreet call of 'Garcon!', Mortar summoned Brick from behind a screen with a tray held high bearing a snifter of palate-cleansing iced champagne sorbet which he deftly placed with a flourish before the Carpenter, and then vanished behind the screen.

"I'm so sorry, that given the constraints of time, I have only been able to produce an extremely modest repast," apologized Mortar, "but the chef has prepared for you a Vichyssoise with just a kiss of tarragon, rack of spring lamb with rosemary, haricots vertes, salade of mixed greens with a light raspberry vinaigrette, followed by a light-as-air Grand Marnier soufflé. Again, our humble house begs to apologize for so primitive a fare upon which one feeds as if from a trough in the most Spartan of circumstances."

As Jesus offered up thanks to G-d and tucked into the soup, Brick reappeared from behind the screen, but no longer in the garb of a waiter. Now he sported corduroy slacks and a tweed sport coat with leather elbows, a loose ascot at the throat, reading glasses and puffing a pipe filled with cherry flavored tobacco. A large book was tucked under his arm.

Mortar had produced a Queen Anne wingback chair in which Brick sat down. He made a great fuss and show of finding the proper place in his book, earnestly puffed on his pipe, looked up at Jesus and he cleared his throat signaling his intent to begin.

Enunciating his words carefully, Brick gave the title of his recitation, "Your Story."

Your Story

Recommended listening: *If I Had a Hammer*
by Peter, Paul & Mary

Mortar had cleared the dishes from the table and finished his waitering chores just as Brick was about to begin. Their timing was exquisite.

"Your Story," pronounced Brick grandly.

"That sounds interesting," said Jesus, only to be immediately shushed by Mortar.

"Sorry," said Jesus in a small way and he sat up attentively and folded his hands in front of himself on the table.

"As I was saying… before I was so *rudely* interrupted," continued Brick in a very offended tone, "Your Story."

"A short hour ago, you, Carpenter, charged me and my friend Mortar with presenting to you something of our best, both culinary and literary. You've just tasted the fruits of Mortar's labors and now from me you shall hear 'a good story'."

"But I ask you," said Brick placing his forefinger to his temple, "what makes a story good? Hmm?? A good story is one in which we find ourselves. Now how are we going to make this 'your' story? How will you find yourself in this story?" He tapped his finger to his temple as if thinking. He looked up as if thinking, but he wasn't thinking. He was merely pausing dramatically to let his thoughts sink into his listener.

"Let's do this," said Brick to Jesus as if he were changing course, "you, give me three words and I will transform them into 'your' story."

The Rabbi, loathe to speak again and gain Brick's further disapprobation, pointed to himself, tucked in his chin and mouthed the word, "Me?"

"Yes, you," said Brick after rolling his eyes, "Three words, if... you... please." He held up three fingers.

The Rabbi, always a fan of word play, looked upward to search for the three best words for Brick to weave into his tale, and he said, "Mercy" without hesitation. Brick held one finger in the air and repeated the word 'mercy' in an officious manner.

Jesus then pronounced his second word, "banquet" and Brick held up two fingers and repeated "banquet" as the second word.

Fumbling about for the third word, Jesus hesitated before finally saying "Ah... ah.... How about Hammer?"

Raising three fingers our storyteller repeated the third word, "Hammer. Are you sure you want the word hammer? You were slow in choosing it. Are you certain it's the word you want?"

Jesus nodded his assent.

Brick raised his eyebrows to portray a dash of dismay at the supposed difficulty of his task. He turned his head partially away from his listener, but then he quickly whirled forward, sat on the edge of his chair and with a confident air he continued.

"Mercy. Banquet. Hammer. In my own country, far away from here, among my own people, this is one way that we tell a story, but wait, my *own* people, my people, my *own*... Anyone who loves a good story is my '*own*' people. Wherever I find those who love a story, I am among my '*own*' people. And a slave, well, we've got fellow slaves everywhere we go..." He clapped his hand over his mouth instantly wishing that he could recall those words.

"Slaves," said Jesus in surprise, "You didn't say you were slaves!"

Brick was ashamed to admit that he was a slave and that he had let this slip from his tongue, (this was the second time already that his tongue had caused him trouble) but he was also defiant because he knew that slave or free was no guarantee of a good heart or a good mind and he also knew his history. So, he shot back, "Your people were once in slavery, if memory serves; and although you have your own kings, you might still be classified as slaves to Rome, no offence intended. With my own eyes I have seen slaves to money, slaves to pride, slaves to just about everything!"

"Don't worry. I won't turn you in," said Jesus, pleased at this spirited response and he sat back in his chair and gave a slight wave as if to say 'continue with your story'.

Brick eyed Jesus somewhat suspiciously, not sure whether he could trust him now that Jesus knew he and Mortar were slaves, but he continued. "Now, what meanings from these words can we bring together that will give us a meaningful story, which serves to entertain as well as to inform?"

"Mercy, banquet, hammer. Banquet, hammer, mercy. Hammer, mercy, banquet. Let's throw them into the air and see where they land and what we can divine from them." He made a mime of tossing three objects into the air and letting them land on the ground before him.

"Mercy is your first word. Does that make mercy your most important word? But deeper than the words themselves are the untold relationships, the unspoken meanings and the assumptions that each person brings from their backgrounds... For example, take the word 'circumcision'. Take it and keep it! To a Jew that connotes your covenant with Abraham, but to a gentile like me, I cross my legs and tell you to get away from me with that knife!" Here he mimicked his actions and gave out a little girl's scream, "Ahhh!"

Jesus emitted a slight chuckle.

"Or take the word 'mercy' and pair it with the word 'god' and in my lands, mercy does not belong with the word god; you may as well say 'weakness' or even 'character flaw'."

"Banquet. A formal affair. Dinner. Good food and wine. Hmm... check this out: To the banquet a king has invited the worthy people of his kingdom to celebrate a wedding, but his guests declined his invitation on one or another pretext."

In a whiny voice he continued, "'My son has fallen ill and I cannot leave my house.' And "I have bought a new field and must go inspect it," and the ever popular "I must wash my hair this night."

Jesus laughed at Brick's thin, high mimicking.

"And the word 'hammer'!" and Brick clapped his hands loudly and forcefully once.

"Your last word, the word that you paused before uttering not sure that you wanted to have it in your story. You Jews associate 'hammer' with Judah Maccabee, your liberator, whereas we might hear the word 'hammer' only as a blunt instrument which pounds. And then again, it may mean 'one who hams' and when I hear the word 'ham', I'm already on my way past the pig to the skillet! And to you, 'bacon' will mean nothing clean! But, I digress."

"The king was enraged at these excuses and so he sent his messengers out to the streets and roads with instructions to invite all and sundry that they meet and bring them to the banquet. And his messengers went out and brought back the sick and lame, the hungry, the thirsty, the poor, the unimportant, the invisible and the sinners!"

"Oh, my goodness, the sinners! A cavalcade of sinners of every stripe and tint! Rogues, scoundrels, cutthroats, rascals, ne'er-do-wells, scamps, scalawags, culprits, malefactors, crooks, cads and miscreants. The greedy, the lust-filled, the cruel, the fornicators, the bitter, the ungrateful, the drunks; don't even get me starting listing the lawbreakers!! And did I mention that there was going to be wine?! So, it's like this, if you want to have a fun party, you don't invite a bunch of religious nuts, right?! In fact, it begs the question. Do you even *like* religious people?"

"Well, I...," demurred Jesus cautiously.

"No, no. It's a rhetorical question. Don't answer," said Brick.

"Speaking of religious nuts and hammers, you yourself, Carpenter, are something of a hammer. You crack those nuts on the head! But you've also got a streak of mercy a mile wide. You forgive. That's what you do."

But all the while he had been speaking, his mind kept stealing back to the thought of being turned in to the Romans as a fugitive slave and that thought would stick in his craw and he decided to weave into his story an appeal to the mercy of this man.

"There have been many uprisings by slaves and I suppose that as long as men are enslaved they will continue to yearn for freedom from their bondage. Your people cried out to a G-d who took mercy on them and led them to safety. Not many of the gods are willing to do that!"

"About 100 years ago a gladiator slave named Starcapus led a rebellion. Thousands of slaves ran away from their masters and joined him. They won several battles against the Roman legions, but in the end, they were defeated and 6666 slaves were captured. It would have been better for them to be killed in battle for these survived to 'decorate' 160 miles of the road to Rome with their crucified bodies – 42 men crucified for each mile of the road. Their bodies were left on the crosses for years as a sign, as a deterrent to other slaves."

Warming to his topic with his vivid imagination fully engaged Brick began a discourse on the horrors of crucifixion detailing especially the nails and how they pierce the hands and feet to hold the wretched victim fast to the cross.

Jesus winced at the description and he noticed something of a change in Brick's eyes. He was just about to risk commenting on it when Brick suddenly began to speak as if not quite himself, the words simply coming to him and him releasing them from his mouth and he said, "You are Mercy. You are Banquet. No more Hammer. You are the Mercy of G-d. You are the Banquet of life. As you've given up carpentry, you must give up the hammer leaving only mercy and banquet. You will liberate without the hammer."

Brick shook his head and returned to the moment and proclaimed, "Your Story! Live it and breathe it, Carpenter!" Brick seemed slightly confused as if he himself did not know what had happened to his recitation, but it struck him as confused and disordered and possibly pointless. Maybe his listener had made something of it more than he himself had.

Jesus had been captivated by certain thoughts and he was staring into space when the recital concluded. His head jerked ever so slightly with an illumination which also brought him back to the present moment and with a polite golf clap, he congratulated Brick on his story and Mortar on his meal, and said jokingly, "So, you boys would like to butcher and scribble, food for the body and food for the soul?"

"As you put it, butchering and scribbling is rather a crude characterization, but you've got the seminal idea," said Brick.

"Eat, drink...," said Mortar. But Brick cut him off and cried out, "...and be literate!"

"I'd be honored for you two gentlemen to be my very first two Para-Apostles," announced Jesus grandly.

"Wow! Really? D'ya mean it?!" cried the Brick.

"Well, yes, I do indeed," said Jesus.

"Wow! Really? What's exactly a *para*-pustule?" asked Mortar, slightly confused.

"Para-*apostle*. It's like an apostle that's in training," explained Brick to Mortar's query.

"Oh. I knew that," said Mortar unconvincingly.

"And," Jesus hastened to add, "your former 'status' is a thing of the past."

PART II

Annunciation

Under water in a spirit sea, Mary holds her breath. Cheeks puffed, a few bubbles escape her lips. Why had she jumped in? She isn't afraid, but everything now is changed. The sun shines radiantly above the surface and she swims towards it easily. She breaks the surface into a new existence.

The breaking light of dawn found Mary wide awake and feeling distinctly radiant, but now uncomfortable... and... then panic... Did I dream that? Was it real? Her senses jumped to the edge. She slipped into hyper-sensitive, and suddenly to 'greatly troubled.' Wait! 'Highly favored one?'

Mary felt a sinking feeling, like dropping through the floor. Something had happened in the night and it was coming back to her now. And the emotions of the night replayed in her heart. She turned her head to the side to as if she could bring more clarity to her memory; as if there was some way to find the meaning in all this so that she could begin her day. Dread, followed by wonder, followed by ecstasy, followed by peace.

She knew she hadn't dreamt it, and so it wasn't a dream, she reasoned. So, if it wasn't a dream, then... was it real?

Shards of memory, like a broken pot, now returned to her. He said his name was Gabriel, "Call me Gabe." The look of wonder and expectation on his face. The delight in his voice as he translated his message to her. She could sense a certain relief after she acquiesced, after she said, 'Let it be done to me as you say.'

She gathers all this, like moisture from a dream that must be remembered before it evaporates. He said the Holy Spirit will come upon you; he said the power of the Most High will overshadow you; and he said you shall conceive... long moments of pleasure so exquisite, a surpassing goodness, acceptance, union, entirely in love – His whole being and her whole self. With child. How sweet!

Now the precariousness of her position hit her. With child. Joseph. Would he be displeased? Would he break the betrothal? Was she to become an outcast? How could she explain this? Would he understand? And yet peace prevailed over her soul, and in the end, Joseph, an exceedingly good man, saw and understood the peace that he saw in her eyes.

But he had said that he must sleep on it. He slept and he dreamt. And the Spirit of the Lord came to him in sleep and said, 'Take Mary for your wife, for she has conceived by the Holy Spirit.'

Joseph awoke from sleep and with the dream in his heart, he knew the same peace that he had seen in Mary's eyes, and he took her as his wife.

Be Not Afraid

Ka-boom! Pop! Pop!

"Ooh! Ooh! Ooooh!"

Sizzle! Bam!

"Aah! Aah! Aaaaah!"

Crackle, crackle, crackle!

"Wow, wow, woooow!!!"

Boom!

Fireworks have always been a means of announcing significant births. Of course, a statement like that is problematic because each birth is a significant birth, and they are rarely accompanied by fireworks. But the Almighty, pleased as man with man to dwell, couldn't resist a little fanfare to counterbalance the meanness of circumstance of this particular birth.

The reverberations echoed across the hillsides and lights flashed in bright colors. Roseate patterns shivered in the cold night air and then disappeared. The extravagant display started slowly, almost intermittently, and then began to build in brilliance, frequency and intensity. The bursts became almost constant and the surrounding countryside was lit up by the ethereal hues as the bursts formed the shapes of angelic heralds.

As the last of the echoes faded away across the remote hills and the colors erased themselves from the black sky, a single near-blinding pinpoint of light descended from the highest heavens and seemed to rush straight for the witnesses of this awesome display.

Horton, Morton, and Norton, night watch shepherds by trade and social critics by inclination, identical triplets, which was rare in those days, and rarer still for shepherds to be characters in any literary blockbuster such as the Bible, *and* with speaking parts, had been minding their own businesses when on the heels of a fireworks display the likes of which had never before been seen, an Angel of the Lord appeared, which was something quite out of the ordinary.

Horton spoke first saying, "Oh, look, my brothers, something quite out of the ordinary!"

Morton spoke next saying, "Yes, brothers, do look. It is *indeed* out of the ordinary."

Norton as always spoke last saying, "Yes, brothers, but don't look directly at it. I've just ruined my night vision."

And the Angel of the Lord spake unto them saying, "Fear not."

Horton spoke first again saying, "I have not taken fright."

Morton spoke next saying, "I'm not afraid."

Norton spoke last saying miserably, "I've soiled myself."

And again, the Angel of the Lord spake again saying, "I bring you good tidings!"

Horton spoke first again saying, "Do tell."

Morton spoke next again saying, "Yes, speak."

Norton spoke last saying, "What's tidings?"

And the Angel of the Lord continued saying, "A Savior has been born unto you this day, in the City of David. He is Christ the Lord. And you shall find him wrapped in swaddling clothes and lying in a manger. Now, what questions have ye?"

Horton spoke first saying, "It's crystal clear. No questions."

Morton spoke next saying, "Ditto."

Norton spoke last saying, "Can I see some identification? You can't just come waltzing in here, pretty as you please, announcing such-and-such, and so-and-so! This could be some kind of identity theft scam!"

The Angel of the Lord brightly and suddenly flashed out at Norton while simultaneously increasing the volume on the audio track. The three brothers fell back upon the ground and covered their faces, so fearsome became the aspect of the Angel.

"Go check it out for yourselves!!" growled the Angel angrily, "you'll see that the Almighty has stretched out his right hand to save his people. And no more sass from the Peanut Gallery!!"

And then suddenly a multitude of the Heavenly Host appeared with the Angel of the Lord singing Glory to G-d in the Highest.

But Norton couldn't let it go, and he raised his head slightly, so that his lips wouldn't be in the dirt when he spoke, and he timidly inquired, "Did you say it was a boy?"

"Yes, a baby boy," replied the Angel. And he hastened to add, "lying in a manger."

"What's he doing in a manger?" asked Norton, "He's not poor, is he? Another baby born into poverty?! Now that's real news?! It can't be the proper place for a Savior!"

"Well," demurred the Angel of the Lord, "it's hard to find a nice room on such short notice and with the Census in town, it was just impossible! It was the best we could do."

"I hope you got double reward points at least," cried Norton.

The Angel of the Lord merely harrumphed Norton dismissively.

Horton, Morton and Norton got to their feet and stood gazing at the brilliance of the angels of the Heavenly Host and admired the gowns of these beings.

"Say," said Horton. "I just love your sashes emblazoned with the *Gloria Dei*."

Morton, in wonder, spoke next saying, "Impeccable tailoring!"

And Norton blew out an appreciative whistle saying, "You guys really know how to accessorize! No offense to you gals up there. What exactly are you? There seems to be some gender-blendering. Not that there's anything wrong with that."

"Off with you to Bethlehem!" said the Angel of the Lord, shooing them off to greet the newborn king. With that, the Angels disappeared, leaving the three brothers to themselves and their sheep.

After a short pause Horton spoke first saying, "That was out of the ordinary."

Morton spoke next saying, "Very much out of the ordinary."

And Norton spoke last saying, "My night vision is ruined now, so we might as well go and see this thing that has been made known to us."

Something Out of the Ordinary

With all due haste Horton, Morton and Norton made their way to the nearby little town of Bethlehem to see this out-of-the-ordinary phenomenon which had been told to them by the angels.

"What are we going to say when we get there? Angels? Are you nuts? They won't believe us. We can't tell them that angels came to us and told us. They'll say Angels? You? What? Were they lost? Did they stop and ask you for directions?"

"We could say that we just happened to be passing by and noticed the gigantic star standing over your stable and being members of the neighborhood watch committee, we decided to have a look-see to make sure that everything was all right."

Arriving in Bethlehem and following the star which clearly marked their way the three brother shepherds stood before the stable which contained the out-of-the-ordinary phenomenon of a child birthed of a young woman.

The Three tried to enter the narrow doorway all at the same time; however this was physically impossible and after a short, 10-minute discussion about who ought to enter first, Horton entered first by virtue of the fact that he had pounded the crap out of the other two as his most forceful argument and also by virtue of the fact that the other two were lying on the ground, having been knocked on their cans during the discussion.

"Hello, is this the Savior we were told about, or should we keep on looking?" inquired Horton politely.

"Baby boy, check. Manger, check. Mary and Joseph, check. It checks out," declared Norton.

"Hey, what say we praise the Lord by doing a traditional shepherd's dance?" suggested Horton.

"Capital idea!" agreed Morton.

"Wait just a dog-gone minute. Shepherds dance?!" said Norton.

"Spring and dance about with abandon, or without abandon, as you please!" said Horton.

"Why wasn't I told?! Did you know that? I would have worn my dancing shoes!" whined Norton.

"Yes," stated Morton flatly.

"Why wasn't I told? Nobody ever tells me anything!" cried Norton.

"We thought it was common knowledge. Everybody knows that shepherds dance, for G-d's sake," said Morton and none too apologetically.

"I didn't know! How was I supposed to know?!" wailed Norton.

"You may not want to parade your ignorance in front of the newborn King and the others. Just follow my lead," said Horton.

So, off danced the shepherds, Horton, Morton and Norton, from the stage of history, happy to have had at least bit parts in one of the greatest dramas ever produced. They, however, would only have the glimmer of an inkling, based on the angels and the fireworks.

Joseph and Mary raised up their son with the usual joys and concerns of any parent. They experienced his first word, which, by the way, was, oddly, *Woman*. They watched him take his first steps at exactly one year from his birth. As baby Jesú suckled at her breast Mary wondered at the words of the Angel Gabriel when he said "So the holy one to be born will be called the Son of G-d."

Her son, Jesú? Son of G-d? This baby? This boy whose diapers need changing? This boy who cried day and night when his teeth came in? Mary's memory went back to the night of Jesus' birth. They were alone so Joseph had to help her birth the child. And then those goofy shepherds came saying they had seen angels, angels of the Lord. They certainly described a vivid and terrifying experience, that if it was anything like what they told, it would have been frightening indeed. If it *didn't* happen at all like they said, it would have been some game they were playing! Shepherds leaving their sheep? Not likely!

But this baby, as soon as he learned to sit up by himself, had begun rocking back and forth as if in prayer. He would do this for hours, contentedly, and sometimes babble away in conversation with some unseen person or personages. Sometimes he would be perfectly silent and at other times he would shriek with joy. But he would always keep his eye on what his mother was doing. As a toddler, he was a mama's boy, no doubt about it.

When he became able to help his father Joseph with his work, he took great interest in wood. He could sit for long periods of time almost lovingly buffing or sanding the things his father made and he could do it in a way that brought out the natural beauty of the wood, showing its grain to best effect.

This capacity for bringing out the best in things or in people was something he seemed to be born with. The other children who played with Jesus just didn't cause any trouble when they were around him. And they didn't behave well in a grudging manner but rather, it was as if they truly wanted to be good when they were around Jesus. Some children you can't leave to themselves for even a minute before there would occur some form of mischief. It was uncanny. Other mothers remarked on this often.

Every mother and father believe their own child to be the greatest gift to the world. Every mother and father are convinced that their own child is precocious, exceptional, and unique - and indeed they are! Mary and Joseph, no less than others, believed that their son, Jesus bar Joseph, was all of that and more - and indeed he was!

Gypsy Boy

Once back in Nazareth, all this goodness was tempered by the whispered slurs of their neighbors. This family's happiness was envied by the neighbors, neighbors who got it in their heads that this family of Joseph, Mary and son Jesus was somehow undeserving.

Even though the neighbors couldn't quite put their fingers on it, something was *different*. Joseph was going to divorce that girl, wasn't he? That's what I heard. For some infidelity? And then apparently, he changes his mind and takes her anyway? Why did he change his mind? Who is the boy's *real* father? So, they go to the census, Bethlehem, I hear, and after that they go to Egypt? A foreign country! No, he wasn't born in Nazareth, but in Bethlehem. What was that all about? And those awful stories about children being killed by Herod! Maybe this boy isn't even the one that Mary birthed! Maybe he's a gypsie!!

Tooth and Yoke

By the age of eight Jesus grew to be a dark-skinned youth and somewhat skinny or wiry and he would horseplay about the house grappling with his brothers (Catholic readers have permission to understand this word 'brothers' as meaning 'cousins.'). But the future John the Baptist, a large, rangy youth himself with exceedingly large hands, gave his cousin more than a scrap. They would often wrestle, first one wrestling as G-d Almighty and the other as Jacob, and switch roles for the next round.

Once, however, the two were engaging in their grappling sport in Joseph's workshop and the two, John holding Jesus in a side-headlock, crashed against the workbench, face-first, and then to the floor. Both came up laughing, but Jesus also came up holding a bloody front tooth and displaying a gash that developed into a scar that he carried throughout his life.

Joseph pretended displeasure and he said sternly, "Two fine young men with so much energy need work to occupy their time. Come, take this yoke; it is ready for my friend in Cana. We will take it there."

The boys eagerly accepted the challenge of the task and the chance to visit another town. They found that lifting the yoke was a chore worthy of them and carrying it was not easy. By the time they reached Cana, the boys were huffing and puffing, sweating and groaning.

When finally, able to set the yoke down before their father's friend and customer, the boys' relief was immense. They both felt light in their bodies after performing their grueling task.

Grilled Cheese Jesus

And, lo, it came to pass one day when the youngster Jesus had reached the age of eight years, two months and 22 days, that Mary, the mother of Jesus, was preparing *pita velvita frita* for Jesus and the other children (Catholics: read 'cousins.') and one portion was left too long on the fire. She snatched it out almost burning her fingers in the process and handed it to Jesus saying, "Be careful you don't burn yourself. It's hot!"

Jesus took the pita gingerly in his fingers and returned thanks, but before he could eat of it, Little Simon, sitting next to him, exclaimed, "Jesú! Look at your pita! There's a picture on it!!"

"Where?" cried Jesus. "I don't see anything." The other children crowded in to see the image.

"Oh," cried Judas and Joses in unison. "It's a face!"

"Heavens to Bethsaida!!" cried James. "The face of a man!"

"What face?! I don't see anything!" said Jesus, keen to be in on the fun of this wonder.

"Oh, I see him!" cried one of the girls. "See, beard, moustache, long hair. His nose is that real dark spot."

But Jesus, frustration showing on his face, said, "I don't know what you're talking about. I don't see anything. It's just spots!"

"It's plain as day," said James with a yawn, already tiring of this because it wasn't his own piece of bread.

"I can't see it!!" said Jesus who was beginning to get angry with himself.

"I think the man is laughing," said Joses.

"Don't play with your food," admonished Mary. "Thank you, Abba, for this bread. Here. Take. Eat. All of you."

Each of the other children took a piece of sandwich and returned thanks, but instead of eating, they all carefully examined both sides of their bread to see if there were any miraculous images on their own pieces.

Jesus lifted his sandwich high up in the light and examined it minutely and from different angles; screwing up his eyes made them water a bit and for a fleeting moment he thought he saw something, but, in the end, he was unable to see what the others saw in the bread.

He hmphed hard through his nose, then held the sandwich right in front of his eyes and slowly moved it away from his eyes, hoping in that way to see the image. Still nothing.

"All of you!" insisted Mary. "Eat!"

Gradually, each child gave up the search for images in their sandwiches and ate.

Mary softly sang a song as the children ate.

"Bread is Life.

Life is Bread.

Abba is Bread to the hungry.

Come to us, oh Abba, as bread for the eating.

May we hunger for You, dear Abba, as we hunger for bread.

May we hunger for Your righteousness as we hunger for bread.

You do mighty things for us, oh Abba, give us our daily bread.

Parting the Jordan River

In the spring of the year both Jesus and John the future Baptist, cousins (cousins, not brothers), had reached the age of eight. The boys wandered far from Nazareth and along the Jordan River just south of the big lake, they decided to play 'Let My People Go' featuring Moses and Pharaoh. Little Johnnie the Baptist as Moses, cried out in a loud, raspy voice, "Let my people go!" spraying spit as he spoke. And Jesus, as hard-hearted Pharaoh, replied in a harsh voice, "You mangy dogs, you slaves! No, no, no! Pharaoh has spoken, so let it be done."

"Well, my G-d will show you something!" shouted Moses, a.k.a. Little Johnnie the Baptist, with flecks of spit flying and he pushed his way past Pharaoh Jesus and marched up to the edge of the river bank.

"On't-Day Are-Day Efy-Day Y-May Ecree-Day! (Don't dare defy my decree!)" shouted Pharaoh Jesus in Pig-Latin to Moses' back. Meanwhile Little Johnnie was facing the water, hands raised just like the real Moses and shouted this command:

Sparkling water, clear and bright
Cleave apart before G-d's might.
Save your people. Set them free
From accursed slavery!

So forcefully did he communicate despite the spitting, that they almost expected that this water should obey his command. As Little Johnnie issued his command, Jesus, in his mind's eye, saw the river parted and, with just the slightest bit of intention he rolled back the waters of the flowing river. Roll, Jordan roll! Had they recovered from their shock at the parted river, they might have crossed to the other bank dry shod.

"Mother of G-d!" gasped Jesus incredulously.

"Holy smoke and hell fire!" spat Little Johnnie.

Mouths agape and eyes wide as pita bread, the boys looked aghast at one another. And Little Johnnie cried wetly, "I didn't do it. I was only pretending!"

Jesus, slipping out of his Pharaoh role, was amazed, learning that he had no small authority even over the physical laws of nature.

The Almighty Father from his throne of glory in Heaven happened to look in on his son and his future prophet at that very moment, and in a flash decided to teach them both a lifetime lesson. So, G-d held the parted waters in place and prevented them from returning to their customary course.

Little Johnnie waved and flexed his arms in a frantic effort to return the waters, but, alas, to no avail. Jesus, concerned that this might mean real trouble, set his child's mind and his child's faith to work, but, again alas, he too, was unable to cause the water to flow again in its riverbed.

Jaws hanging open, both boys blinked hard several times in disbelief. Then Jesus took a cautious step down into the riverbed, but Johnnie stood rooted to his spot on the bank.

"Come on, let's look," encouraged Jesus.

"I can see it from here."

"No, c'mon!"

"No!! My *no* means *no*!!!"

"It'll be okay."

"NO!!!" He said it so strongly that he surprised Jesus and even himself at the strength of his statement. Then Johnnie shamefully admitted, "I am afraid of water."

"There's nothing to be afraid of," said Jesus holding out his hand.

"I c-c-can't," said Johnnie.

"What do you mean, 'you *can't*'?" asked Jesus.

"I can't swim," confessed Johnnie.

"You don't have to swim," said Jesus brightly. "Come on, take my hand."

So, Johnnie, overcoming his feeling of dread, clasped Jesus' hand and timidly stepped off the bank into the riverbed.

Fear soon gave way to healthy curiosity and they gazed at the parted waters and then ventured down into the riverbed to see this wonder at close hand.

They marveled at a school of silvery fish just inside the sparkling blue-green waters of the lake. A turtle with its stubby little legs swam across the downstream side of water.

When they reached the bottom of the riverbed, the Almighty released his grip on the waters. The pure, clean torrent, obeying his laws of nature, rushed downstream in the manner prescribed from the Beginning. And the wild rushing of the water, held back for too long, released its pent-up energy on the boys, tossing them about, throwing them heels overhead. The wave engulfed the boys and held them under the surface for an extended sabbatical.

Under the water Johnnie's little heart began to pump wildly and he saw a terrifying tunnel of burning flames which reached all the way up to heaven.

Out from the heaven end of the tunnel stepped a white lamb and a giant, booming voice said, "Behold the Lamb of G-d, who takes away the sins of the world." As the lamb walked easily and slowly through the tunnel its shape changed to that of a man, a man that was nailed to a cross, crucified in the Roman fashion. The man raised his head with difficulty and looked at Little Johnnie. In his eyes showed all the pain and agony of all the world.

The crucified man then lowered his head, giving his spirit up to G-d, and he died. But out of the tunnel of fire flew a pure, white dove, and the bird flew down and perched on the crossbeam. The dove spoke to Johnnie saying, "Prepare ye the way of the Lord." Then the dove began to grow larger and larger and glowed with increasing intensity to the light of a thousand suns. Reaching down and clutching the man by the arms, the dove flew back through the tunnel of fire. As the dove reached the end of the tunnel, the fire consumed itself and the tunnel vanished.

Then Little Johnnie's head broke the surface of the clean water and a gulp of air found its way to his lungs.

Having managed to maintain their grip on each other by the hand, G-d only knows how, Jesus hauled his cousin out of the rushing waters and collapsed on the riverbank. They both huffed and puffed, sucking in the good air. Johnnie, after sputtering water out of his lungs, gasped out, "I saw a lamb! Under the water! I saw a dove! I saw a man crucified!" Jesus listened to these extraordinary claims and said nothing, which was a very grownup response. Breathlessly, Johnnie tried to explain, "he was a lamb, he was crucified; he was a dove; he looked at me; he told me, 'Prepare the way'."

Still, Jesus said nothing, which upset Johnnie, thinking that his cousin didn't believe him.

"Didn't you see the fire down there?" asked Johnnie, not believing that what he had seen could be missed by anyone with at least half an eye. Jesus just shook his head no. "Don't you believe me?" demanded Little Johnnie.

"I didn't see anything, not even fire."

John harrumphed hard and shook his head in disappointment.

"Wait," said Jesus, trying to recover the situation, "I just had an idea! Next time you go in the water, I've heard that if you wear a camel's hair garment and a leather belt, it will keep you floating, that it acts like a... a... a saver. Camel's hair clothing keeps you floating! But only if you wear a leather belt with it."

"You can keep your camel's hair and leather belt because I'm never going near the water again!" cried Johnnie, and remembering Jesus' words before they stepped into the riverbed, he said in a mocking voice, "*you don't need to swim*! Sheesh!"

That evening, in his prayers before sleeping, Jesus thanked his Abba Father for the valuable lesson he learned that day and, for once, he immediately fell deeply asleep.

And Little Johnnie, in his nightly prayers thanked Almighty G-d for escaping a near brush with death. He also thought of all the things he had seen under the water and he wondered at the phrase, "Prepare ye the way of the Lord." He held those words in his mind like a boy might hold a pretty rock, turning it over and over to examine it from different angles.

And then a light came on in his head. He sat up smartly on his mat and said, "Great balls of fire! Prepare... out of the water... Jordan River... cleansing... a sign of repentance... new life...Prepare ye the way of the Lord, water... fire... water..."

Then in his mind's eye he saw a limitless expanse of watery deep and he feared greatly. Breaking into a cold sweat, Little Johnnie clapped his hand to his forehead in dismay and cried out, "Oh, Lord, no! Not in the water! I'll drown!!!"

The Lord persisted, however, and explained that water was definitely a critical component of Johnnie's vocation.

Johnnie begged on his knees for no water.

But the Lord was insistent and He reminded Little Johnnie of Jesus' advice to wear a camel's hair garment with a leather belt for buoyancy.

This happy thought brought some relief, but still Johnnie was paralyzed by fear, so Abba Father relented and suggested a lovely place on the Jordan River, a site with water and with dry land. This thought assuaged the mounting panic in Johnnie's heart and the word 'saver' also came to his mind bringing comfort as the Lord made straight the path of Little Johnnie's vocation. Abba was also pleased because riverfront properties always command a higher resale price.

Abba Father also waited until this last moment to slip in the clincher. "The long-awaited Messiah is coming!"

"I haven't waited long; I'm only seven," said Johnnie in all innocence.

Abba Father clapped his hand to his forehead in dismay, but said nothing, which was a very grown-up response.

Little Johnnie was very tired when he heard this but he was certain of what he heard. He thought again of the crucified man and his haunted eyes and he thought he saw a familiarity that he should recognize, as if on the tip of his tongue, but he just couldn't make the connection. Despite his exhaustion he slept fitfully with all these ideas and images a swirling maelstrom in his head.

And that is why our Savior, instead of swimming across the lake, was walking on the water on his way to meet his disciples. He had indeed learned a valuable lesson that day: Always swim with a buddy.

Historical note: (Actually, 3 historical notes)

1. Standing close to the Baptist while he was speaking frequently resulted in a thorough wetting of his audience, so much did he spit.
2. Every single survivor of John's baptismal rite attested that they were held under the water long enough to experience a similar revelation as that in the Baptist's childhood. By contrast, those who merely observed his baptismal technique from afar were left with the impression that the flailing arms and kicking feet of those immersed were induced by an overabundance of religious fervor or paroxysms of ecstasy. In any event this flailing and kicking during

baptism eventually gave birth to two sects: the Shakers and the Quakers.

3. John the Baptist caused to have erected signs near the site of his baptismal ministry which were inscribed in three languages, Greek, Latin, and Aramaic, the words: Always swim with a buddy.

So was it done, so let it be written.

Night Terror

Each breathing the breath of life in their own rhythm, all the others of the house were sleeping soundly as people do when the nights are cool and blankets are heavy. Many were curled up next to another, sharing the heat of their bodies. Jesus lay back to back with his mother Mary, but he wasn't sleeping. Despite the warmth of his mother's body, he felt cold and shivered yet again. His eyes were wide open capturing all available light, for light, as is well known, drives out fear. He didn't want to see in his imagination the images that so terrified him. If he were to close his eyes, the images might return, so he thought to keep his eyes open as long as possible, so that if he were to fall asleep, it would be sudden, with no time of closed-eye wakefulness before slipping into the oblivion of sleep.

As usually happened Jesus' mind drifted along and inevitably caught on death. He had seen with his own eyes how the bodies of the dead were quickly prepared, wrapped and laid away inside tombs. The stench from the moldering bodies seared his nostrils and he was only too glad when the stone was rolled back into place across the tomb's entrance and the terrible stench of death dissipated.

In the night many things seemed to move including things that weren't supposed to move. Jesus' hyper-vigilance only served to heighten the apparent danger. The fear that assailed him on most nights was the fear of being assumed dead and then being buried. Buried alive!

Here's how it usually happened. He would be knocked on the head, knocked unconscious. It would be presumed that he was dead. His body would be prepared for burial and he would be laid in a tomb far from the village. When all the mourners had departed he would regain his senses in the cool and dark of the tomb, just like the cool and dark of this night. Macabre corpses with deathly grimaces would mock him. He would be unable to budge the stone covering the entrance to the tomb. And then it would only be a matter of time before he really died, weak, alone and terrified.

A flash of lightning rent the night sky and the thunder's boom cracked. Several of the others awoke, looked around and lay back down. Jesus listened attentively as the first large drops of rain pelted the roof above his head, and presently, with the steady drum of rain sounding in his ears, he drifted into a heavy exhausted sleep.

The Burning Bush

A glorious apprehension or balanced tension had always existed between them. Among other things, he had taught her to read and write. She had taught him to play and relax. And despite the cultural separation of adolescent males and females, the two managed to see each other often.

During this time frame Jesus often prayed and as often found himself distracted by the thought of her. Yet he would return in prayer to his Father and confess "Father, I think I'm in love with her."

And his Father would reply, "Well, that wouldn't surprise me."

"Yes, but... Yes, but this complicates things," said Jesus.

"Complicates?" returned the Lord of Heaven.

"You're not helping!" complained Jesus.

"Did you think you'd be human without being in love?" countered the Lord.

"But what about my wife, I mean, my *life*, my mission?" asked Jesus, correcting his pre-Freudian slip.

"What about it?" asked the Lord.

"I can't even think about anything, especially when she's near me," said Jesus. "I've tried talking to my Mother about it, but she only smiles and sings her praises. What I need is a clear head about this, but..."

"But what?" asked the Father.

"Have you seen her?" asked Jesus.

"Yes, I have," said the Father.

"Do you know if she likes me?" asked Jesus anxiously.

"Yes," replied G-d.

"Yes, she likes me?" asked Jesus.

"Yes, I know whether or not she likes you," replied G-d.

"So, tell me. Spill!" demanded Jesus.

"No," said the Father.

"C'mon, tell me!" begged Jesus.

"No," insisted G-d.

Jesus sighed deeply and said wistfully, "It's like the burning bush: aflame, but not consumed."

Secrets Aborning

Just a short time ago, the young Magdalene saw her father's steward take a furtive look around before entering the storehouse. He came out of the storehouse after only a minute and walked through the courtyard, out the gate and into the road.

Why was the Magdalene watching the steward come and go from the storehouse? She was watching the steward come and go from the storehouse because she was certain that the steward was stealing from her father and for a second, more personal reason, as well.

The second reason was that she had 'developed' a taste for the red drink; a taste with a passion, a taste that spoke to her soul, a taste that had become an obsession. Each day her desire grew. And each day she drank more and more, all the while keeping a wary eye out for the steward. But this day she drank even more than she had intended and she drank it faster than she had intended and the small numbness began to grip the back of her head. Her forehead acquired the feel of a dense woodblock and stopped functioning with the precision that she was accustomed to.

The wine burned in her belly for she hadn't eaten yet that day.Her sense of balance was subdued and she sank wearily onto the bags of wheat stacked in the storehouse. "I'll lie here for just a few minutes," she thought and she closed her eyes as her mind swam in a sea of images, some pleasing and some frightening and some enticing in lurid ways.

She felt out of breath and her stomach began to churn. She rolled onto her side which gave some relief to her stomach.

Suddenly the door to the storehouse opened and the blinding white shaft of light that penetrated her reverie was now blocked by the figure of a man that stepped into the storehouse and closed the door behind him. She tried to shield her eyes with her hand but the bright afternoon sun that briefly illuminated the room now left her with dazzling spots before her eyes and unable to see.

Immediately she felt a hard fist hitting her in the face and then a hand tightly clasped about her throat, causing her to gag. Another hand grabbed her forearm and the man lay down on top of her. She thrashed wildly beneath the man who released his grip on her wrist but he continued to choke her and he again began to hit her in the face. She continued to strain in his grasp but the wine had robbed her strength and she was unable to resist. He tore at her clothing. She couldn't breathe. She lost consciousness for a short time but was brought around by the man's hot breath against her neck and the searing pain in her groin. She felt that he was literally tearing at her most intimate self, as if he had the power to reach into her deepest self to bring ruin. The man's body stiffened and then sagged with release. He seemed to grow angrier and he slugged her more viciously than before. Finally, he got up to a kneeling position and he grabbed her by the back of the neck lifting her face to his and growled like an animal saying into her face that if she spoke a word of this to anyone that he would kill her, that he would tell that she was 'spoiled', that he wasn't the 'first'.

He got to his feet and straightened his robe and warned her maliciously, "Not a word, my little lush!"

Mary feigned illness for the next two days and irritably refused any concern for her. Never had she felt ugly. Never had she felt filthy. She found herself scrubbing and scrubbing but unable to get clean.

Of course, the thought was a mother of the act and the Magdalene plotted and planned from the first to take her revenge. For two years did she seethe with anger. For two years did she endure the repeated depredations of the steward. For two years did the grapes of her wrath ripen into bitter hatred.

When the rotten tree bore its hateful fruit in season, did the knife in her hand dispatch the author of her shame. So cleverly was the deed done that it was impossible to discover by whose hand the steward came to grief. He was buried and soon forgotten by all but the one who felt his last breath in her face.

Only the wine remained constant for her. It comforted her saying, "you only took back what was yours. He took your life and now he has paid for it. Let him rot in hell."

"Rotting in hell," said Mary softly, "but why must I, too, rot in hell."

Throwing Stones (Jesus at 12)

Inside the synagogue the elders were deciding the fate of a woman caught in adultery, caught in *the very act*! There wasn't much discussion.

Outside the synagogue the air buzzed with the tension of dread expectations, solemn and lurid. Jesus was there. Everyone was there. The woman herself sat limply on the ground, softly weeping, enduring the scoffs and taunts bestowed upon her by the good people of Nazareth.

As the Holy Scriptures say, it was "a time for gathering stones", neither too big, nor too small. The boys of Nazareth had begun gathering together stones, assessing each one in the way their ancestor David might have done, considering their heft and likely impact. Those boys who had reached manhood, but were too young to be admitted into the deliberations, were the most fervent gatherers. If they couldn't participate in making the judgment, they would certainly ratify it with their stones.

Thunk! Thunk! Stones crashed into the trunk of the tree as some practiced their aim.

An older boy, with a crooked tooth, grabbed Jesus' hand and filled it with a stone. "Try! Throw at the tree!" he commanded. Jesus stood still. "Throw!" the older boy commanded more loudly, this time loud enough to catch the attention of the others. Jesus hung his head, but even though his eyes were on the ground, he knew that everyone was looking at him to see what he would do.

But before anything else could happen, the elders burst out of the synagogue shouting, "Stone her! Stone her!"

The circle of leering spectators milling around the woman on the ground widened allowing for safety from errant stones. All who had been practicing their aim at the tree now came running, keen not to miss their chance to throw their stones while the woman was still conscious. Hands all around the circle filled with stones. A tense silence fell on the crowd as they stood ready to execute the judgment of the elders. The woman softly sobbed in her last breaths.

The boy with the crooked tooth who had bid Jesus practice his throwing, waved his hand in the air as if taking command, and called out to all, "Throw!" One of the elders took a stone in his hand and hurled it forcefully at the woman and hit her in the shoulder. She began to cry out in pain but her sobs were soon drowned in the exertions of the crowd as stone after stone crashed into her body.

Stones lay all about the woman's body, many of them touched with her blood. The crowd sucked in the air breathing heavily and the boy gave Jesus a shove and demanded, "Throw!" All turned to look at him now.

The boy shouted at him, "Why don't you throw?" Tears formed in Jesus' eyes. The crowd held its breath.

"Oh, do you love her?" mocked the boy.

"You love her! You love the adulteress! You love sinners! Throw, dammit!" Cursing this way in front of the crowd made the boy feel even more like an adult, for no one corrected him.

"Are you a man? Or are you a child?" shouted the boy. The crowd stood waiting for Jesus to say or do something.

"Are you one of us?!" hotly demanded the boy, fairly dancing in rage.

Jesus' knuckles had turned white from his tight grip on the stone. With a defiant gesture he sprung his fingers from around the stone and it fell to the ground.

"You're not a man!" cried the boy and he swung his fist and smashed Jesus across the mouth, drawing blood. Several others among the crowd laughed at this humiliation. One person in the crowd half-heartedly rebuked the boy saying, "That's enough. Leave him alone."

The crowd breathed out a sigh of relief and began to disperse having satisfied itself that its duty had been fulfilled and that G-d's justice reigned in Nazareth.

Jesus stepped over to the woman's body, knelt down and began to remove the stones from the woman's head and face. She was barely alive, struggling to say something important enough to keep her tenaciously grasping at life. Finally, she gathered her last strength and breathed the word, "Pearl." The woman's last connection with the living was through the eyes of Jesus and she desperately needed him to understand her plea before she could go. But it was a desire unfulfilled and she suddenly slipped away, her soul fleeing her body together with her breath.

Presently the woman's relatives came to remove her body. Jesus wept, kneeling at her side, and was pushed away with disdain. A small girl, perhaps three years old, holding the hand of a relative, stared at Jesus as he sat in the dirt, as her family lifted the woman's body out of the stones. The girl turned to watch as the woman was wrapped in a shroud and unceremoniously slung over the shoulder of a large man in the family.

The family walked away, keeping close to each other in their fear and grief. The small girl had turned around and again fixed her gaze on Jesus, trying to comprehend what had happened and what he had to do with her mother's death. But as the group retreated, she had to be pulled along, awkwardly, and with brows knitted in confusion, she still stared at Jesus.

"Come, Pearl," coaxed one of the women.

Finally, she turned and walked away with her family, but not without a backward glance.

Jesus put his hand to his mouth and felt the cut he sustained. He looked at his finger with the blood from his mouth and he wiped it away, but then he noticed some dried blood from removing the rocks from the woman's face, blood covering blood. Did blood always have to be shed to achieve justice? And what had just happened? The sin of adultery. One person stoned to death. The other person unnamed but not unknown. Was this justice? Was Nazareth now a better, safer place? Is this what G-d wanted?

Roll Away the Stone

A large stone, roughly cut and resembling a wheel, stood covering the doorway to the tomb. Jesus and his half-brother James crouched low, found good handholds on the stone, and rolled the stone away from the tomb's mouth. A close relative was to be buried in the family's tomb.

A foul, moldy stench assaulted the nostrils of all present, but especially those closest to the tomb's opening. The stench of death was so strong that Jesus' eyes watered. From inside the tomb a stark, white skull grinned grotesquely at him. Bits of rotten tissue still clung to the bones. As he looked on the earthly remains of Joseph, he had to blink his eyes several times to relate these bones and rotted flesh with his stepfather and when he had remembered all the kindness with which Joseph had raised him, tears of memory replaced his tears of irritation from the stench.

The orbital sockets of Joseph's skull stared at Jesus. Gone were his father's kindly eyes which had always been comforting to the boy as he was growing up. Joseph's eyes had seemed to Jesus to be soulful with mixed joy and melancholy, lit by the wisdom that comes of discipline and obedience to the will of G-d.

The speck. Jesus' memory flashed back to the speck in his eye. Joseph had first told him to stop rubbing his eye. Next, he stood behind the boy and gently tilted his head backwards. Then using his left thumb and forefinger, he held the boy's eye open and he moistened the tip of his right forefinger and spoke as he performed the action. "Your finger needs some moisture on it so that the speck will adhere to your finger... and there it is!"

Joseph released the boy who turned around to inspect the speck proudly displayed on the tip of his father's finger.

"Wow," said Joseph with mock astonishment, "look at the size of that thing! That's no speck, that's a plank!!"

After he had rubbed his eye to relieve the itch of the splinter, they had laughed heartily at his father's comparison of the speck to the plank.

James and Jesus laid their uncle Solomon into the tomb, next to his brother Joseph. Then all the mourners returned to the village.

For some time after they sealed up the tomb, the stench of death clung to Jesus' clothing.

Identity Crisis

"Mom?" said Jesus.

"Yes, my dear," said Mary the Mother of G-d.

"I don't know how to say this, so I'll just come out with it."

"What's on your mind, son?"

There was a long pause as Jesus struggled to put things in just the right way, but settled on this.

"W-Who am I?"

Mary drew in a long breath and released a long sigh before answering. She had always known that this question would be asked at some point. She also knew that the answer wouldn't be simple. She could conceive that the answer might take some time to grow on her son. Mary could state some simple facts from her own perspective that would shed light on the answer, but she also knew that the best answer would come from Jesus' own heart. She knew that the best answers would be like bread - when she adds water to the leavening for bread. The leavening by itself was one thing. The water by itself was an entirely different thing. Both substances were separate and distinct entities.

Yet when they were combined, they created something entirely different – a new entity. This new entity was added to flour and became bread for eating – for life. Bread gave life. Her own son was both water and leavening that would change the nature of flour and that together all three items would combine into bread. This was how she understood her son.

The time had come when the absolute best of her own self-understanding would help her son to understand who he was, but she didn't respond just yet.

"Sometimes, I think I'm going cra-cra."

"What? 'Cra-cra?

"Crazy, Mom." And with a shrug of the shoulders he said, "Everyone knows that."

"I guess your mother isn't as hip as everyone else is."

"Sorry, Mom."

"Continue, please."

"I have thoughts that make me think I'm not who I appear to be. Thoughts that I'm different from everyone else. It's hard to explain because I think I'm like everyone else, but I'm also more – or something - than that. I'm not sure how to put it."

"Can you describe your feelings?"

"Well, I know that G-d is our Father, that... that He's the Father of all.."

"Yes, He is."

"And we are all flesh and blood, sort of unlike Him, but, even more than having a soul, like everyone, I think, I feel that there is something more – much more."

Jesus thought more as he spoke. Just saying the words out loud to his mother seemed to cast a different light on his feelings.

"I know that you've told me stories. Stories about my birth and the shepherds; about staying behind in the Temple to talk about the Law with the Elders; but even more than that, I am learning that I can do things – powerful things, good things, but I don't know where this comes from or what it means. I mean, am I a son of G-d in some special way – in some more or different way from others?"

Just expressing his thoughts aloud to his Mother made him feel better. His Mother seemed to understand everything in a way that other people didn't. He loved his Mother.

Mary gazed lovingly on her son just as she had when he was a baby. And now, before her very eyes, he was growing into a man. Where had the years gone? She thanked G-d in her heart for such a son, much as any other parent who loves their children. She wanted the best for him, but she also carried the notion that this child, her own son, her boy, was destined, or marked out for G-d's plan of saving His people Israel.

It was time to reach into the treasure chest of her memory, to share things with him that would help him grow into the man that G-d wanted him to be.

"On that night, the night I conceived you, an angel came to me and he said that I would bear a son that would be the hope of salvation for G-d's people – all G-d's people."

She paused before continuing. As she looked into his face, she knew that her sensitive boy understood everything so far, and she was determined to go on, knowing that she could trust him with her own, deepest secret.

"You, Jesus bar Joseph, were conceived of G-d's Holy Spirit, blessed be the Name of the Lord." Here she began to sing a song of her very own, a song from her soul and heart, a song for those who love G-d, and a song for the ages.

" My soul doth magnify the Lord,

And my spirit hath rejoiced in G-d my Savior

Because He hath regarded the humility of his handmaid: for behold from henceforth

all generations shall call me blessed.

Because He that is mighty hath done great things to me, and holy is His name.

And His mercy is from generation unto generations to them that fear Him.

He hath shewed might in His arm: He hath scattered the proud in the conceit of their heart.

He hath put down the mighty from their seat, and hath exalted the humble He hath filled the hungry with good things, and the rich he hath sent empty away.

He hath received Israel His servant, being mindful of His mercy.

As He spoke to our fathers; to Abraham and his seed forever."

Jesus recognized in the beauty of his Mother's song that the words spoke truth. The words of the song conveyed to him that she was speaking of a relationship with the Almighty that the prophets of old had longed for, had only hinted at. Here was intimacy of heart with the Ineffable, with the Transcendent Being. Human words were simply not up to the task, and yet, his own Mother knew more than the Lawgiver Moses; she understood more than the prophets; she understood G-d more than the scribes,

Pharisees, and priests; she loved more than even the simplest heart.

Then Mary did one of the most profound things (of course there were many others) in her entire life. She took a piece of bread and said, "Take this and eat."

Jesus received the bread into his hands. He thanked G-d for the bread and for his Mother. He broke the bread and handed a piece to Mary. She gazed into his eyes as he handed it to her. She received the bread back into her hands. A tear dropped from her eye onto the bread. He reached up with his hand and gently wiped away another tear from her eye and he rubbed it onto his own piece of bread. Then they both ate.

A deeper understanding of life illumined both their hearts. Mary realized in a slightly troubling way that bread must be consumed for it to fulfill its purpose. Jesus began to understand that bread must be broken to fulfill G-d's own purpose. As a candle lit in the dark reveals only its immediate surroundings, so this light ignited in his heart a beginning of his purpose. The Almighty, in His wisdom, reveals to women and men not the entire plan but pieces of the plan – enough pieces of the plan to take the next few steps.

Both Jesus and Mary received from G-d some idea of where He was guiding them. Although G-d spoke to them of bread, they knew that He was speaking to them of the paths that they were taking and of their ultimate destinies.

And Jesus said, "Can I have some more? I'm hungry."

PART III

Seven Times Seventy/ The Call of James, Son of Alphaeus

In his mother's womb he was not formed in the usual way. His brain didn't form in the usual way, nor did his hands and feet. Learning to walk had been extraordinarily difficult and when he walked, he resembled a bird with broken wings flapping uselessly and awkwardly. He walked high on the balls of his feet leaning forward and lifting his feet high which only served to strengthen this avian comparison. His eyes drooped and his speech was thick and slow. He was born with the palsy but had managed to survive due to the efforts of his mother who clung fast to the deep conviction that her son was G-d's greatest gift to her, her 'angel-baby'. His father was not able to accept his son and was the first person who looked completely through him; he chose not to see his son and in all practical ways the son became invisible.

For the most part, other people did not see him either. If they gave any thought to him, it was to wonder who had sinned, he or his parents, to be so punished by G-d. A common reaction to this person who looked different and spoke differently was ridicule and mean-spirited mimicry. What they didn't know, was that his heart was also not formed in the usual way, but was exquisitely fashioned by the hand of the Almighty with great sensitivity to the pain of others and near in-sensitivity to his own pain. He was also given an inordinate capacity for love and forgiveness. His mother had given him the name James, son of his father Alphaeus.

There was a time as James grew up that he thought his name was 'Stupid' because he heard the word so often in reference to himself. His mother explained to him that his name was James and that the word 'stupid' was not polite and that he must forgive those who said it. This happened so often that James himself finally understood that this was happening over and over again and he asked his mother, "how many times must I forgive?" His mother's answer was, "Seven times seventy!" For James this was an impossibly large number, but it stuck in his memory and when someone would try to hurt him with their words, James would blurt out, "Seven times seventy!" in his thick and slow manner. Of course, his verbose assailants did not understand his meaning and would leave him alone rather than begin to feel stupid themselves.

In her slow dying days, James' old mother had not objected when he formed a fast friendship with the young Rabbi Jesus, for she knew she was not long for this world and that James must find his way in a largely hostile world. She wished, however, that the Rabbi wouldn't spend so much time with sinners. She was fearful of the way they might treat her angel-baby James. Jesus had come to her one evening and she had earnestly enjoined him to take care of her son, for she had seen at first-hand how cruel people can be to others, especially to those at a disadvantage.

And the Rabbi took her hand in his and assured the old mother saying, "he will be with us and he will be one of us, you can be certain. But I will not call him to take care of him. I will call him because he has so much to teach us, if we will choose to learn from him."

Struggling to push out the words, James' mother said, "Forgive me, Rabbi, I wasn't a very good mother to my son."

"Dear Woman," said Jesus, caressing her cheek with his hand, "you've taught James to love; you've taught James to forgive; and you've taught James to be faithful to the Lord."

At these words tears began to flow from her eyes and peace descended upon her soul. She breathed in deeply and exhaled so completely that Jesus and James thought she had died, but after a long pause she opened her eyes again.

"Is this Heaven?" she asked.

"Our Abba Father will welcome you into Heaven as a good and faithful servant," assured Jesus.

At the very last James' old mother looked upon her son and more tears came to her eyes and she mouthed the words, "I love you," and "Seven times seventy." James took her hand in his and pressed it hard to his chest and eternal mixed with temporal and Heaven and Earth momentarily merged as James' Mother took her leave and shed her body made from the clay of the Earth.

The old woman was buried. James's grief was profound and he cried and cried for his mother, but then, all at once, he stopped grieving and made ready to embark on his life as a disciple of the Rabbi.

James, when presented to the others as a disciple, cried out thick and slow, "Seven times seventy!" and laughed. After a long, awkward moment as the men considered their new member, James cried out, "Seven times seventy," and again he laughed. All that Simon Z was able to mutter in reply was, "Yes, seven times seventy! Big deal. Four hundred...ah...ah... fifty." And to punctuate their understanding, James cried out again, "Seven times seventy!"

Simon Z, at a loss as to how to take this statement, looked to Jesus for an explanation and the Rabbi said "It's something his mother taught him."

Jesus Meets Smokey

Jesus was in prayer telling Abba Father that he'd come to a decision; that he'd soon announce his intention to preach the Good News that the Kingdom of G-d was at hand. Carpentry was out he'd said, but that it was something he could fall back on if things didn't work out.

"I just don't want to burn any bridges," said Jesus, not entirely at ease with his decision, not certain of where it would ultimately lead. He considered asking G-d for a sign, but thought better of it and said, "Well, that's it, I guess."

Said the Almighty, trying to be a good parent, "I will support you fully in your decision." He didn't want to be too pushy with His Son and pressure Him into something that He didn't want to do.

There was a pause while each collected their thoughts and intentions.

Absently rambling, Jesus changed the subject saying, "I've noticed that people frequently take Your word and misunderstand, misquote, misuse, etc., etc. I'm a little bit worried about that."

And Abba Father agreed, "Yes, I know exactly what you mean!"

Jesus asked hesitantly, "How - How do You deal with it?" It's not always easy for a son to ask his father for advice, even if He is the Almighty.

"Well, besides writing it in stone, there's not much you can do about it," lamented Abba Father. "Even then they get confused! Strive for consistency. Repeat, repeat, repeat."

"Yeah," said Jesus pensively.

The Almighty's attention strayed to another matter and both were lost for a time in their separate thoughts.

Coming around again to His Son, Abba Father changed the subject, "I noticed you're spending a lot of time alone, and that's not always so good. I could send you a help meet... someone to love and adore you... someone to always put your needs first... someone to always stand at your side... someone to...."

" So," Jesus broke in, "are You talking about a...?"

And at that moment precisely, for no one's timing was better, Jesus felt a cold, wet something touch his exposed ankle and he jumped five cubits into the air, so startled was he. Upon his return to the ground, the erstwhile carpenter sustained minor scrapes hip and thigh.

The owner of the wet nose had shrunk back fearing that the reaction that he had elicited was of danger to him.

"Holy Moses, you scared the bejeezus out of me!" said Jesus gasping deeply and clutching his hand over his pounding heart. The dog, for the owner of a cold, wet nose must be a dog, began to wag his tail as if he enjoyed his little stunt.

Jesus saw that the dog meant no harm and he held out his hand for the dog to sniff, which he did.

"Where did you come from, boy?" Jesus inquired of his unexpected guest.

The dog did not reply, but merely gazed steadily at Jesus.

"What's your name, boy?" asked Jesus.

The dog was silent.

"You look like a nice dog," offered Jesus.

Still the dog said nothing.

"Cat got your tongue?" asked Jesus somewhat snidely.

The dog cocked his head to the side as if in an effort to understand.

Jesus reached into his sack and pulled out a small piece of bread that he held out to the dog.

The dog approached cautiously, then took the bread and gulped it down in one go.

Jesus reached down to pet the dog, who first sniffed at his hand and then allowed him to pat his head.

Through the succeeding days, the dog continued to show up at Jesus' prayer time and Jesus continued to share his bread with the dog. And Jesus asked the dog, "What is your name, boy?"

With the routine established the dog finally felt confident enough to confide in Jesus that his name was Smokey.

"Oh my chips and shavings," said the former carpenter, "It's not every day that you meet a talking dog!"

And Smokey replied that, as a matter of fact, it *was* an everyday occurrence since all dogs could talk, but that most humans could not understand.

Jesus, impressed with the dog's quick wit, said, "Why don't you stick around with me and let's see if you can learn some new tricks."

But Smokey reversed the proposition and suggested that Jesus might learn some new tricks if he was to hang around with him, like, for instance, how to get acquainted with people by sniffing their butts.

"I'm trying to do things in the conventional human way," was Jesus' polite rebuff to that kind offer.

Smokey persisted, suggesting that Jesus use all of the tools at his disposal.

Jesus didn't respond to that and Smokey just let the matter drop, for the time being.

Smokey came to spend more and more time with Jesus and in his own way he became the most devoted of Jesus' disciples. He seemed to sense Jesus' moods and respond in a manner that was neither over solicitous nor dismissive. He knew instinctively how to lay up against Jesus' back for warmth during the nights. But more than anything and more certainly than any of Jesus' friends and disciples, Smokey had the gift of discernment. He would let out a low growl if anyone with an evil spirit were to pass by, and he felt that it was his duty to keep Jesus informed of this traffic in the land.

When Jesus mentioned to the dog about going to a friend's son Michael wedding in Cana, he coaxed, "Smokey, why don't you come along with me, boy?"

Smokey jumped and turned in circles of excitement at the chance for a road trip but told Jesus that he didn't like being patronized with that 'boy' language. Would he be so kind as to put a cork in it?

Jesus, mindful of the dog's feelings and esteeming him greatly, vowed to clean up his language.

Not to change the subject, but Smokey thought it odd that Jesus was taking his bag of carpenter's tools with him.

"Well, I was taking them just in case this doesn't work out," was Jesus' reply.

It didn't exactly inspire confidence according to Smokey's way of thinking, and he suggested that Jesus take a page from Cortez and burn the ships so there'd be no going back.

"But I don't have any ships," puzzled Jesus.

Smokey pressed his eyes shut tight to keep from making a sarcastic remark, and said that he was speaking figuratively, that the tools represented the ships/tools as a means of returning to carpentry as a way out of difficulties.

"I knew that," insisted Jesus unconvincingly. And then he said, "Well, I can burn the wooden parts, but not the metal parts."

Smokey explained patiently that the gesture was the important thing, and not the fact that metal parts would remain. And he gave Jesus a piece of advice that was to prove incredibly valuable through the trials that lay in the future, for Smokey said that sometimes you have to give up everything before you could move on to new things, that if there be no 'escape' option, then you must go forward.

In the failing light of day Jesus quickly built a small fire and they sat side by side and surrendered the valuable tools one by one into the care of the flames. The smoke issued both sorrow and expectancy, but before the embers had completely died, they fell asleep and in the cold light of morning, the remaining metal parts of the tools looked much like large nails among the ashes of the fire.

After thanking the Almighty for another day, Jesus was anxious to get moving. He longed to embark upon his new life despite his misgivings.

"C'mon, bo... I mean, c'mon... friend," said Jesus, catching himself. "We've got a wedding to go to and I want to get there early." He slung his bag, now lighter without the tools, over his shoulder and took the first step on his journey.

Smokey, ever mindful of potential dangers, admonished Jesus that people do strange things at weddings and that if there was to be any alcohol, then people do *really* strange things.

The Wine at Cana: The Modest Water Saw Its G-d and Blushed[1]

Suggested listening: *Red, Red Wine* by UB40

"Woman, what have I to do with thee? Mine hour is not yet come," said Jesus.

"Don't you 'woman' me!" cried Mary. "A Son of Man must always concern himself with his mother."

The newly-minted Para-Apostle Mortar tasted the wine that the head steward had proclaimed the best wine saved for last and he cried out, "Sacre bleu! (Holy Shit!) Exquisite! Chateau LaTour '61, n'est pas?! (Isn't that right.)"

And the steward, who heard Mortar's identification of the rare vintage, replied, "Oui, monsieur, c'est cela! (Yes, sir. That's it exactly!)"

---

1 Epigrammatum sacrorum liber (1634). Translated by John Dryden from Crashaw's Latin original: "Nympha pudica Deum vidit, et erubuit (The modest Nymph saw the god, and blushed)", *Complete works of Richard Crashaw* (1872), edited by Alexander B. Grosart, vol. 2, p. 96.

The servant who had served Mortar leant over and told him, "Better than that. A few short moments ago it was but water. Monsieur Jesú turned the water into the wine."

"You don't say." said the Mortar.

"Yes, I do say. In vino veritas! (In wine is truth.)" replied the servant.

"But wait! You can't serve it immediately! First, the wine must breathe!" cried Mortar, "And the..." He broke off mid-word when it was obvious that no one was listening to him.

Mortar then worked his way over to where Jesus was sitting and he said, "Jesú, my man, A votre santé. (To your health). And he clinked glasses with Jesus. "If my palate's not mistaken that's a genuine Chateau LaTour '61. How did you do it?"

"Du rien, (it's nothing) Mortar, du rien." said Jesus deprecatingly, "it was a favor to my mother."

"'Du rien', he says. Can you, ah, do this 'nothing' again?" questioned Mortar earnestly, "Maybe a little bit of the bubbly this time, a nice Merlot or even a little aqua vite, or..."

"Say that again." said Jesus quickly.

"Say what, bubbly, Merlot, aquavit?" said Mortar.

"Yes, that. Aqua-vite. The water of life. Water... life. Life water. Life water. *Living* water. My man, you're a genius, I think you're onto something. Let me write that down. Tuck it away for future reference," said Jesus with a thoughtful look. Jesus pulled out his notebook and quickly scribbled a few words and he quickly returned the notebook to his satchel.

"Never mind that!" exclaimed Mortar. "Bigg, I mean B-I-G-G bigg idea! We could open up a little wine bistro and with your 'logistical capabilities', shall we say, we could keep the overhead real low. I do the cooking and you keep the bar! You've got the makings of a great bartender. It'd give you a chance to sharpen your people skills. The rest we can train you for. Maybe we can get Matthew to keep the books for us. Martha can wait tables." Mortar put one arm around Jesus' shoulder and with the other made a wide, sweeping gesture with his other arm as if to conjure in the air an image of this instant dream. "We could call it 'M & J: A Little Wine"

"Whoa, Mortar, slow down." Jesus said, "My head is spinning and it's not the wine! We'll talk about it later. C'mon let's go to the Cigar Club tent. Bring your glass. By the way, did you hear about the man who sat on a grape? It gave out a little whine!"

Words Count

Ahem." The bridegroom from Cana, Michael, cleared his throat awkwardly to announce his presence as he entered the tent where his new bride awaited him. Michael had just been entrusted with the secrets of a happy marriage from the friends of his father in the Cana Cigar Club and he earnestly desired to put that advice into practice from the very beginning of his married life.

Recently discovered texts, among them the Q, have shed light upon the Jewish marriage customs in the early 1st century in Palestine and scholars have pieced together what appears to have been a custom known as 'Words Count'. This custom welcomed newlywed bridegrooms into the ranks of married men and into cigar clubs. Each member of the group or club provided his best marital advice in the fewest words possible.

By the way, in some quarters this text has been taken as decisive proof that Jesus was a married man. (The fact that Jesus frequently went off alone and prayed at length might be even better proof that he was a married man.) How else, they ask, could he have gained entry to the cigar club, a venue in which most men were married. Others take pains to point out that not all members of cigar clubs were married men and that, in and of itself, is not proof that Jesus was married. These comments, however, miss the important point that he smoked cigars.

Jesus, Brick and Mortar, and some of the future disciples gathered themselves to smoke and welcome the new man into their number. After congratulating the young bridegroom and complimenting him on the beauty of his bride, spiritual and otherwise, the men settled themselves down and lit up.

(Translator's note: Research shows that the Messiah usually chose a Churchill in a Maduro wrapper, but the Para-Apostles were wont to change up their choice of smokes. Frequently the men also enjoyed a certain ritual entitled 'Scotch' of which much is known to modern-day scholars and laymen.)

"Well, let's get started," cried Peter, "First of all, Samuel, as the Father of the Bridegroom must provide the prize of a fine cigar for the contest winner at the next meeting of the Cigar Club. As we are sitting in my sumptuously appointed tent, I proclaim myself to be judge and jury, all judgments are final, and remember gentlemen, *Words Count!*"

Ever the impatient adventurer, John, who had even lit up first, held up four fingers to gain everyone's attention and said, "I'd like to go first, to set an impossibly high standard for my comrades with their wagging tongues, and my four words of marital advice are these: 'This too, shall pass!'" Dry laughter followed this dry comment so typical of this dried-up wit. Samuel couldn't refrain from this comment: "Our friend John has become an optimist in his old age! He's lived too long to be a pessimist!" This remark provoked an outburst of mirth.

Bartholomew held up three fingers and waited for silence before he said, "Guard your tongue."

Oohs and aahs of wonderment greeted this sage advice from so august a companion.

"When I guard my tongue, I find it best to keep it in my mouth!" quipped John.

Laughter again broke out among the men.

"That will be very hard to beat," said judge and jury Samuel, "The words of a prophet to profit us all!"

And Jesus added this comment, "Three simple words to guide a man for a lifetime. A simple commandment, but rarely kept." He kept that thought in the back of his mind for future reference.

Simon Zealot grinned in self-satisfied manner and held up two fingers to draw everyone's attention. Eager to pronounce his words, he could barely wait until the men were silent before he ejaculated, "Frequency. Vigor." With his words he gave the young man a matching nudge and wink.

Knowing looks and laughter rocked the tent.

And Samuel protested, "Foul! This contest's object is marital advice, not bowel movements." Again, laughter filled the tent.

But the Carpenter had yet to take his turn and he was becoming known more for his teaching than for his carpentry, more of which later. (No doubt he got plenty of his best material from his Cigar Club friends.) And so, it was with some trepidation that our short-winded gents looked to the Carpenter to see if he might come up with a one-word zinger.

To their dismay, the Carpenter Jesus held up just one finger and when everyone's attention was riveted and straining to hear, he said in a whisper, "Listen…" And he paused for so long and so confidently that some thought that 'listen' was his one word of advice, but after the long, long pause he continued loudly, "to all of these men except for John. His advice may hold good on most occasions, but not today, which even he will admit. But especially pay heed to our brother Bartholomew. Guard your words well for verily they do come out of the heart and go into the heart. And three cheers, or rather two cheers, for frequency and vigor! Sorry, far too many words from me."

Judge and jury Peter, proclaimed Simon Zealot, with his two words 'frequency' and 'vigor', to be the winner of the contest and the fine cigar.

Now the young man Michael, of high intellect and true heart, or true heart and high intellect, treasured the pearls of wisdom that he was given by the men of the Cigar Club. He understood that life can be short, that 'this, too, shall pass'; it reminded him to always 'listen' to his bride, and in speaking to her to 'guard his tongue' to ensure the 'frequency' and the 'vigor' in their love, and he vowed to himself to always remember that *Words Count.*

The Magdalene and the 7 Demons

Suggested listening: *Bottle of Wine* by the Fireballs

Freely flowed the wine at the wedding in Cana. There is evidence to suggest that not only did Jesus change water into wine, but that upon Mortar's suggestion, he also changed water into the champagne used to toast the bride and groom and even into Grand Marnier that was imbibed only in the cigar tent. The guests had the added stimulus of rumors swirling about the Carpenter/Rabbi who had just moved from Nazareth to Capernaum. He was going to make a big announcement. What could it be? It was the event of the season! It has come to be one of the most talked about weddings ever, as well it should be, because of the immense importance that... well, I'm getting ahead of the story.

As the young bridegroom at Cana, Michael, ran out of the tent where the Cigar Club was wrapping up their session, he bumped squarely into Mary, "the Magdalene", who was carrying a glass of wine in either hand.

(People called her "the Magdalene" employing the article 'the' because she had no real friends that might call her Mary.)

By some miracle she managed to fall flat and heavily, but without spilling a drop of the wine. She was drunk as a Phoenician sailor. Her garment came slightly undone in an immodest posture, but she didn't notice that.

"You shonofabitch!!! 'ook wha chu did!" she screeched, the wine having made her more the enraged lioness than usual.

Michael helped her to her unsteady feet and copiously begged pardon. All the while she heaped on him the vilest forms of abuse, so her words related in this passage might be characterized as kind by way of comparison. "Nex-sht time watsch where you're going! Shonofabitch! I hate weddings!!"

Michael quickly departed to his bride's tent, very much in a hurry to..., well, never mind.

Smokey had gotten to his feet and exited the tent when he heard the commotion outside. He noticed what Michael in his hurry and the Magdalene herself hadn't noticed: that her robe had bunched up in a funny way that completely exposed her derriere. Smokey interpreted this as a cordial gesture of friendship and politely poked his cold, wet nose between her cheeks and sniffed.

Now the wine was launched into the air. When the Magdalene had finished screaming and returned to the ground she saw Smokey cringing from the reaction he had so innocently provoked. She clumsily got to her feet as she cursed, "Shtupid dog! You shpilled my wine!!!" and then she growled and snarled at the poor beast. But she lost interest when she remembered what she came for.

She turned drunkenly around, a complete circle, before reorienting herself outside the entrance to the Cigar Club's tent, and called out, "Jezhus! Je-e-zhus! I know you're in there."

Hands on hips she waited, oh, three seconds, before she decided to go in after him. She might have just as brazenly entered the Holy of Holies in Jerusalem's Temple. At first, she couldn't see, what with the low light and the fog of cigar smoke lazing in the air. But as her bleary eyes adjusted to the light she saw on the men's faces that by stepping across the threshold of this tent she had committed a faux pas of the first magnitude, which didn't displease her.

Peter, Simon Zealot, Samuel, Bartholomew stared at her, simply stared. How dare a woman, any woman, even this woman, violate the sanctity of the Cigar Club?! Always quick thinking, the Magdalene straightened up and stood defiantly in the middle of the tent. "Give me a chigar! And a drink!" she demanded.

(Some historians maintain that this incident marked the beginning of Peter's animosity for the Magdalene.)

Jesus jumped to his feet but before he could speak, Brick broke this impossible indignity by saying, "Mary the Magdalene, would you please sit next to me and I'll get you a cigar." This courtesy shown her in one of her worst moments would be ever remembered by the Magdalene.

"At leash there's one gentleman in thish group." The words sloshed out of her mouth.

Brick, with a flourish, furnished her with a small and slender cigar appropriately feminine, which he lit for her and then passed to her. The Magdalene took it awkwardly between her thumb and forefinger nearly dropping it, and started puffing away, proud that she had regained her poise and imposed her will.

The men remained silent, except Brick who in an effort to break the ice politely said, "Nice wedding."

"I hate..." and here a belch escaped her lips before she continued, "I hage, I mean I *hate* weddings. Wha' were you talking about? In here. Wish all this smoke," she demanded, waving her arm in front of her before slumping forward. The folds of her dress hung loose nearly exposing her breasts. The men averted their eyes and said nothing. Jesus hung his head and clapped his hand over his brow in resignation and sighed deeply in exasperation.

Picking up her head, the Magdalene looked around contemptuously into the men's faces and said viciously "Jezhus, I don't know why you shpend any time with these worthless shits!" And she looked to each of them spitefully, defiantly, and then inhaled deeply on the cigar and blew a long spout of smoke before her head fell again to her chest.

Jesus got to his feet again and said wearily, "Mary, why don't I escort you to your house."

"Yeah, this wedding sucks anyway and I'm getting dizzhy. Jezhus, I wanna go home, take me home. Now!" she demanded drunkenly.

The Carpenter said politely to the men, "If you'll excuse the both of us, it's getting rather late, or should I say early, and we have to be going."

He helped her to her feet which nearly gave way. "I'm alright. Don't tousch me. I shaid don't tousch me! I can get up by myshelf. I want to get away from theshe limp dicks," she scoffed. Just before leaving the tent she turned to the men one final time and pointed her finger rigidly in the air, and then slowly curled her finger down and then she laughed wickedly as she groped her way out of the tent.

Outside it was a beautiful night, warm and starlit and infinite with possibilities. The Milky Way was a brilliant white sash across the velvet fabric of black space, the heavens glorious in formal attire for the wedding.

"I don't feel sho good," said the Magdalene weakly as Jesus helped her along. She was, however, exceedingly and bitterly drunk and she slipped and fell to the ground on her butt, legs splayed apart. "I'll just shit down and resht for a minute, jusht for a minute."

There are those moments when a surfeit of alcohol can actually produce lucid thoughts, when truth is exposed, the heart laid open. The problem here is that such drunkenness also leaves no memory of the piercing clarity and so is lost, unless a sober friend is there to witness it.

One of those moments was now granted to the Magdalene and, indeed, the truth spilled out of her own mouth, "I hate this fucking place. I hate my fucking life. I hate what I do and I hate what I don't do. I hate everyone. I hate my fucking self. I hate, I hate, I hate..." She slipped into a babbling state, only clearly enunciating the curses that poured out of her mouth.

Jesus picked her up bodily, held her around the waist, and as he did so, torrents of sour smelling vomit began to issue from her mouth. Her body was racked with spasms, expelling the wine and all the fear and hate, all the bitterness, restlessness, the insecurity, the rancor and savageness that had taken root in her heart.

Somehow, he produced a gourd of water for her to drink, which she grabbed with both hands and gulped down greedily. It washed away the worst of the awful taste in her mouth.

He carried her to a place under a nearby olive tree and he sat down on the ground against a rock and held the Magdalene in his arms. She smelled of vomit and had passed out.

Jesus held his hand on her forehead and prayed, commanding the seven demons to depart from her and not to return. Jesus' body tensed with effort and concentration and he commanded, "Get out and stay out." The seven demons obeyed grudgingly, kicking and screaming as they went, convulsing the Magdalene's body. Spit dribbled from her mouth and her breath came in gasps that made her whole body heave.

And there came over him a temporary respite of melancholy resignation, a powerlessness wherein every tension is relaxed, every anxiety is relieved, and every concern is relinquished. In this state with his Magdalene in his arms, he too slept deeply.

The burnished gold of dawn found her in Jesus' arms. Instead of a severe headache and the old familiar hates and fears gnawing at her insides, the Magdalene opened her eyes afresh in the bliss of new freedom and peace, her head against his chest. Immediately she sensed that something had changed. What, she didn't know yet, but everything she saw was fresh and new.

And she remembered the reason that she went into the Cigar Club's tent and asked, "You made some announcement last night? Are you going to marry me?"

"Well, no. I said that I was giving up carpentry," said Jesus.

"Giving up carpentry? And nothing else? Nothing about us? Nothing about me?" she asked.

Jesus replied to her, "I'm going to see my cousin John the Baptist and then I must go to the desert for a time of proving. Wait for me and pray."

She watched him head down the road toward the south side of the lake – to the Jordan River. It seemed that he was carrying all her hopes and dreams away with him. Smokey had run along after him, but walking a respectful distance behind.

The Magdalene's Clarity

Suggested listening: *I Can See Clearly Now* by Johnny Nash

Jesus headed down the road to the desert and now, for the first time in a long time, in fact, the Magdalene couldn't remember when, last, she had a clear head with which to think, and she undertook a mental inventory of her situation. Her head now was as clear as a cold, gray dawn in the desert, no shimmering to blur the landscape, no wine to blur her outlook.

Back in her home, she poured herself a cup of wine merely out of morning routine, but she let it sit and she watched it. She grew thirsty. The red liquid shimmered and beckoned, shyly yet coyly, making promises and cooing with all the passion of a lover and the Magdalene longed to drink.

"Come, Mary," said the wine, which, as a courtesy, called her by her name. "We've spent so much time together, you and I. We belong together. I promise this time will be different. I have what you want."

With sobriety simply handed her, the Magdalene felt a sadness in receiving something for which she hadn't worked or earned. She didn't feel worthy of it and the wine mocked her, demanding, "where's your self-respect? Do you think you can trust that carpenter friend of yours? That's why he's gone to the desert! I'm all you've got left." The wine began to storm in the cup, to viciously berate her, "You worthless bitch! You're nothing! Remember the steward? He knew what you are. Jesus doesn't want you. If you were a woman worth your bride price, he would stay with you and he would love you." The voice of the wine suddenly changed pitch and murmured softly, "but I won't leave you. I'll always be here for you. I'll wait until you are strong enough to drink again."

Prickly sweat broke from her brow and her hands twitched slightly before starting to shake. Nausea gripped her stomach. Her muscles tensed. She raked her fingers through her hair to scratch out the confusion in her mind. The Magdalene let her head sink into her hand and she rubbed her forehead. Although it seemed ages ago, she was certain that last night the demons had left her and now she decided that she must leave her demons.

And then she had that awful feeling, that same awful feeling from so long ago in her father's storehouse and how her father's steward, curse him, had stolen so much more from her than material wealth. Her stomach fell inside her to the depths where this horror lay hidden, surfacing when she summoned it for examination and sometimes just bursting out of her. Her head began to spin just like that day her head had spun. The pit in her stomach was still just as deep as always. The nausea was just as severe.

She began to hiccup nearly belching at every hic. They became so violent that now she nearly vomited every time.

(hic)

G-d, grant us the...

(hic)

Serenity to accept things we cannot change,

(hic)

Courage to change the things we can, and the

(hic)

Wisdom to know the difference

(hic)

Patience for the things that take time

(hic)

Appreciation for all that we have, and

(hic)

Tolerance for those with different struggles

(hic)

Freedom to live beyond the limitations of our past ways, the

(hic)

Ability to feel your love for us and our love for each other and the

(hic)

Strength to get up and try again even when we feel it is hopeless.

(hic)

She dashed the cup of wine to the floor and strode with purpose out the door. She would not return to the oblivion of drunkenness. She would not return to her numbing wealth. If he was giving up all that he possessed, then so would she.

She was as good as any man, and we know for a fact, as good as any that he chose to become his disciples.

Where was she going? She knew that she could not simply sit and expect her life to be different. She knew that she wasn't happy with the way things were. She knew that it was time to move. But she didn't know where she was going. And she didn't know what she'd do. So, she followed Jesus and he was headed into the desert.

So, You Want to Be a Rabbi

Suggested listening: *Sympathy for the Devil*
by the Rolling Stones

Far in the shimmering distance of the desert rose a great cloud of dust. Jesus sat in the heat and the glare, sweating and praying fervently as one in a trance. Smokey, lying on his side in the shade of a large rock, gathered his feet beneath himself and crouched, waiting for this, whatever it was, to make its entrance. First his right ear cocked and then his left as he weighed the potentialities. Jesus didn't look up; he knew who it was.

The dust obscured the top-heavy figure which swayed back and forth. It was quite close before it was distinguishable. An elephant? By G-d, an elephant! A gigantic elephant! It was rather fearsome to Smokey, who hadn't the luxury of having seen one in a zoo or even in books before this encounter.

The behemoth itself featured a howdah, or passenger box atop its broad back, which was fancifully decorated with gilt curlicues and doodads.

The dingle balls on the canopy shook with each prodigious step of the behemoth. A matched set of four, grey feet pounded ploddingly throwing up clouds of dust, but sitting up top in the howdah, the recumbent Passenger rode in relative comfort, with two bronze-skinned beauties, twins in fact, who fanned him with broad leaves of palm and attended his every whim. He was sipping a gin and tonic garnished with a freshly cut slice of lime speared through with a small, pink umbrella.

Sitting astride the neck of the gargantuan beast and driving him, sat a small, but fearsome looking monkey of a man, who served as both mahout and bodyguard.

The entire equipage came to a halt in front of the Son of Man.

Monkey man nimbly slipped to the ground and then assisted the Passenger and the bronze-skinned beauties to dismount the elephant.

"Nice ride," commented Jesus wryly, but he smiled for there was a certain panache required to make one's entrance astride a beast of burden.

"So, what's this I hear about you giving up carpentry?" Lucifer smirked slightly and gave a wink to no one in particular as if to say that he was in on the joke. "At least you'll have something to fall back on!"

Smokey got to his feet and went sniffing about Monkey man, the women, the elephant and finally Lucifer. Upon catching the scent of this entity, he gave out a low growl. Lucifer absently kicked at the dog to shoo him away.

"How can I help you today?" Jesus remained polite and tried to avoid Lucifer's bantering tone, because in spite of himself, he did enjoy a give-and-take discussion.

"Well, first, a small matter. I had something. Now I find it gone. And I think you have it, er, her, to be exacting..." said Lucifer evasively.

"If it's gone, how could you find it? It? Her? Maybe you could express yourself more clearly," said Jesus.

"Why, it's the Magdalene. You've 'evicted' some friends of mine and now she's gone her own way," said Lucifer. "I want her back." He added parenthetically that a guy could father some children with that woman, if you catch my drift. If I were human, that's what I'd be doing. Maybe that's what you should be doing.

"Anyway, I'll offer you these two in trade for the Magdalene," he said indicating the twin bronze-skinned beauties.

"You can't go around trafficking in people," said Jesus reprovingly.

"Isn't that what you do?" retorted Lucifer.

"I tell them the truth and I give them their freedom," said Jesus.

"And, I suppose," said Lucifer, "You're all agog over truth and freedom, or some such, like truth equals freedom." He dismissed the idea with a wave of his hand.

"Truth equals freedom," said Jesus thoughtfully, "I like that."

Smokey had taken up a stance behind Lucifer, lifted his leg and urinated on the back of his legs.

"Damn your dog!" Lucifer cried, lifting first one then the other foot out of the urine that rapidly soaked into the desert sands. He swung his cane, a bull's pizzle, at the dog, but Smokey was too quick and scampered away

"He's not my dog. Smokey is my colleague. He cherishes his freedom," said Jesus evenly. He reached up to his mouth and gently fingered the scar at the side of his mouth, remembering that just such a cane had caused his scar.

Lucifer looked around at the bleak surroundings and commented, "Tres non civilisé, so to speak." And he conjured a small table with an umbrella and a chair for himself. He sat down, settling himself comfortably in the shade of the umbrella. A fresh drink appeared on the table. The women flanked him on either side to fan him.

And Lucifer turned to him and said, "So, you want to be a rabbi. That's a very noble calling. I hold clergy of all stripes in very high regard indeed. And if it doesn't work out, you can always fall back on the carpentry." Lucifer tried his line a second time without success and he looked to Jesus for some kind of reaction. Getting none, he continued.

"You know it takes a lifetime of study. But you're not afraid of that. I've watched you growing up. No, you're certainly not afraid of that," said Lucifer in a toadying fashion.

And from Jesus no reaction was forthcoming.

But Lucifer grew impatient. His time was beginning to seem to him unprofitably spent.

"There's just one aspect of your 'rabbi plan' that doesn't sit well with me, and when I point it out to you, I think you'll find that you probably agree with me. I'm not sure how to put it, so I'll try to be delicate." He paused to let that sink in.

"It's just that it seems to me, and maybe I'm the one who's wrong here, but, well, one rabbi is just like another. There! I've said it. It's not so bad, really, is it? There really isn't much to distinguish one rabbi from another. You've seen one, you've seen them all. What will you do or say to distinguish yourself from all those other rabbis?"

Lucifer wanted to pause again to give Jesus time to consider before he continued, but his impatience got the better of him.

"How many towns are there in the Galilee? 100 or so? 100 rabbis or so? And they're all the same! Ask the same question of any of them and you'll get the same answer from all of them. More or less. More than likely, one just like another. Wouldn't it be something if you were different from the rest? If you, say, had something truly novel to say and not just a twist or a variation on a theme? Because when you get down to it, I know what you're going to say." And again, the devil tried to pause for a reaction and again Jesus did not rise to the bait.

"Well, then, let me humbly offer a few suggestions." continued Lucifer. "You're going to tell people that they must love G-d and that they must love each other. I've heard it all before. It's no big deal. It's nothing new. It's not *original.*" Lucifer's patience was becoming a bit frayed. This silent treatment from Jesus wasn't what he had expected or wanted. He had expected and wanted a spirited debate or a lively discussion on the merits of what Jesus thought would be his new and exciting offering. This was tedious and upsetting. "Don't you want to tell me about the Golden Rule? Love your enemies? You're just recycling messages of past prophets. Why can't you give me some new and original material to work with?!" Lucifer's voice was gaining in volume, but Jesus remained quiet. "Why don't you fight back? Are you so weak? Are you so meek? Can't you rise to the occasion?" Now Lucifer was losing his patience. He was indeed running out of time because Jesus wouldn't be fasting forever. "You'll have to come up with something much better than this. Something original, something new, something... Don't you want to be different from all the rest? Don't you want to be better than that whole mediocre lot? They're nothing!! But you, you've got talent! You've got that certain 'je ne sais pas'. You have to use it. You won't let it go to waste!!" Lucifer looked frantically around and saw nothing. Jesus was still sitting with his head down. Lucifer took a deep breath and tried to calm himself, to regain his composure. He rubbed his chin and offered with a conciliatory spirit, "We could work in tandem, you and I. Like a team of oxen yoked together plowing the same field."

This caught Jesus' attention and he looked up. Lucifer was caught slightly unaware that his ploy had worked and he hastened to follow up his initiative by saying, "Yes, that's it, we could work together. I could.... we... I meant to say 'we'... even work with the same personnel. In fact, that Judas fellow seems very talented. He could be of some use to me, er, us."

"But I'm getting off on a tangent. You're the one I want to talk about. You're the brains of the outfit. You know, whatever your message, and that's not my main concern, really it isn't, you're going to have to make the move to the big leagues. You're going to have to turn pro. I'm talking Jerusalem! I'm talkin' High priest! You've got what it takes, but you need a little guidance. No one makes it in any religious hierarchy without a little help from his friends, so to speak, without a little help from me. And you're no exception."

"Jerusalem," repeated Jesus thoughtfully.

Every lie contains some particle of truth, so they say, and Lucifer was right about one thing: Jesus would eventually have to go up to Jerusalem.

Changing the subject, Lucifer returned his to his original point of concern, the repossession of property.

"Well, if it's all the same to you, I'll retake possession of the Magdalene..." the devil trailed off hoping that his attempt at recovery would slide by unnoticed, but Smokey garnered the attention of both Jesus and Lucifer with a sharp bark.

"You are to keep your claws off my friend Mary," demanded Jesus sternly.

"Your *friend* Mary?" mocked Lucifer. "Not even for these two incredibly beautiful, eager, more than *friendly*...."

His ingratiating tone and implications were more than Jesus could stand, but before either of them could say anything more, the dynamic of the interview underwent a change, brought about by the approach of another.

The Desert Gets Crowded

It would be wrong to say that Jesus and Lucifer concluded any business, having hashed out the details of an agreement, but their 'interview' had reached an impasse and there was nothing more to be gained when Smokey issued a sharp warning bark as the Magdalene appeared through the heat and glare of the desert.

"Well, speak of the devil! It's the She-Bitch in person!" scowled Lucifer as the Magdalene approached. "We were just talking about you. In none but glowing terms, I might add."

"Mary, what are you doing out here?" asked Jesus.

"I must go where my Lord goes. I must drink the cup that my Lord drinks," said the Magdalene solemnly.

"Oh, isn't that delicious," said Lucifer mockingly. "...must drink the cup...yes... you know your cups, don't you? A-ha, a-ha!"

"Lucifer, shut up!" demanded Jesus.

"Touchy subject? I've seen this before. The Magdalene will display great resolve and talk the talk for a few days but then the desire will gradually reassert itself and then she'll take 'just one small cup of wine' because she can 'control' it now."

Now Lucifer turned to address the Magdalene directly, "How many times have you quit drinking in the past? It's more than you or I can count. It's practically a habit! A habit of quitting!"

"Lucifer! Enough! Torment Mary no more! Be gone!" commanded Jesus and in a whirlwind, the elephant and howdah, twins and Berzerker the Mahout, and Lucifer himself vanished, leaving much more expeditiously than when they came.

Jesus turned to the Magdalene, who had fallen to her knees on the rocks and sand of the desert and began to weep bitterly, and he said, "It doesn't always have to turn out like that. Let your weakness be your strength in the Lord of All."

"I don't understand," she sobbed. Her tears fell to the ground and were immediately gobbled up by the thirsty desert.

"Learn to trust in the Lord. He cares for the sparrow. How much more does He love and care for you?! And I. I will be with you, too," said Jesus.

Not much more time was spent in the desert. Jesus had 'considered' and rejected various alternative approaches to his work of proclaiming the nearness of the Kingdom of G-d. Both Jesus and the Magdalene would continue their journeys in faith for the foreseeable future.

Jesus and John the Baptist

Ever since the parting of the Jordan River, John the Baptist had been fascinated by fire. It wasn't often that he needed to have a fire. His diet of locusts and honey didn't require any cooking and the place where he "resided" – you can't really say that he "lived" somewhere –was merely a matted spot down by the Jordan River. It was the very spot where years earlier he had seen the Messiah in a vision under the water. Vision may not be the right word.

At night he would crawl in among the reeds and lie down to sleep, usually in the same spot as the night before but sometimes not. There was no house, or shack, or shelter. The main thing for him was to be out of the wind. And speaking of the wind, it rivaled John's eloquence, often carrying away his words more surely than his audience.

As night fell John and Jesus sat on the riverbank by a small fire that Jesus had built. John kept poking into the fire with small sticks and twigs and when they would catch fire he'd hold the stick up and stare with wonder at the small yellow flames. He would turn the stick this way, and now that way, to see how the little magic yellow flags would respond. More than once he nearly burned his fingertips for holding a burning stick too long.

He sometimes lapsed into a sort of trance and affecting a deep, booming voice, the way G-d speaks, he'd say, "I-I-I am that I am-m-m-m. T-T-Take your shoes off-f-f-f. Th-th-th-is is Holy-Holy-Holy Ground-d-d-d." But now, not entranced, he said, "You are the Anointed One of G-d."

Jesus rolled his eyes and suppressed a smirk, and then he said, "I wish G-d would always speak clearly like that."

"He does," asserted John the Baptist.

That comment raised Jesus' eyebrows and he said, "That's not been my experience. How do you know who the Messiah is?"

"Let my people go!" said John the Baptist, cupping his hands around his mouth to more closely resemble the voice of the Almighty, calling to mind their childhood game. He scratched his head, but he wasn't thinking because, according to him, faith and belief weren't things that you had to think about. They were certainties in his life. His own mission had been a certainty from his youth. So, playing his cousin's game, he replied with a question, "How did you know that you should be baptized by me?"

"I will answer your question when you have answered mine," said Jesus, "who told you to start baptizing in the first place?"

"Who told you to start healing?" retorted John.

John was absolutely confident that he was doing just what G-d wanted him to be doing, and when his cousin Jesus was around, he felt even more certain in reaction to Jesus' apparent uncertainty. All this he couldn't put into words and instead he said, "I'm older than you."

"G-d frequently chooses the younger for reasons that aren't always clear at the time," said Jesus.

"The mission G-d has given me is crystal clear: make a highway through the desert straight for the Messiah. 'Prepare ye the way of the Lord." He gave a wide sweep of the arm as he spoke as if brushing away any obstacle that might bar the way. "And here's the bottom line: I saw you under the water."

"What?" asked Jesus.

"Remember when we were kids and parted the river?" asked John. "Well, I nearly drowned that day, but I saw the Messiah and now I see clearly who he is."

"How can you be so certain? I didn't see anything that day." asked Jesus, truly puzzled.

"How can you doubt?" said John, shaking his head in reproach.

"G-d seems to be more evasive when I ask Him what I should do. He moves in mysterious ways, you know," said Jesus.

"No, there's nothing mysterious about it. Men know exactly what they must do for G-d, and if they don't understand, send them to me and I will help them sort things out," said John with complete confidence.

"Do you know what the Messiah should do?" asked Jesus.

"He should save his people from sin... and the Romans! That's an easy question," scoffed John the Baptist.

"I thought only married men are so certain," said Jesus.

"Maybe you're not *really* listening. Maybe in your very, very heart of hearts, and I mean your really, really, *really* deep self, maybe, just maybe, sin crouches at your door. Maybe sin stands at the door and knocks waiting to be let in." John was unbelievably sincere and earnest.

"I doubt that I've sinned," insisted Jesus.

"Maybe you've blasphemed the Holy Spirit!" cried John aghast at the thought.

"I've always wanted to know what that means. Do you know?" asked Jesus

"No. No one knows," said John.

"Then, how can I do it if I don't even know what it is?" said Jesus in frustration.

"Then go and sell all you have and give the money to the poor," said John triumphantly.

"There's a thought," said Jesus. "It couldn't hurt to try, but it's not going to be very much."

"It's hard to give all for anyone. And just when we think we've given all, we find something that we've kept back. Oh, and by the way, don't tell anyone. Your Father who sees everything will know and you will have great treasure in Heaven." John enjoyed getting in the last word; it reconfirmed for him his status as the elder cousin.

Jesus watched as John poked another small stick into the dying embers and several yellow bits of flame rose up. The reeds along the river rustled in the breeze that had come up. Night had fallen without a moon and except for the embers of the fire, it couldn't have been darker.

Literal or Figurative Language?

Blood streamed down between the man's fingers - the hand he held to his face and he was obviously in pain. He clutched something carefully in his other hand.

He was asking for the Rabbi, and people pointed in the general direction of the shore, and he ran up to one of the men right at the shore and he fell to his knees before him and his story spilt out of him like water from a gourd.

"Oh, Rabbi Jesus, I plucked out my eye. And then I smashed it. The hole really hurts.

I was just doing what you said, 'If thine eye offend thee, pluck it out for it is better to go to heaven without one eye than to go to hell with two eyes.' I looked at women with lust in my heart, but the eye is easier to get at than the heart. And I suppose if I had plucked out my heart I'd be dead. Oh, G-d, what have I done? Wait. You're not him."

"There is a certain logic there, but, you're right. I'm Judas, Judas Iscariot, not the 'Ramblin' Rabbi' Jesus. He's over there, by the fire, eating. Probably not going to have much of an appetite after he sees you." said Judas.

The man scrambled again to his feet and ran over to Jesus and fell to his knees before him.

"Oh, Rabbi Jesus, I plucked out my eye. And then I smashed it...."

"Yes, yes, I heard what you said over there." said Jesus. "We'd better get right to it. What do you want me to do? You've extracted and smashed your eye, I believe you said?"

The man held out his hand with the pitiful eye looking sad and smashed with grains of sand and dirt stuck to it and blood all over. Reconstructive surgery seemed out of the question. Only a miracle would suffice. "I see." said Jesus, "Oh, sorry, but how incredibly Oedipal!"

Jesus looked at the mangled eye in the man's palm and then up to the eye still in place in the face of the man, and he said very earnestly, "First of all, don't do *anything* to cause injury to your remaining eye, no matter what I say! Take my meaning quite literally *this* time."

"Well, ok, but I did it because you said if 'your eye offends thee, pluck it out!'" said the man slightly offended.

"Don't you see, oh, sorry, but if everyone who heard that took it literally, a good portion of them would be blind if they had courage like yours. But do you think there might be a deeper meaning to my words?" asked Jesus, a bit exasperated.

"Well, I suppose." the man stubbornly admitted, "but why'd G-d make so many pretty women *and* give us eyes? Ain't it sort of inevitable that men, being the way we are, are going to lust? Ducks swim. You might as well tell the moon not to shine."

"Now you want to blame G-d for beautiful women?" asked Jesus. "G-d gave us eyes and He *gave,* so to speak, us beautiful women because He has faith in us." Jesus said.

"I don't get it." said the man, "and can you, are you going to do 'something'?"

"Yes, of course, I am." and as Jesus spoke the man already began to feel less pain. "Look at it this way – oh, sorry again – G-d gives us a world full of beauty and ways to enjoy it. And He trusts us to enjoy it in ways that are respectful of others. It's simple, really." said Jesus. "Here's what I hoped that you might have learned from my words: Remove," said Jesus making quotation marks with His fingers, " *fig-u-r-a-tive-ly spea-king,* from your hearts or eyes that which causes you to treat others disrespectfully."

"Oh. I see," said the one-eyed man, reluctantly admitting that his own wisdom was apparently not of the highest order.

"Here, the least I can do is to stop the bleeding and relieve the pain." Jesus touched his face and the man was healed.

Calling over his shoulder, "Hey, Susanna, could you help us here. This gentleman could use an eye patch." And turning back to the man, Jesus asked, "What's your name?"

"Thaddeus" replied the man, "Jude Thaddeus." He offered his hand to Jesus, the hand not holding the eye. They shook hands. "Guess I won't be needing this anymore." he said. He turned and threw the smashed eyeball into the lake.

Judas, standing nearby and watching the entire scene said somewhat amusingly, "Eye-zy come, eye-zy go."

Introducing himself the Rabbi said, "Jesus of Nazareth, student of G-d and student of Humanity."

"I know who you are," replied Jude Thaddeus.

"By your actions I'm not sure that you do," said the Rabbi gently, "but join us and find out."

No-More-Sick-of-the-Palsy

Brick and Mortar had followed all the villagers of Capernaum to the house where Jesus was speaking, but they were unable to get inside to hear the Rabbi. They were wondering who the shaky old man was who came out of the house with a rolled-up sleeping mat.

Once outside the house, No-More-Sick-of-the-Palsy sayeth unto himself, "Whither go I? For this man hath the words of life and I shall stay and listen as he holds forth."

So, No-More-Sick-of-the-Palsy tarried by the door, whereupon the disciple Thaddeus, trying to keep the door clear in compliance with local fire codes, sayeth unto him. "Didn't the Rabbi tell you to go home? He holdeth forth not for his own health, you know. I'm sick of all you fakers comin' round and interrupting Jesus just to get healed."

"Shut the hell up. I'm staying," said the No-More-Sick-of-the-Palsy, "It's a free country and anyway, you're not the boss of me."

Thaddeus, suffering not this affront to his authority, gave No-More-Sick-of-the-Palsy a shove that knocked the man to his backside in the dust. "Now get outta here!" said Thaddeus.

No-More-Sick-of-the-Palsy scrambled to his feet and rushed headlong at Thaddeus who easily side-stepped his assailant, giving him a kick in the leg and he tripped head-first into the wall of the house, knocking loose bits of white plaster, and crumpled into a heap on the ground.

"Stupid bastard!" said Thaddeus contemptuously as he wiped the dust from his hands.

"You've broke my leg!" cried No-More-Sick-of-the-Palsy, grabbing his leg to himself and feigning great pain.

"Get outta here before I break the other one!" threatened Thaddeus.

Meanwhile, Jesus had grown aware of the commotion outside the house and he made his way to the door, where he said, "What's going on here?"

"He tripped on the steps and now he's lying on the ground. He prefers it down there," said Thaddeus innocently.

"Do not!" protested No-More-Sick-of-the-Palsy, "He pushed me! Twice!"

"He's a faker. Who you gonna believe, me or some bum who just learned to walk?" asked Thaddeus, grabbing No-More-Sick-of-the-Palsy under the arms and standing him up on his two feet.

Jesus turned to Brick and Mortar who had witnessed the scene and asked, "Did you see what happened? Did this guy fall?"

"No, sir. I mean, yes. Sir," said Mortar.

"He didn't fall? Or he did fall?" asked Jesus.

"No, yes, sir," said Mortar.

"What Mortar means to say is that's not technically correct," explained Brick. "He merely obeyed the law of gravity by embracing the dirt following his loss of balance, which was precipitated by the hand to his chest and the foot to his leg. Gravity and physics, I suppose, laws of motion, that sort of thing. Simple really. Oh, and not merely once, but twice."

"Balance? Physics? Gravity? Motion? Twice?" asked Jesus incredulously.

"Yes, twice. Once after being pushed to the ground and once after being tripped," said Brick.

"Yes, I quite agree, twice. I mean I don't agree twice; I agree this happened twice," confirmed Mortar.

Thaddeus glared at the two newcomers and ground his teeth.

And Jesus said in a tone that brooked no argument, "Thaddeus, we'll talk after I finish speaking inside."

Jesus said to No-More-Sick-of-the-Palsy, "Go in peace."

"Now," said Thaddeus, "You heard the Rabbi. Off you go. And don't forget your mat."

"Thaddeus," said Jesus when the man had departed, "You are a lost cause. Try to be a little more gentle, please. We've got to smooth off those rough edges of yours."

Jesus went back into the house and Thaddeus gave Brick and Mortar the stink-eye and curled his lip in anger as he scowled, "A couple of wise guys. We'll see if you're smart enough to get lost before I get you alone."

The Waiting Father

And it happened that a certain man was called home by the Almighty Father. In the early heavenly morning the man arrived at the Gate of the Eternal Kingdom and was bid entry into paradise. The man, however, said, "I can't enter in as yet, for I must wait and pray."

At mid-morning, the gate watchman said to him, "Good and faithful servant of G-d Most High, you may enter as soon as you wish."

"Thank you," said the man, "but I must wait and pray for my daughter."

At noonday as the guard changed, the man was again invited into the Kingdom, but again he declined, saying, "I fear for my daughter, and so I must wait and pray for her."

The same occurred again in the early afternoon and again before supper. Each time the man demurred, preferring to wait and pray for his wayward daughter.

At eventide, as the watchman was about to close the gate, the Savior himself came to the gate and said to the man, who had fallen to his knees before the Lord, "Good and faithful servant, why can you not enter into my Kingdom? Why do you tarry here at the gate?"

"Thank you, my gracious Lord, but my joy cannot be complete without my daughter, for my children are my heart," said the man.

"I myself will summon your daughter," and indeed, at the Lord's word, the daughter appeared before them.

Seeing the Lord and her father, the daughter fell on her face and averted her eyes, begging, "I have despised you in life, My Lord, and I do not deserve to be here."

And the Lord replied, "My love and favor are bestowed freely as gifts; no one among you *deserves* the portion they receive, but all receive the gifts of love and peace."

"I must depart My Lord, for I am among the worst of sinners. I chose sin and loved it," cried the daughter.

"I love even the worst of sinners and call them unto myself," said the Lord of Hosts. "Verily do I honor your father for his faith and his prayers, for nothing is lost to those that love the Lord. When the 10th plague was visited upon Pharaoh and the Egyptians, did not the destroyer pass over the houses of those with the blood of the lamb on their doorposts? Was not the entire house and all those therein preserved from harm? Likewise does the hand of the Lord save those of a faithful man's house. Enter in with your father and forget your shame."

And indeed, there was much rejoicing in the Kingdom, for another sinner was brought safely home.

Jesus Heals... Sometimes

Cupping his hands around his mouth to further project his voice, Thaddeus cried out, "Everybody form a line! Everybody will get a turn with the Rabbi."

But the people heeded him not, and all clustered round the Rabbi, refusing all entreaties to form an orderly queue. They clamored to be next and made loud noises.

"I said," cried Thaddeus thoroughly indignant, "form a frickin' line! Can't you people listen?! I swear to G-d!"

Meanwhile, the Rabbi was talking softly with a person before the laying on of hands and the solemn, healing moment, and above the murmurs of the crowd, a cougher coughed, loudly expectorating. Cough, cough, cough. Gross!

The Rabbi looked over to see who was coughing, but then the cougher fell silent, so the Rabbi returned his attention to the person at hand. Just as he was about to continue his ministrations, the cougher coughed again, wretchedly retching. Cough, cough, cough, cough, spit. Again, the Rabbi was distracted by the cougher. Ahem. Relative silence again reigned. And Jesus returned to his ministrations, again. Not more than five seconds later the cougher coughed again, this time more wretchedly than before and more prolonged than before. Cough, cough, cough, cough, cough, spit, sputum, cough, retch, cough, sigh, cough. Cough. Ahem. Double gross!!

The Rabbi's concentration was lost and admitting defeat he called aloud, "Would the cougher like to come forward now, please."

An old crone came limping, coughing and sputtering forward, and scolded the Rabbi saying, "I ain't no 'cougher'! I'm a lady with a cough. There's a difference, you know." Cough, cough, cough, etc. This woman was short and stooped. A wart grew out of the end of her nose and long hairs grew out of her chin. She was the second cousin of a rotten old potato.

"My bad," said the Son of Man.

And he was just about to lay hands on her head when the cougher, I mean the lady with the cough, fell into another fit of coughing, so long and so sustained, spraying this way and that, cough, cough, that the Rabbi recoiled from her. But he was too slow and a generous gob of spit and mucous caught the Rabbi on the left hand. He looked at the mucous projectile that landed on his hand; then he looked about him for a wipe and seeing none, wiped the sprayed sputum at the hem of his garment.

The crone smiled and tilted her head in apology and said, "Sorry. Couldn't help myself." Jesus quickly took advantage of the moment, laid hands on her head, healed her, just as she drew a deep breath prior to coughing up another lung, but alas, none was forthcoming. Healed, just like that. (Finger snap.)

And Thaddeus, the traffic cop, doorman and bouncer, tried to hustle her along for many people had come to be healed, but she protested saying, "I come about my leg. The cough I coulda lived with."

"Well, what's wrong with your leg, then?" asked Thaddeus.

"I'm not tellin' you! What, think you're a specialist? I come about something else, too," said the crone.

"Just trying to be helpful," muttered Thaddeus.

"Well, why don't you try shutting up? That would be helpful," wheezed the lady with a former cough.

And turning to Jesus she asked in a coy voice, "Can you make me pretty?"

"That would truly be a public service, if you can manage it, my Lord," said Thaddeus sideways.

"I told you to shut up, if you please," said the crone rounding on her antagonist.

"Maybe she don't need that voice o' hers, too?" said Thaddeus to Jesus.

The old woman swung her cane at Thaddeus, but deftly ducking, he avoided the blow.

Jesus, the healing rabbi, turned to the woman and said, "Beauty is in the eye of the beholder..."

The old woman cut in on him and said, "But nobody be holdin' me on a cold night! Old babes want love too, ya know." And she shook her cane at Jesus to emphasize her earnestness.

Jesus, trying to keep things on a professional level, said, "Dear Woman, I don't perform what may be termed as 'elective' procedures."

And the old crone reached out with her cane and smartly rapped Jesus across the knuckles.

"You holy men are all alike. You don't understand a bit about a person's life. You give what you *think* we want, not what we *really* want!" ranted the old woman.

And as she limped off, she fake-coughed to draw one last look from the healing Rabbi and his disciple Thaddeus.

Black and White

Next in line after the cougher, uh, er, sorry, the lady withOUT the cough, were two men. So engrossed were they in their interchange that they didn't notice that it was their turn to talk with the Rabbi and, oblivious, they continued so:

"I'm telling you, I heard what I heard!" said the first man.

"I was there! I heard it, too!" protested the second man.

"But you've got it all wrong," cried the first.

"No, I was there! I heard what he said!" insisted the second.

"Yes, so did I and he said, 'it was black' confidently stated the first.

"I can't believe what I'm hearing! He said, 'it was white'" said the second with complete assurance.

"It's good you don't believe what you're hearing, because he said 'black'," said the first.

"It was 'white' plain as day,"

"You must be stupid in the head! Black!"

"Who're you calling stupid, stupid?! White!"

"Let's ask him. He's right here!"

"Fine. Let's ask."

"Greetings, Rabbi. We were engaged in a ah, ah, discussion of your words this afternoon and it seems that this knucklehead here..."

"Knucklehead, yourself..."

" - ok, this *listener* of yours here can't remember correctly what you said. Somehow, he got the impression that you said 'white', when it was so clear to all that you said 'black'."

"Could you re-tell him your words on black and or white?"

"I believe that I said 'every shade of gray between black and white'," said the Rabbi.

"Aha!! I knew it. Black it is!!" cried the first.

"Yessss!! White!! I know what I heard!!" exulted the second.

And the two listeners with ears to hear retreated, heatedly and happily explaining to the other the error of his ways, for nothing is so sweet as exposing the errors of others to their faces. That's a partial explanation of why so many young people go into teaching.

Let him who has ears listen.

Naked Crazy Nate

Ssshsssh! Please be very quiet.

Naked Crazy Nate was hiding and didn't want to be seen just yet. A large entourage approached the cemetery where Naked Crazy Nate lived.

Why was he living in a necropolis (that's a fancy word for cemetery)? Because he was possessed of demons and accepted modality of therapy for such an affliction was to be chained up by the local populace, in a city of the dead. Naked Crazy Nate, however, would have none of such treatment and although able to break bands of metal and chains, he was unable to break these demonic bonds. So, living among the tombs seemed natural enough, or was minimally acceptable to the locals. He had one unfortunate vice: he liked to scare passersby.

Crouching like a lion Naked Crazy Nate allowed his prey to come on, closer, closer, closer...And then leaping wildly out of his hiding place, he screamed and shouted and made threatening gestures.

All the approaching group save one recoiled in fear, but Jesus kept on talking as if he had neither heard nor seen anything out of the ordinary. His disciples, loathe to interrupt the Rabbi, were pointing at Nate and fear of this one, naked man showed on the faces of the Dozen and the Others.

Finally, slowly, Jesus stopped talking and turned to calmly face Naked Crazy Nate, who continued to try to frighten him. Defeated, Nate stood still and Jesus suddenly faked a lunge at him and Nate fell back in fear.

The demons in him called out, "What do you want of me, Jesus of Nazareth, Son of the Most High G-d?"

"Did you hear that?" cried Thaddeus. "I can't believe that! It's just impossible!!"

"Believe what?" said Nathanael, a bit alarmed by Thaddeus' vehemence.

Jude Thaddeus turned to Nathanael with raised eyebrows, questioned, "It's just impossible! From Nazareth?! I didn't know Jesus was from Nazareth. Did you know that? Nobody tells me anything?"

"Don't torment me!" cried the demons.

"I'm not tormenting anyone," replied Thaddeus, even though the demand was not addressed to him.

"You torment everyone, dumbass! But that's not what we're talking about," scoffed the demons.

"Who're you calling a dumbass, dumbass?!" demanded Thaddeus.

"Don't send us into the waters, for we can't swim!" pitifully whined the demons. "Suffer us to enter the pigs!"

"Don't call my disciples 'pigs'," protested Jesus.

"Not them, but those pigs over there," clarified the demons, pointing to a herd of nearby swine.

"Oh," said Jesus apologetically, "my bad. Okay, into the pigs with you, then." And straightaway the demons left Naked Crazy Nate to lodgments in the pigs, who promptly stampeded into the lake and drowned.

"Ah, I hate to tell you, but pigs can swim," said Thaddeus.

"Does that look like swimming to you?" asked Jesus coolly.

"But pigs *can* swim!" countered Thaddeus.

"Don't ruin the moment," said the Rabbi.

Naked Crazy Nate's demeanor changed immediately upon the departure of the demons. The Dozen scrounged some clothing for the man, for he was naked, not due to an anti-fashion fetish, political statement, but a lifestyle choice. He begged Jesus to go with him.

"No," said Jesus, "I've got my hands full with these guys." And Jesus looked meaningfully at Jude Thaddeus. "But go and tell what G-d has done for you!"

"What?!" spat Thaddeus. "I'm no dumber then them others!"

"Well spoken, my friend," said the Rabbi.

I Hate That Story

He also said to his disciples, "There was a certain rich man who had a manager. An accusation was made to him that the manager was wasting his possessions. He called him, and said to him, 'What is this that I hear about you? Give an accounting of your management, for you can no longer be manager.'

"The manager said within himself, 'What will I do, seeing that my lord is taking away the management position from me? I don't have strength to dig. I am ashamed to beg. I know what I will do, so that when I am removed from management, they may receive me into their houses.' Calling each one of his lord's debtors to him, he said to the first, 'How much do you owe to my lord?' He said, 'A hundred batos of oil.' He said to him, 'Take your bill, and sit down quickly and write fifty.' Then he said to another, 'How much do you owe?' He said, 'A hundred cors of wheat.' He said to him, 'Take your bill, and write eighty.'

"His lord commended the dishonest manager because he had done wisely, for the children of this world are, in their own generation, wiser than the children of the light. I tell you, make for yourselves friends by means of unrighteous mammon, so that when you fail, they may receive you into the eternal tents. He who is faithful in a very little is faithful also in much. He who is dishonest in a very little is also dishonest in much. If therefore you have not been faithful in the unrighteous mammon, who will commit to your trust the true riches? If you have not been faithful in that which is another's, who will give you that which is your own? No servant can serve two masters, for either he will hate the one, and love the other; or else he will hold to one, and despise the other. You aren't able to serve G-d and mammon."

***

Later that day, Jesus and the Magdalene sat alone quietly reviewing the day's events and the conversation turned to the parable of the unscrupulous steward. With a visceral tone in her throat the Magdalene said irritably, "I hate that story."

"Oh," said Jesus, taken aback by the strong reaction from Mary.

Already she was unhappy with their conversation because to continue only meant revealing herself more than she felt ready to do, and she said glumly, "It just doesn't make sense."

Jesus said nothing and waited for her to continue.

"I mean, who would commend that thieving bastard for his behavior! He should've gotten his master's debts plus interest. It doesn't make sense." The words 'thieving bastard' received a vehemence that was unwarranted by the context of their conversation and Jesus noted this with a sense of concern.

But he said "I know. It *doesn't* make sense. I slipped it in to see if anyone was paying attention. Some people don't question anything. They just take what is said as if it all makes perfect sense; just as if they understand perfectly."

The Magdalene could scarce believe her ears and a look of astonishment passed across her face.

"You try coming up with a corker off the cuff, even with lots of preparation, it's not as easy as it looks!" challenged Jesus. Then abruptly he changed the subject.

"Mary," said Jesus tenderly, "Abba loves you, no matter what you've done, no matter what you are." A mist of deep emotion covered his eyes as he looked deeply into her, looked deeply into her very soul.

All of Mary's longing for love and compassion rose in her body and caught in her throat. She began to shake and to comfort herself she drew in her arms and covered her face with her hands. She broke into sobs that came from her deepest self, sobs so filled with pain that for some time she couldn't speak. Jesus put his arms around her and held her close to himself absorbing her pain and shame.

Finally, Mary pushed him away and was able to compose herself, wiping her eyes and nose, she retreated behind the hard exterior and spoke devoid of emotion. "When I was a girl I was raped by my father's steward." She spoke these words in an almost casual tone as if she had practiced speaking them before, but the edges of these words were razor-sharp and they continued to lacerate her insides.

Jesus' eyes widened at this and understanding of her pain dawned in his heart and a tear rolled down his cheek.

"Why are *you* crying?" she asked bitterly.

"I'm crying because the image of you that I hold in my heart is clean and pure and perfect in beauty," said Jesus.

"But that's because you're good." Her lower lip began to tremble.

"And you are good as well," replied Jesus. "Abba gave you great beauty in your heart and in your soul."

This was more goodness than she could bear and she snuffled back the tears that wanted to be released. She sucked in a deep breath in an effort to forestall any tears, but her emotions and memories conspired against her. She sat stiff and erect, a fortress unto herself.

Presently, Jesus said, "Stay with the pain. It's trying to teach you something." Then he got up and left Mary to her thoughts.

"That man is a gift from G-d." Her heart told her that.

Unbelief in Nazareth

The man with the crooked tooth rose to speak and he greeted Jesus with sarcasm-drenched words, "Well, the prodigal son of Mary returns to his hometown. Do you expect us to run to meet you with open arms? 'Jesus has returned! Put a ring on his finger! Put a fine robe on him! Kill the fatted calf!'" The men in the synagogue laughed in accord with this characterization.

These comments sparked a thought in the mind of Jesus, but he stood as still as a house built on rock withstands wind, rain and flood.

In a vein of mockery, the man with the crooked tooth continued, "Did you think we missed you? Did you think we couldn't get along without you? Did you think that goodness in Nazareth went with you when you left? And who are these *heroes* that form your merry band? I see you've got an idiot, I'm sorry, I meant to say 'intellectual' (he was referring to James); a Judean (at least he's a Jew); some erstwhile fishermen; I won't even mention the scandalous women, including your mother Mary, who follow your camp; and lastly, probably 'leastly', a pair of suspicious foreigners of dubious virtue."

"The Kingdom of G-d is at hand," said Jesus, "to those who humble themselves."

"Why don't you just walk humbly out of our town. We don't need whatever it is that you are selling."

The others in the synagogue unleashed a hail of catcalls and insults. At the door of the synagogue, Jesus stopped, turned to face them, and shook the dust from his feet. This elicited another round of shouts and insults. The townspeople gathered round and with much jostling, 'escorted' Jesus and his followers to the edge of the town.

As Jesus and his entourage left the village of Nazareth, Mortar gave full vent to his indignation, saying, "What a bunch of yokels. They don't know *merde* from pudding! Pardon my French."

"Jesus, he don't get no respeck!" said Brick, trying to make light of the situation.

Jesus was murmuring to himself something like, "Son of Mary, prodigal, son; there's a story in there somewhere."

"You knuckleheads shut up!" said Thaddeus. He was peeved by the reaction of his countrymen to the Rabbi, but would tolerate no outsiders commenting on the matter. "I don't know why the Rabbi tolerates the likes of you."

"My, my, my goodness! Such harsh words from an Apostle, one of the Elect! I thought you might be adhering to a higher standard of behavior than us mere mortals, Thaddeass," taunted Mortar.

"Shut up, you butchering meat head!" said Thaddeus spitefully.

"I don't know why you've got to impugn the dignity of my vocation," cried Mortar, "but my wits are as sharp as my knives, and they're more than a match for the likes of a slab of bacon like you! Talk about pearls before swine!"

"Take that back, you frickin' foreigner," spat Thaddeus as he made a lunging feint to draw Mortar into a move. And it worked too well, for Mortar not only reacted, but landed a punch on Thaddeus' kisser that split his lip. Thaddeus put his hand to his mouth, then looked at the blood on his hand and saw red, so to speak, and launched an offensive of flailing fists.

The Mother of All Conflicts

Their engagement was quite vigorous, like unto that of a married couple, featuring side headlocks, scratching, gouging, swearing, biting, kicking, pulling hair and choking. No holds were barred. Mercy and quarter were neither asked nor given.

The others quite enjoyed the excitement before anyone felt the impulse to intervene. After all, this tempest had been a'brewin' and there was some need, it was felt, to let the steam blow itself off.

There isn't much to say about why they didn't like each other. It was the way they looked *at* each other and the way they looked *to* each other, merely a matter of prepositions!

Jesus came up just as the others were pulling apart the flailing combatants, still displaying a fighting spirit far from quenched, a spirit befitting that of gladiators fighting to the death.

Brick, being in the center of the circle, and deeply partisan in his feelings for Mortar, was the last to become aware of the presence of Jesus and was caught by the Rabbi in mid-sentence, "Bite him...."

And Jesus incredulously repeated back to Brick his words, "Bite him?!"

Brick shrank into himself and mumbled something apologetically about being caught up in the excitement of the moment.

Jesus, with his arms akimbo, gave him a stern look of disapproval.

Thaddeus, spit and blood hanging in a long thread from his mouth, fished in his mouth and pulled out a tooth. Was it his own? Yes, well, it would no longer serve him and he threw it to the ground.

Both fighters sustained minor lacerations about the head and face. Both gave as good as they got. And there's the rub – there was no clear-cut winner.

Jesus grabbed both contestants by the scruffs of their necks, he being no wimp and not averse to taking control of situations.

"Stop! No further! You two stay here, right here, in the road. Resolve this issue betwixt you or it will remain a stumbling block and you will learn nothing more from me. We are going back to Capernaum. When you resolve this, return to me and we'll talk," commanded Jesus.

Mortar and Thaddeus sat on opposite sides of the road, Thaddeus in the hot sun, Mortar in the shade of a mustard bush. Their mutual glaring was more searing than the hot rays of the sun. Desultory cursing broke out disturbing the monotony of the Galilean morning.

Finally, Thaddeus, thinking it was stupid of himself to suffer the heat without benefit of shade, spoke to his antagonist, "Mortar, don't take this to be an offensive movement, but I wish to sit in the shade of the mustard tree that you enjoy on that side of the road. I'm not asking your approval. I'm merely informing you of my intentions."

To which Mortar replied disdainfully, "'Tis a free country." And he sniffed his nose at Thaddeus.

Thaddeus got up and moved to Mortar's side of the road and sat in the shade as far from Mortar as was manageable while still enjoying the shade of the tree.

Silence reigned and both men glared at the rocks in the road. 'Ere long the sun's celestial journey across the sky left Mortar sitting in the glaring sun and Thaddeus comfortably ensconced in the middle of the mustard tree's shade. Some would say, "Everything happens for a reason."

"Good brother," said Mortar, "as you may have noticed I am now sitting in the sun and in order to enjoy the shade of our good tree, I must remove myself to your other side, whether 'tis your right or left, I can never remember, but I mean over there," as he pointed with his finger. "If I move, please don't mistake that for an offensive act."

"I will suffer your movement as you, with a good spirit, suffered mine," said Thaddeus.

Mortar thought he sensed a certain softening in the demeanor of Thaddeus and he told himself that he must be careful to exploit any openings that may occur. He also reminded himself of the great discomfort of his present circumstances, not the least of which would be in the near future when he must report to Jesus and explain his behavior. This current stand-off might be the least of his worries and might it not be wise to cut his losses here in this dusty road and save the best of his personal resources for his inevitable meeting with Jesus?

Thaddeus, for his part, had not been idly enjoying the shade. He, too, had been making calculations of the sun's angles and the height of the tree and the length of the shadow, and how all this might be used to his advantage against his adversary Mortar. But amid his calculations Thaddeus, too, understood that when this knot was untangled, whatever the outcome, he would still have to meet with the Rabbi, and the Rabbi wasn't always much concerned with who won the fight, but with the effect of the fight on the hearts of the contenders.

Indeed, it could be said of both men that they had some good understanding of their Rabbi and the kind of man that he was.

And it was Mortar who first ventured to observe, "It doesn't matter if you're right, or I'm right, does it?"

"You're right," said Thaddeus, who knew exactly what Mortar was talking about. "What say we un-ass this place, begin our walk to Capernaum, resolve as best we can our differences on the way, report to Jesus and get this business over with?"

"I must admit that it's hanging over my head like the sword of Damocles," said Mortar.

"Don't you mean 'Maccabean Sword?!"

"No. Sword of Damocles."

"That's Maccabean."

"Damocles."

"Maccabean."

For now, the two men had to content themselves with argument.

The Resolution of the Mother of All Conflicts

Mortar and Thaddeus presented themselves to Jesus who was sitting in the shade at his house in Capernaum. The two men hadn't even washed their faces and hands and still wore the dust of the road and the sweat of their exertions.

"You wanted to see us?" they inquired of their Rabbi.

"Yes, I did. Please sit down in the shade," beckoned Jesus.

Some of the other Apostles, Para-Apostles and hangers-on, seeing that something of possible interest was about to pass, moved unobtrusively nearer to catch whatever morsels of gossip that might fall from the Master's table, all, of course, under the guise of trying to avail themselves of the spiritual instruction that was sure to be administered to these two wayward followers. What they secretly hoped for, was that Jesus was going to open up a super-sized can of whoop-ass on these two knuckleheads and that they'd have a story to tell around the well tomorrow. And so, Jesus' gentle invitation to Thaddeus and Mortar to sit down in the shade was the last thing that the others expected.

"How was your journey back to Capernaum?" inquired the Rabbi politely.

"Fine," said Thaddeus suspiciously.

Mortar only shrugged.

"Please sit down. Join me. Can I get you some wine? Cigars? Yes?" asked Jesus.

"Sure," said the two men uncertainly, wary of a clever trap. This Rabbi was just unpredictable enough to do something, well, unorthodox, to say the least.

The Rabbi himself served Mortar and Thaddeus wine and gave them the best cigars he had available and this further heightened the sense of their uneasiness. The lookers-on began to grow uneasy as well. The spectacle they had hoped would develop into a gossip bonanza was simply not living up to its billing. And finally, Jesus made a loud announcement to no one in particular in which he said, "Those who remain nearby for the benefit of their souls will be offered the opportunity to prove the effectiveness of their training by undergoing an extremely rigorous trial by fire." It wasn't long before all extraneous personnel had departed the operational area.

Jesus lit a double Maduro Churchill and began puffing away, content to let the tension rise and Mortar broke first saying, "What are you going to do?"

To which Jesus replied, "What am *I* going to do? I think the question should be turned around. What are *you* going to do?"

This perplexed both men who expected a severe dressing-down. This wasn't at all what either man had expected and they were simply at a loss.

"I've talked about love of enemies and a man's enemies will be of his own house. I didn't really expect that I was speaking so prophetically and so close to home," said Jesus. "I have great faith in both of you, but it makes me doubt my own judgment in choosing the two of you."

Thaddeus sensed the uncertainty in his Rabbi and said, "Ever since this foreigner and his bean-pole friend showed up with their cigars and their bacon, you've been, well, you haven't spent any time with us. And they're not even full Apostles! And they're not like us!!"

"What do you mean, 'not like us'?" asked Jesus with suspicion.

"Well, they're some sort of Gentile, but they're certainly not Jews!" cried Thaddeus.

Mortar, for once, had the good sense to remain silent as Thaddeus dug his own hole deeper and he felt right proud that he had proved to be such a thorn in the side of his adversary.

"This isn't about what these men are or are not," said Jesus. "The G-d of Abraham, Isaac and Jacob is the G-d of all men, not just of us Jews. He's the G-d of the living – all the living."

"Well, then, why don't you let everyone and anyone be your followers! Next you'll be letting women in!" said Thaddeus bitterly. His anger at Brick and Mortar had darkly clouded his judgment and now he was saying things that he was surely going to regret later.

"Yes, why don't I?" repeated Jesus thoughtfully. "Thaddeus, you might be onto something there. And of course, you're aware of my fondness for the fairer sex and so why not women? Yes, women especially."

"Oh, my G-d! Now who's not being careful of the words coming out of his mouth!" said Thaddeus in reproach to his Rabbi.

"I think it's time to take a breather," said Jesus. "Hot heads are speaking hot words."

"I wouldn't mind one of those cigar things," said Thaddeus, "if it's all the same to you."

"Yes, please help yourself," said Jesus.

Thaddeus chose a short cherry flavored cigar, bit off the cap, spit it on the ground and lit up. The smoke soon soothed his temper, but he decided to bide his time and hold out for a complete and resounding victory. Determined to hold the upper hand, he apologized to Mortar for his intemperate words, saying, "There are two kinds of people in the world: those of us big enough to forgive, and all you others. I will pray for you."

Mortar, set his jaw and growled through his teeth, "I forgive you, too, for your stupid, insensitive, unfair, mean-spirited and completely unfounded words. I pray that you will more closely follow the Rabbi's teaching and become a better man."

As Jesus puffed away on his cigar he realized that he was in effect talking to two drunken men about the virtues of sobriety, he said aloud and to no one in particular, "Gentiles, too? And women?"

And Women?

Abba? What do you think of women?" asked Jesus.

"I am very fond of them, in fact, they might be my finest creation. I think most men might agree with that. Remember back before you became a man - there was that one girl who took hold of your heart. Something about Moses' burning bush, if I recall correctly."

Jesus blushed. He remembered all right, just as most men will fondly recall the first time that they were in love. Purely and innocently. It marks the soul in a good way.

Jesus let out a deep sigh.

"See! Right there! You were just thinking about her. Your pulse quickened. Your pupils dilated. You felt a shiver deep inside. Apparently, you like them as much as I do, but more to the point, women are every bit as intelligent as men are. From observation of all of them, I'd have to conclude that they are more in tune with their emotions than men are, generally. I should add that their gifts are underappreciated."

"Yes," said Jesus, "but their role in society..."

"Their role in society should change. If I asked you right now, who understands your message so far?"

"Right, so far, I'd have to say that my Mother has the best understanding, and then, the Magdalene, and James the Less."

"Perhaps we could say that the least 'qualified' persons, women and a man without all the standard abilities, are your best 'students. I'm proud of you, Jesú. You are growing beyond the limitations of your era. You will not be 'successful' if you do not use the women in your midst according to their gifts. Don't get me wrong, I like your guys; they were chosen well, but some of them have a lot of work to do before they will be ready for the work."

PART IV

We Need to Talk

James, the brother (Catholics may read this word as cousin) of the Lord, was adamant. "Mary, we have to do something about your son Jesus."

"What are you saying? 'Do something?'" Mary looked up from her sewing. When the phrase 'your son' was used by someone she knew the comment following this phrase was always negative.

"Many others have come to me about it," said James. "They say, 'You're the head of the house. Do something."

"Do something? What?!" asked Mary. "What others?"

"They say 'he is out of his mind.' He's going around talking about... crazy things. He's healing... he's done it more than once! Even lepers!" His consternation was tinged with admiration.

"Well, there's nothing wrong with that," replied Mary

"Nothing wrong?! Nothing wrong?! He's casting out evil spirits, too!" cried James, who was getting heated up.

"That's a good thing, isn't it?" asked Mary.

"Of course, it is, but.... but... but.... he's casting out evil spirits!! How can he do that!! He's my half-brother!!! He's your son!!! And I'm responsible!!! Every time he does something, people come to me. Jesus did this or Jesus did that!! Are they right: *is* he out of his mind??!!"

Mary said nothing and waited while James, breathing hard, subsided into himself.

"James, I want you to calm down because there's something I haven't told you; and I think it's going to be very hard for you to hear," said Mary evenly.

"What?!" said James sullenly.

Mary began uncertainly and James interrupted several times at first but in the end, he listened for a long time before he spoke again.

"Oh. G-d of our Fathers! May He be forever blessed." said James in disbelief. Then he cocked his head and said, "I don't know if I can believe that..."

Mary said nothing.

James looked suspiciously toward Mary, his father's second wife. He had always known her to be truthful and practical; he loved her and he loved his younger half-brother, Jesus; but this was rapidly becoming a test of his loyalty and of his belief instead of a check on his half-brother's sanity.

"Well, that's just... that's just..." he left off speaking before he said anything that might offend his mother.

Mary still said nothing.

James looked down at his feet for a long time. He looked up at Mary and winced before he said, "That means that... Jesus... is...Jesus... is..."

Mary finished his sentence, "Jesus is my son."

This time James said nothing.

"I don't want you to tell anyone," said Mary.

"You don't have to worry about that!" said James. The sarcasm was more than James should have allowed himself in speaking to his father's wife. He shook his head in quiet self-reproach.

So, James and Mary agreed that, for the moment, it was best to 'collect' Jesus, bring him home and discuss the matter.

There were so many people at the house where Jesus was speaking that they couldn't get near him. For a time, they stood outside and listened. Jesus' voice was barely audible and was often interrupted by outbursts of laughter. Then Jesus' tone turned serious and not a sound was heard from his listeners as they strained every effort to listen and hear every word.

Thaddeus, standing in the doorway as was his habit, brushed away several attempts of James and Mary to get his attention. He shushed them loudly several times before he finally looked around and saw that it was the mother of Jesus and the half-brother, James. James whispered his request to Thaddeus who with an exaggerated rolling of the eyes and a shoulder-shrug communicated to them that although he didn't understand the request, he would, nonetheless, comply with it and he began weaving his way through the crowd to where Jesus was standing and speaking.

The whispered interruption was unwelcome by the audience judging by the murmuring and shifting of seats. Jesus himself seemed slightly perturbed.

As Mary and James waited outside they heard these phrases clearly: "Who are my brothers and sisters? And who's your Daddy?" And they wondered what he was talking about that so enthralled his listeners.

Finally, Jesus appeared backing out of the doorway still talking. Apparently, no one wanted him to leave, but Jesus apologized for the interruption and called out to them all, saying, "Remember! Who is your family?! And who are your mothers and brothers and sisters?!" As soon as Jesus disengaged from the house full of listeners, a loud rumble of voices broke into discussion that signaled debates and commentaries on what they had heard.

Jesus, as he turned to James and his mother, clapped his hands together and rubbed them briskly. He was exhilarated by the reception of his listeners, but now he saw that James and his mother were in earnest and his face took on a look of concern for them, and he said, "Has someone died?"

James said tersely, "We need to talk." They walked home in silence.

***

Sitting just inside the gates of the house, far from those who were already asleep and in nearly complete darkness, Jesus broke the silence, quoting an unnamed source, "'He is out of his mind.'"

"I don't know where that came from," mumbled James looking to the ground, but then he gathered himself and said accusatorily to Jesus, "Do you know what your mother told me about you?!"

"Yes, she's told me that, but it doesn't make me anything less than you," said Jesus.

Words were becoming obstacles for James and he stuttered. "I-I-I wasn't thinking l-l-*less*. But if it's true, then...."

James' voice trailed off and the unspoken words lodged in his throat. Things weren't clear to James and now he felt more confused than ever. He clung desperately to their family status, eldest son, his father's second wife, and his father's younger son. Compared to what he had just heard, the family's blend of relationships which of late caused him much consternation, was the epitome of prosaic.

Raising his head, James looked at Mary and Jesus and started to speak, but only stuttered, "S- s-s-s..." but no actual words were forthcoming, so blindly was his mind racing to assimilate what he had heard.

"I didn't want to believe it at first, either," offered Jesus. "I wanted to be like everyone else, but that's simply not possible."

James fumbled to find any meaning. He blinked his eyes several times and said, "So that means...."

"Yes...." said Jesus, waiting for James to understand.

"Well... well..." said James. "It means... that... you...

"Yes, I am..." allowed Jesus.

"But you're Mary's son! Aren't you?" asked James, needing to confirm what he already knew.

Jesus nodded his assent.

"A-a-and you're my half-brother..." said James uncertainly.

"Yes, I am, but..." said Jesus.

"And G-d is... is...." stammered James.

"You've got it!" cried Jesus.

James caught himself about to say something, mouth open wide, but no words came out. He lowered his eyes in intensive thought. Then his eyes snapped wide open as if realization had slapped him on the forehead. He looked at

Jesus in shock and slowly reached out to touch him, verifying the flesh and blood of what he had heard. He stood up mumbling that "I've got to sleep on this," and he took his mat to lie down.

Jesus and Mary were left alone to ponder in their hearts. James now was the only other person who shared their secret, besides Joseph, who had long been in the grave.

"He'll be alright," Jesus whispered to his mother.

"You're a good son, Jesus," said Mary.

"And so is James," replied Jesus. He laid down on his mat and the conversation with his brother and his mother began to weigh on him as the implications of their words began to sink in. He was suddenly struck with the realization of how difficult it must be for his mother and brother to have a family member of such uniqueness and ambiguity. Yes, ambiguity! For if he were truly the Son of the Living G-d as was understood in those days, he would have taken on a much more political persona, not to mention a military or perhaps even a bid to become the High Priest, though he was not of the correct family line. Such was the longing of Israel for G-d to deliver them from the tyranny of the Romans that a humble rabbi from the Galilee simply was not considered.

***

After sleeping fitfully, actually, you might say that after lying awake restlessly punctuated by short and fitful periods of thin sleep, Jesus arose very early and left the house. It was still dark with a lighter colored ribbon of gray marking the horizon. Jesus made his way easily in the darkness; easily because he had so often taken this path to his favorite spot overlooking the lake.

"You're worried," said Abba.

"Yes," replied Jesus gloomily.

"Spill," said Abba.

Jesus' words spilled out quickly. "I don't think that I am what people really want."

Mortar Employs His Prerogative

This had gone on for too long. Why, after all, had he purchased a slave in the first place? He had best bend her to his will, and the sooner the better. His self-respect was at stake. What was the point of freedom if you couldn't do whatever you wanted to do? The Rabbi had some crazy ideas about slavery and freedom, but those were easily discounted. He wasn't a slave and he hadn't ever been a slave. What did he know?

Mortar made a show of standing, stretching and yawning in a big way. He announced to no one in particular, "I'm feeling particularly manly tonight. I own a slave and her heartfelt desire should be to please her master in any way that she can."

Brick looked up and thought, "Here he goes." But he wouldn't dream of interfering with another man's property.

"Sweetness, come with me," commanded Mortar imperiously and she followed looking askance at him.

From the darkness muffled voices were heard in disagreement. Someone was demanding something. Someone was emphatically refusing something. Neither was pleased with the others' response. Sounds of a scuffle were followed by a loud thump as if someone had struck and split open a watermelon. After this came a high staccato whimpering. Some thought it sounded like Smokey whining in deep distress.

Presently Mortar came crawling back to the fire, sucking in shallow gasps of breath. He rocked back and forth in exquisite agony, his hands protecting his crotch.

"How was it? Did you give her the ol'...?" Brick made an obscene gesture, the vernacular for a sexual encounter characterized by the male partner driving the interchange with force and vigor.

No intelligible answer was discernible through the pain-induced babbling.

Finally, he managed to assume a precarious sitting position, mostly sitting on one haunch and leaning to his left. His breathing slowly returned to normal and he said in a high-pitched falsetto, which male readers will understand, "Maybe getting a slave wasn't such a good idea."

Slave or Free

"A slave to all'?!" These words of the Rabbi were insulting. What did he know of wearing chains and slavery?! She had always hoped to run away, but this had made the situation all the more repugnant.

Holding her hood close, Sweetness slunk away from the camp. Her senses were hyper-alert to the slightest sound in the inky blackness of the moonless night.

She heard something. She froze in her tracks. Her pupils widened to admit as much light as possible in order to sight the source of the sound. Her nostrils flared as her nose attempted to provide information to her brain to identify this potential threat. She looked first left then right. Something was out there but she didn't know yet what or where?

Suddenly a sound broke the silence of the still night air. It was just at her feet. She jumped in the air as a startled bird takes flight with a burst of flapping feathers and wings. At least her hand holding close the hood managed to stifle the scream that tried to escape her lips. The adrenaline coursed instantly through her veins, her heart began pounding furiously, pumping blood, especially to the parts of her body with which she would effect her escape. Her lungs gulped the night air's oxygen to fuel her muscles in their flight. Every sense and sinew strained as she fought the impulse to run, and then she saw, not what, but who had elicited this fight or flight response from her.

It was the Rabbi! A shimmer ran through her body as it released the tension induced by fear.

He now began to murmur his prayer, reciting:

"The Spirit of the Sovereign LORD is on me,
because the LORD has anointed me
to preach good news to the poor.
He has sent me to bind up the brokenhearted,
to proclaim freedom for the captives
and release from darkness for the prisoners,"

She scoffed at him. "Freedom?! You proclaim freedom for captives?! There are slaves all over the world – in your own camp – for G-d's sake! – and you do nothing! How can you proclaim freedom?!" The adrenaline in her blood had fueled her anger.

"There are many who consider themselves free, but they are slaves just the same.

"But they don't have these!" She cried fiercely as she held aloft the chains that bound her wrists.

The chains suddenly slid from her wrists and from her ankles onto the ground. Just like that! They just slipped to the ground. Her jaw dropped in astonishment. Her eyes opened wide in disbelief. She looked in shock at the Rabbi, who hadn't moved a muscle, and then she looked back at the chains lying on the ground, regarding them warily as she might a coiled serpent. She overcame her dismay and picked up the chains which were completely intact and unbroken or unbent.

She looked around to see if anyone had been awakened or alerted to the sound of the chains as they hit the ground, but the camp was completely still.

"What do you want?" whispered Sweetness cynically as she eyed the Rabbi.

"Nothing," said the Rabbi simply. And everything."

"Nothing?! Everything? Talk in riddles to your band of knuckleheads. If you've got something to say to me, then say it."

"I give you your freedom. Do what you will."

"Real freedom doesn't mean running and hiding, but I thank you for removing my chains," said Sweetness. "But I remember you, Rabbi. You killed my mother. You were with those who killed my mother. I saw you. I remember you. I remember!" Her words were spat out with passionate hatred.

Jesus had already felt the sting of opposition to what he said; that was nothing new. He enjoyed the give and take of a good debate, after which, those in disagreement could still be respectful, but this visceral, throbbing hatred was new and it cut him to the core. It left him stunned. He racked his memory, 'I killed her mother?'

And with that, Sweetness vanished into the night.

Swine Before Pearls

And it came to pass the next morning that Jesus was awakened to a smell that he had never smelt before, tantalizing, intoxicating, extraordinarily tempting. He sat up and looked around him and saw all the disciples standing in a cluster around a small fire heatedly arguing. He walked up to them and when they noticed that Jesus was present, they all fell silent. Thaddeus stood with arms folded on the edge of the group close enough to listen, but far enough away to display his obvious displeasure.

There in their midst sat Mortar and Brick. Mortar was frying something in a pan, Brick was eating something in his mouth and his disciples looked expectantly to the Rabbi.

And Peter spoke saying, "Master, good morning to you."

"Good morning to you, Peter, and to the rest of you," said Jesus. "What is the topic that has gained a hearing this early in the morning and in such vigorous tones?" And he looked back to the pan that Mortar was busily tending, and he added, "Son o' man, that smells good!"

"That's the problem," said Peter. "It's called... What's it called again?"

Mortar looked up from his pan and said brightly, "It's bacon! Ba-con. It's part of a nutritious and delicious full English breakfast."

"It's unclean," cried Thaddeus, "and we can't eat it without defiling ourselves!"

"Where did you get it?" asked Jesus.

"From them drowned swine. Such a waste of good meat! I fetched me out the lake a porker and dressed 'im out and voila! Bacon!" said Mortar. His pride was evident.

The Rabbi rubbed his chin in a thoughtful way as the disciples watched for any sign of how he might pronounce.

"I got enough for everybody if Brick here don't eat it all first," said Mortar. "Please help yourself, Master."

And Peter, trying to hurry matters along, put in, "I say we eat it." And he sniffed, inhaling deeply in anticipation.

And the smell of bacon entranced them all, even the reluctant ones. Even Thaddeus.

"No!" several of the others protested rather weakly, "It's unclean. It's against the law!"

And the smell! The smell of it was heavenly, thick-sliced bacon cooked over a wood fire.

And the Rabbi, still rubbing his chin looked skyward and thought for a moment. Then he sniffed, and then he smiled. And then he said, "Not that which goeth into the mouth defileth a man; but that which cometh out of the mouth, this defileth a man." (Matthew 15:11)

"Yes!" cried most of the disciples while at least one lapsed into sullen silence.

And the Rabbi speaking to all said, "Mortar, our laws forbid us to eat this meat."

Mortar wrinkled his forehead at the disturbing thought of not eating bacon and he said wonderingly, "You mean to tell me you've never aten bacon?"

Jesus continued, "No, but I will not refuse your generous hospitality. Some, perhaps, cannot eat, and they must be allowed to follow the dictates of their consciences."

Mortar handed Jesus a rasher of perfectly fried bacon that he ate with a closed-mouth grin and closed eyes in epicurean ecstasy. Then Mortar served all the disciples, some of whom ate with trepidation, but most of whom ate with gusto.

And Brick said in a loud voice for the benefit of everyone, "Thaddeus, I stuck up for you yesterday."

Thaddeus took the bait, "*You* stuck up for *me*?"

"Yes, someone, I don't want to give the name, said you weren't fit to eat with pigs!"

Thaddeus' brow furrowed and his eyes narrowed, ready to take offense at this comment.

Then Brick delivered the punch line for all to hear, "But I said you were!"

The men laughed heartily over this while Thaddeus bit his tongue. He didn't want to get into a verbal fray in front of the Rabbi, but he began to plot his revenge.

One disciple who shall remain nameless, broke off a small piece using a leaf to avoid actual contact with the bacon lest he become unclean, and pretended to touch his lips with the bacon. He feigned some chewing and said softly, "I don't really like it. Would anyone like to have mine?" It was snatched from his hands before he finished his sentence.

Jesus had finished his bacon and it occurred to him that something was amiss. He made a point of looking around, searching for something, someone, and then he said loudly, "Has anyone seen Sweetness?"

"She's not here," mumbled Mortar without looking up.

"I wonder where she went," said the Rabbi.

"Last night, I gave her her freedom," said Mortar, still not looking up.

"Mortar, I'm so pleased with you. You've taken my words to heart and acted upon them!"

"Yes, well, once you've been a slave yourself, you understand these things," said Mortar quietly.

"Bullshit!" One of the Dozen fake-coughed into his hand.

But inside Mortar was annoyed with himself. He was annoyed with Jesus. And he did a very natural and human thing: he took it out on those closest to him, saying,

"Brick, you dumbass, get over here and clean these dishes."

Hey! Homo!

As Jesus and the Dozen made their way from one place to another, a certain, again unnamed member of the group, had lagged behind and when all of the others were ahead of him, he called out in a loud voice, "Hey! Homo!"

Another member of the Dozen turned around to look more quickly than the others, after which his face reddened involuntarily, conditioned to sensitivity as he was by this taunt. Most of the others, many of whom did not even turn around to look, continued on their way after little more than fleeting looks of consternation passed across their faces. One of the Dozen mumbled weakly, "Leave him alone," but there was no more than this.

The one at the back who had called out this mischievous and malicious slur laughed in a nasty way at the imagined cleverness of his own trick.

But Jesus, knowing who had shouted this comment, turned to the group, and when all had closed up behind him, and he said these words as he held up three fingers:

"There are three kinds of people in the world: victims, bystanders and perpetrators."

Peter counted on his fingers the three types of people, saying under his breath, "victims, bystanders, perpetrators..."

The Rabbi looked hard at all the group, and he paused briefly before saying while holding up two fingers, "No wait. There's two kinds of people in the world: sinners and assholes, although some people can be both."

Many of the men and women were taken aback by the Rabbi's use of the word 'asshole' and the vehement way in which he had pronounced it. But before anyone could speak, the Rabbi held up one finger and said, "No wait. There's only one kind of person in Heaven: the humble."

The unnamed disciple who had begun all this with his hateful taunt ground his teeth as he hung his head after suffering a serious look of disapproval from the Rabbi.

Very late that evening, Jesus was apart from the group, praying alone, when one of the Dozen approached him and sat down beside him. Jesus nodded in welcome and waited for the man to speak.

"I am hateful to myself," he said. After a short pause he continued, "I am hated by my own family, by my own people. I'm different from the others." The pain in his voice was palpable and Jesus reached out and put his hand on the man's shoulder.

Speaking in a low voice the Rabbi recited the words of the psalmist saying,

"For you created my inmost being;
you knit me together in my mother's womb.

I praise you because I am fearfully and wonderfully made;
your works are wonderful,
I know that full well.
My frame was not hidden from you,
when I was made in the secret place.
When I was woven together in the depths of the earth,
your eyes saw my unformed body.
All the days ordained for me
were written in your book
before one of them came to be.
How precious to me are your thoughts, O G-d!
How vast is the sum of them!"

The man pondered the words of his Rabbi and finally said, "Thank you, Rabbi. You're too good for the likes of us."

"This teacher loves his students, you no less than any of these others. The Almighty is G-d of all the living, not just those who think they own Him. Be at peace in your heart for you are loved by G-d."

Greatly heartened by these generous words, the man found the strength to forgive his tormentor; but more to the point, he began to forgive himself for his own self-loathing.

Jesus' First Nightmare

"MaryMag," said Jesus, "I had a very bad and disturbing dream a few nights ago." And he told of his dream in this way: there was a very dark place lit by torchlight and men in black robes were torturing my mother saying, "You're really just a Jew, aren't you?!" And Mother, crying, says, "He is my son." And the men insist, "but you are a Jew, are you not? Do you worship the Christ, or do you worship your Father of Lies?" And they hit her in horrible ways. I don't want to describe it; it's so... ugly. And she says again, "He is my son, he is a Jew and I am a Jew." And they hit her even harder. They hit her on the head. It's terrible. And then she turns to look at me, to look at me for help, her eyes are wild with fright. And in the dream, I feel responsible, as if I am to blame for them hurting her."

"How does the dream make you feel now?" asked Mary.

"I feel awful, terrible," replied Jesus.

"What do you think it means?" she asked.

"Sometimes I worry that people will take the things I say, they'll take them the wrong way," he said, "but I can't control them. I can't make anyone think, or act or believe a certain way."

"I'm not sure that you can be held responsible for the things that other people do. You can influence them for either good or evil, but everyone's responsible for their own actions, and that's the truth," said MaryMag.

"What is truth?" asked Jesus.

"Here's what I know of the truth: I've found the truth in many places and not always with those who claim to possess it. The truth is not something that is owned. It is not locked away in a trunk. Truth is active, it is lived, it is roughed up; it is exercised and used. Truth is practiced and refined or perfected. And what poor vessels are we, whom G-d has chosen to carry the truth. He must be so disappointed to give so much beauty and yet he must so rejoice whenever it changes even a single heart. G-d must be an optimist else he long ago would have done with us women and men. How else could he stay his hand of justice against us, for we deserve no less. And this: You are the Truth."

Mightier Than the Words

"Oh, Rabbi Jesus, I'm glad I caught you. I've been putting a few thoughts to paper for you to use. I wonder if you could take a few moments to look it over," said the Wordsmith, Para-Apostle Brick.

"Of course, I can. Let's have a look-see," said Jesus.

Brick handed Jesus his script and sat back with a look of great satisfaction, for he knew that what he had written was pure gold.

As Jesus read over the script his eyes widened in disbelief and then he laughed which was not a reaction that Brick seemed happy to have elicited.

"What's so funny?" he asked the Rabbi just a little indignantly.

"Perhaps my English isn't the best," said Jesus, "but 'the penis mightier than the words'? I'm not sure that I understand your meaning there."

"Wait, wait, wait. That's not what I wrote. Let me look at it again," demanded Brick. He hastily snatched the script back from Jesus and closely scrutinized the text and, sure enough, he hadn't left enough space between his words 'pen' and 'is', and as it stood, it read 'penis'.

"Damn! Oh, pardon me, Rabbi," said Brick, "your English is good enough. It's me penmanship that's wanting." And he made the correction on the spot by drawing a line between 'pen' and 'is'. "Now then, try again," said Brick.

"So," said Jesus, taking the script back from Brick and continuing to read, "it should read, 'the pen is mightier than the words'? I'm still not sure that I get it."

"The pen," explained a slightly peeved Brick at having to explain the brilliance of his thought, "has the potential and therefore is more important than the actual words it writes. Now," said Brick with a hint of condescension, "do you get it?" And he thought that sometimes the Rabbi could be a little... well, thick. "For gosh sakes, it's like explaining a joke. The humor is lost," he lamented.

And Jesus replied patiently, "If I could offer a small suggestion, take the 's' from 'words', move it to the front and make 'sword'. Then you'd have 'the pen is mightier than the sword', but I don't know English that well and, of course, you're the Man o'Words."

"What?! This ain't no scrabbling scramble of words! This is high art! I'm tryin' to upheave the level of discourse," said Brick, huffing off and thinking, "That Rabbi's got some work to do if he thinks people are going to remember any of his words."

Fling Open the Gates of Mercy

"Fling open the Gates of Mercy!" cried Jesus lustily. He threw his hands wide apart.

"Hey, J.T., what are the Gates of Mercy?" asked Mortar.

"Well, they're... they're... they're... the Gates of Mercy! You know... everyone knows... the Gates of Mercy..." said JT uncertainly. Then with certainty he turned to Jesus and boldly asked, "What are the Gates of Mercy?"

"The Gates of Mercy?" said Jesus repeating the question. "Why, the Gates of Mercy, that's the doorway into Heaven, not to be confused with the Gates of Justice, which is the doorway to Hell."

"Why are the gates of Hell called the Gates of Justice?' asked Mortar.

"Something like 'abandon hope all ye who enter here' should be inscribed over the gate," said Brick.

"That's a good thought, but all who enter Hell pass under the inscription that says 'the judgments of the LORD are true and righteous altogether'," replied Jesus. "and each, as they enter, will never admit the Truth of it. But over the Gates of

Mercy is the following inscription: 'Lord have mercy on me, a sinner', and each, as they enter, will ever admit the Truth of it."

Smokey on the Water

Recommended listening: *Smoke on the Water*
by Deep Purple

Out of the mist and fog covering the lake came a small disk that seemed to hover in one spot before changing course and slowly beginning to return back into the obscurity of the fog from whence it came. But before that, a black dog raced from out of the fog, leapt high and caught the disk in its mouth and landed on all fours on the surface of the lake. The dog wheeled around and returned running into the fog. Four of the Twelve from their position in the boat saw this clearly but could not believe their eyes. They said nothing, but they kept watching.

Presently the disk reappeared just over their heads, seemed to hover above them and then changed course, returning toward the fog. Jude Thaddeus called the attention of the remaining Eight to the flight of the disk and this time all of the Twelve beheld as again the black dog bounded out of the fog, jumped and fetched the disk out of the air, landed solidly on the watery surface and returned toward the fog, but this time the figure of a Son of Man appeared coaxing the dog with encouraging words and praising him for his deft and well-timed leap.

This Son of Man, looked up and noticed the boatload of wide eyes and dropped jaws, and headed with the dog jumping about him, across the surface of the lake toward the Twelve.

Mouths agape, the Twelve, seeing but still not believing, recognized this Son of Man as their Rabbi Jesus. Jude Thaddeus, in his disbelieverment, stood up in the boat, which caused it to rock even more perilously than it had previously. Peter, the fisherman, lunged away from Jude Thaddeus to counterbalance this sudden movement, but he misjudged and fell out of the boat.

And Jude Thaddeus, given to voicing the obvious, said, "Master, is that you?"

To which Jesus replied, "Well, duh! Who else could it be?"

Peter, who had easily pulled himself up onto the side of the boat, said, "Lord, if it is you, bid me come to you across the water," for he thought this a clever trick.

"Come on, then," said Jesus and Peter took some tentative steps on the surface, in the full knowledge that he was defying several of the Laws of Nature and wondering how it could be.

In a short time, rationality clouded his view of this activity and he began wondering that the waves and wind still obeyed the Laws of Nature while the same seemed not required of him. He began to sink below the surface of the water, but Jesus grasped his hand and pulled him into the boat and Smokey jumped in as well. Smokey, with an enthusiastic shake, wetted the others in the boat.

The astounded men stood or sat and stared, for they were completely unprepared for such a display of... a display of... well, they didn't know the answer. Jesus reached out and lifted Jude Thaddeus' chin to close his gaping mouth. J.T. swallowed hard and found the words to say, "Jesus, are your feet wet?"

"Of course, they are," replied Jesus.

J.T., always finding words, not always the right ones, but finding them nonetheless, said, "Jesus, do dogs come by this ability naturally, because I know that it is not in the nature of men to do this thing naturally."

"Define 'naturally', suggested the Rabbi.

"Well, well..." sputtered J.T.

"It's a deep subject," countered Jesus.

"What?" said J.T.

"I said, 'It's a deep subject.' Get it?" asked Jesus.

"What?" said J.T., even more perplexed.

"A well," said Jesus.

"A what?" said J.T. squinting his eyes.

"A well," said Jesus matter of factly.

This put an end to their need for words and J.T. simply stared at this Son of Man.

Peter looked in dismay.

James and John were dumbfounded.

Andrew was flabbergasted.

Judas was stupefied.

Simon Zealot and Nathaniel were flummoxed.

The others, whatever their names are, were pole axed, aghast, taken aback, astounded and amazed. They had all drawn back away from Jesus. A hand of one of the disciples reached fearfully forward to touch the Rabbi and quickly withdrew after confirming for all that this was indeed a flesh and blood creation in G-d's own image.

All were stone dead silent, having lost temporarily the power of speech and reason. The looks on their faces spoke more eloquently than anything they might have said. But there was the thread of a thought common to them all, a thought, a sounded note that resonates down to our own days, 'Who *is* this Son of Man?

"Always swim with a buddy," said the Rabbi.

There was no response.

"Never swim alone," counseled Jesus.

Still none spoke.

"I learned when I was young that you should always swim with a buddy," said Jesus. "I nearly drowned once. And it wasn't fun."

Professional Development Day

It wasn't a Sabbath, but Jesus invited the Dozen to a day all to themselves, a day of fellowship. There was swimming in the lake, barbeque, and croquet.

Mortar busied himself with supervision of the preparation of the food. Some of the disciples teased him in a nasty way about doing 'women's work'. He suffered no qualms about doing this, taking pains to point out that most of the best chefs are men. Bartholomew, who had taken a special interest in his craft, was initiated into the Société Secret du Barbeque, complete with the secret handshake, monogrammed apron, and the Société's silver spatula.

Mortar made a potato salad without mayonnaise, explaining the dangers of unrefrigerated foods. He talked at length of dry rubs versus marinades. He talked of searing meat and slow cookery. In short, Mortar was a teacher at heart, but he relished too much the superiority that his knowledge bestowed and thought not at all about the responsibility.

Some of the men had erected a small pavilion to protect them from the sun and after a hearty repast, the men all settled down to more wine and cigars.

It was after everyone had settled in that the Rabbi began to talk with them, saying, "How about a polite golf clap for our chef, Mortar, who has served us so eloquently and gracefully the Word of G-d made Food?"

And the Dozen returned the requisite muted applause punctuated by several yummy sounds of appreciation. Mortar basked in the glow of admiration from his fellows, like roasted meat being basted in a rich sauce.

"Hey, guys," said Jesus, "have I told you the one about the Good Samaritans? About the guys who helped me....

"Heard it a thousand times already," said Thaddeus. All the rest nodded their heads in agreement. They would rather have heard a story about the Good Galileans, a story about themselves, rather than a story about the two para-pustules.

"Well, then..." Jesus spoke, saying, "Every day I thank G-d for you guys. I couldn't have asked for better friends, you're better than brothers. Things have gone quite well so far, but from here on out, it's going to get a lot more difficult, for the Son of Man came to serve rather than to be served. You see, men and women don't easily change their behaviors. Look to your own reactions to my words and deeds for the example. And yet I must say that we've all learned a great deal from each other.

An SBD (Silent But Deadly) fart insinuated itself among the men. A quick turn of a head and several sniffing noses tried to ascertain from whence it came. As the fart gained in strength and intensity, it attracted the attention of all, and Thaddeus complained, "By the dry bones of Ezekiel, that was slippery sucker!! 'Fess up! Who dunnit?"

All the disciples protested their innocence and waved their hands before their noses to dissipate the stench and Jesus, making a face, said, "Holy Moly, that's some nasty stuff! Hey, do you know why farts smell?"

"No, why do farts smell?" asked Judas, ever the straight man for the Savior.

"So the deaf can enjoy them, too!" cried Jesus

He waited for the men to return their attention to his words and then he continued, saying, "My words have not made your lives easier. If anything, you've been called to a higher standard of love built on our traditions of fulfilling the law and heeding the messages of the prophets. You have been called to the standard of love, a love that encompasses men and women, Jew and non-Jew, Judean and Galilean, Roman and Samaritan. You have learned that prayer changes the heart, your own heart. You have learned that G-d loves sinners no less than he loves Pharisees. You've learned that there is unity in love, that the G-d of all humanity seeks the lost and the lowly."

Some of the disciples on the periphery had nodded off, what with the bright sun's warm rays and the meal that cast its magic spell over them. Of course, it really was the stomach requiring greater blood flow for digestion, but they weren't encumbered by that knowledge.

Peter looked around and seeing Thaddeus drowse, gave him a playful kick and said, "C'mon, man. Can't you stay awake and listen? Buck up!"

And Thaddeus, behind a closed eye, said, "I *am* listening. And don't kick me, or I'll whoop your ass."

"You and what legion?" mocked Peter. "And somebody kick the Brick over there. Even para-apostles need to stay awake!"

James and John, in like manner, rebuked the others who had fallen asleep, saying, "Come on, you guys! Can't you stay awake for a while?"

"Are you boys quite finished?" asked Jesus in a dry tone. Taking a different tack, Jesus said, "did you hear the one about non-believer who proposed to a good Jewish girl?"

This, of course, captured the rapt attention of the men, and even Thaddeus opened his eye and leaned forward, eager for every word. And Jesus said:

"A young lady came home and told her Mother that her boyfriend had proposed but she had turned him down because she found out he was a non-believer, and didn't believe in Heaven or Hell. "Marry him anyway, dear." the Mother said. "Between the two of us, we'll show him just how wrong he is."

"And just like the Mother and Daughter, we shall show people that the Kingdom of Heaven is right here and right now."

Unpleasantries

Speaking of Heaven and Hell..." said Thaddeus snidely. And the others turned their heads to see what Thaddeus saw. Mary the Magdalene was approaching them with the other ladies following timidly behind her. The Magdalene walked boldly up to the Rabbi and said loudly, "Women are excluded from eternal life with the Almighty."

No one among the Dozen challenged this sentiment. A few of them seemed to weigh the Magdalene's statement in their minds, but with mental shrugs accepted her declaration at face value.

"Sucks to be you," said Thaddeus, looking around at the men for their approval. Several of the men chuckled uneasily, but chuckled nonetheless.

But the Rabbi, not entirely comfortable with this venue for this discussion, said slowly, "well, that's not really true, Mary. Abba Father loves women as much as He loves men..." His voice trailed off in further thought.

Susannah, standing behind the Magdalene, whispered, "Maybe Abba Father loves women *more* than men!" Several of the women giggled, covering their mouths with their hands.

"In that case, women *will* receive eternal life? Is that what you're saying?" said the Magdalene, trying to lead the Rabbi into an unequivocal statement.

"Yesss," said Jesus carefully, "women will enter G-d's kingdom."

"Women?! In G-d's kingdom?!" cried Peter, not believing what he was hearing. "G-d made his covenant with men. We bear the 'mark' of our covenant!"

"Do not think for one minute, Peter, that men are superior to women because you have penises!" cried the Magdalene impatiently. "G-d didn't need to remind us women in such a personal manner to keep his covenant!"

Although shocked by the Magdalene's blunt remarks, the men remained silent. Some of the Dozen even lapsed into thought at her suggestion that women didn't require a physical sign of the covenant and they might have admitted inwardly that she had a point.

"In that case," continued the Magdalene, "we want to sit at the Rabbi's feet and hear the living words while we are alive."

No one moved and no one said anything. Before losing the moment, the Magdalene said to the men, "Move over and make some room under the pavilion in the shade for us." And the men closest to the Magdalene grudgingly shoved themselves over to make room for the women.

Jesus Tells of Abraham Pleading for Sodom and Gomorrah

Tell us a story, Jesus," said James the Less eagerly. "C'mon, tell!"

"What story?" Brick asked of James the Less.

"A story from the Torah," replied Nathanael. "Jesus has a perfect memory for Scripture. He hears it once, and he remembers it perfectly. C'mon, tell about Abraham, Jesus."

"You know all about Abraham," said Jesus, "you tell it."

"No, you tell," cajoled James. "C'mon, tell it."

"Well, let's see. The Almighty decided to destroy Sodom and Gomorrah because of their great wickedness. In fact, if G-d was in the business of destroying the wicked, there would be very few people left and He would be booked for weeks in advance. But Abraham said to G-d, "Far be it from You to destroy the righteous along with the wicked, because You are a merciful and just G-d.

"Oh, yeah," said G-d. "What are you selling?"

"What if there are 50 righteous people in Sodom and Gomorrah, would you still destroy it?" queried Abraham.

"No," said G-d, "I will forbear to deconstruct." This last He pronounced with a lofty air and laid his right hand across his breast, lifting his eyes heavenward as if to pledge his honor.

"What did You say?" asked Abraham.

"Forbear to deconstruct," said G-d, enunciating this time very carefully and rolling his Rs.

"Forbear to deconstruct?" repeated Abraham wonderingly. "You are indeed an enigmatic G-d! But, now that I have been so bold as to speak, I will continue and say, what if there are only forty-five righteous men? Would you still 'deconstruct' those towns?

"Maybe," said G-d, "but cut to the chase. Where's this going? What's your bottom line?"

"What if there are ten righteous men in Sodom and Gomorrah? Would you 'deconstruct' the righteous along with the wicked? Say it ain't so," pleaded Abraham.

"It's very wicked there. I doubt that you could find 10 righteous men," said G-d.

"You're not going to flood the place again, are You?" asked Abraham.

"No, floodwater isn't the sort of PDW that I was hoping it might prove to be," said G-d.

"What's a PDW?" asked Abraham suspiciously.

"Pinpointedly Discriminating Weapon," replied G-d, and then He stated flatly, "Collateral damage, don't you know. But," said the Almighty with a raised forefinger, "I've got an A of D weapon in Research and Development right now that hopefully resolves the issue in an acceptable manner. And did I mention all the mopping up that had to be done after the Deluge? My G-d, what a mess that was!"

"I'm lost again," said Abraham, shaking his head. "What's an A of D?"

"Angel of Death! Don't you keep up with current trends in weaponry?" asked G-d. "We're talking real precision here!"

"Ah, no, but, OK," said Abraham. "I almost hate to ask, but how, then, are You going to do it?" asked Abraham.

"I'm experimenting with various 'media' and this time I'm going to employ H & B from an HBP," said G-d, hoping to sound professional.

"What's H & B from an HBP, or whatever?" asked Abraham.

"Hellfire & Brimstone! And Heaven Based Platform!" cried G-d impatiently. "Do I have to tell you everything?"

"Hellstone and brimfire!! Heaven Placed Batform!!!" cried James the Less overeagerly, for this was his favorite part of the story and he made explosion noises with accompanying hand motions.

"Do you want to tell it?" asked Jesus, raising his right eyebrow a bit.

"No, you go! Tell it!" cried James, totally oblivious to the annoyance of the Rabbi.

"Well," said Jesus, slipping back into the character of Abraham, "where was I? Hellstone and brimfire, I mean, hell*fire* and brim*stone*," said Jesus, correcting himself and emphasizing the correct combination of words. And he continued this way.

"Hellfire and brimstone? Where are you going to get those" asked Abraham, suspicion and doubt creeping into his tone.

"Don't you worry about that. There are huge stockpiles of the stuff and its expiration date is drawing nigh. Use it or lose it," admonished G-d.

"Hellfire and brimstone? That stuff's wicked awful. Why do You have it?" asked Abraham.

"Never you mind that. I have a 2nd Amendment right, you know," said G-d.

"Yes, but You haven't answered my questions. Where will you get hellfire and brimstone and why do you have it, anyway?

"Satan. He owes me," said G-d a touch defensively. "What? You don't think I keep hellfire and brimstone in Heaven, do you? Environmental Impact Statements, Hazardous Materials Handling Training & Licensure, security clearance, background checks, Personal Reliability Program, etc, etc. It's just too much paperwork."

"I'm sure I don't know about any of that," said Abraham a little sarcastically.

"And that's why you're not G-d," retorted G-d peevishly.

"I hate it when You do that!" cried Abraham.

"What?" asked G-d, wary of walking into a verbal minefield.

"You pull rank to get out of answering questions," said Abraham. "If we are to have any future dealings, I'm going to want them in writing. And in plain language, no small print."

"In writing?" asked G-d incredulously. "No small print? Don't you trust me?"

"Should I?" asked Abraham.

"Shouldn't you?" asked G-d, reversing the proposition.

"Look," said Abraham, "trust is a two-way street and the days when a man's handshake sealed a bargain are gone. Any future agreements between us will need to be in writing. Besides, when I tell people that I talk with you, I get funny looks."

"Perhaps that's not such a bad idea. Hmm... in writing. I'll take your suggestion under advisement," said G-d, already scheming as to how He could turn the whole covenant business, currently in the conceptual phase, into a Win-Win proposition. G-d lapsed into silence, so busy was His Mind racing ahead with visions of a vast array of possibilities.

Finally, Abraham broke the silence by clearing his throat, "Ahem. Trust, contractual agreements. In writing?"

Thus interrupted, G-d returned to the present moment, regarded Abraham absently and said, "Ah, I'll get back to you on this stuff. Gotta go. TTFN." And the Almighty vanished in a wisp of smoke (He had been working on entrances and exits and their various effects.) leaving Abraham in mid-sentence, "OK. Good... bye."

And Abraham was left to wonder if the Almighty was one who could be trusted to keep His Word. And he determined to get future agreements..."

"Written in stone!!" cried James the Less with gusto and before he subsided, he repeated to himself for good measure, "written in stone."

"So," said Jesus, concluding his recitation, "so, as you can see, trusting G-d for everything isn't always so easy, as our Father Abraham found out. And of course, that is the seminal thought from which was born what came to be known as the 10 Commandments, which, as we all know, were..."

"Written in stone!" cried James the Less.

"Written in stone," affirmed the Rabbi.

And James turned to Brick and said, "That's what I like about the Rabbi. He puts things in a way that the average guy can understand."

The Water Test

The Rabbi Jesus was teaching the disciples in the shade of a pavilion by the lake. He spake and said unto them, "There are two kinds of people in the world..." And Thaddeus broke in to finish the Rabbi's sentence saying, "Two kinds of people... faith-FUL and faith-LESS. Either you have faith or you don't. One or the other. Not both." And he sat back, pleased with himself for the incisive wisdom that he was imparting to his friends and for saying it better than the Rabbi himself said things, so he thought. He looked around the group to acknowledge their nods to this word, this gem from the storehouse of his genius.

And Jesus repeated, "Faith-FUL or Faith-LESS. One or the other, but not both. Let's give Thaddeus a polite round of applause and the 'Water Test' to see if it really is true."

"That's right!" repeated Thaddeus confidently, "either you have faith, or you don't have faith. Either or. Not both." And then with a voice that betrayed far less confidence he took the bait, swallowed it whole, and said, "Uh, I'm not familiar with this... uh, '*Water Test*'." He made finger quotes around *Water Test*.

"Well, a wise *and* honest man," said the Rabbi, "and since yours is the truth to be tested, you may have the honor of fetching a cup and a skin filled with water for the Water Test." Jesus mimicked Thaddeus by putting finger quotes around *water test.*

Thaddeus grimaced at the thought of fetching anything because it was women's work to perform this sort of drudgery. It was beneath his dignity as a disciple to fetch water, but to show his 'superior-ness' to customs and tradition, like the Rabbi frequently did, he quickly fulfilled the request.

Jesus, taking the cup, turned it upside down to show the others that it was indeed empty, and then held the cup aloft and said, "Empty – faith-LESS." The others, eager students that they were, nodded their heads with alacrity. Then he took the skin, filled the cup and held it aloft and said, "Full – faith-FULL. The others nodded eagerly in affirmation. This wasn't so hard.

"Thaddeus," said Jesus, holding the cup higher, "come and inspect the cup closely to make sure that it is as full as it can be." Thaddeus stepped up, rolled his eyes, glanced quickly at the cup, and said, "Yes, it's as full as it can be." And then he gave a snorting chuckle. He was satisfied that the cup was full and he was satisfied that he had taught the Rabbi something. Jesus wasn't the only smart fish in this pond.

"Thaddeus," said Jesus, "I want you to be really, really, *really certain* that the cup is as full of faith as it can be. Would you kindly inspect the cup more closely?"

Thaddeus looked again at the others, cocked his head to the left, smirked and then bent over, face just mere inches from the cup and was going to loudly proclaim the cup to be full when Jesus, with a timely, well-aimed flick of the wrist, splashed the water from the cup into Thaddeus' face.

Thaddeus sputtered at the water in his face and raised his hands to wipe the water away.

And Jesus held the cup up for the disciples to see and said, "Empty? Faith-LESS? But there's a tiny bit of water still in the cup. Faith-LESS?" Jesus then poured more water into the cup, but did not quite fill it up. He showed the disciples how much water was in the cup and he asked, "Full?" He frowned and said, "No. Neither faith-FULL, nor faith-LESS?" And with a quick snap of the wrist, he again threw the water in Thaddeus' face. Our scholar had still not recovered from the shock of the first splash and the Rabbi was at it again!

Then Jesus took the cup, poured a little bit of water into it, then he again put the proposition to the disciples, "Partly full? Partly empty? Faith-FULL or faith-LESS?" Thaddeus, quick learner that he was, took a step back. Now they sat quietly and waited for whatever Jesus would say next.

Jesus smiled and drank the water in the cup. Then he said unto them, "But here's the real point: From whence does the water come?"

Sarcastically, Thaddeus said, "From the lake."

"From the lake," mimicked Jesus in a squeaky voice and then continued in his regular voice, "I believe that water is serving as a metaphor for faith. Thank you, Thaddeus, you may sit."

Thaddeus did not really appreciate being summarily dismissed and sullenly sat down. A look of consternation passed across his face.

"Now," said Jesus, "let's pose that question again. From whence does the water come?"

No one dared to speak and several disciples put on their thinking faces as if to say that although they were trying to work this out in their minds, they hadn't yet come up with any definitive answers.

"Water, like faith," explained Jesus patiently, "comes as a gift from the Almighty."

"Now, how did you feel when the 'faith' or 'water' was flung in your face, Thaddeus? Don't answer; we could see it on your face," added Jesus quickly. "That is the faith of the 'self-righteous'. It burns others rather than comforting them. Now, however, if we are offered faith as a drink with kindness, it satisfies and refreshes. That is faith that pleases G-d.

Truth and S'mores

This is how the whole thing went down. It was night. It was dark. Therefore it was a dark night. Brick and Mortar had waited for all the disciples to fall asleep. When they thought it was safe, they reached into their traveling bags and brought forth graham crackers, a Hershey's chocolate bar, and marshmallows. The scent of the marshmallows roasting awoke Jesus for he was gifted with an astonishingly sensitive sense of smell.

"I want one of those," said Jesus in a whisper.

"We want a story, first," replied Brick.

"But that will wake up the others," protested Jesus.

"They wouldn't understand anyway."

"There was a man once – have I told you this one? There was a man once. He sought the Truth. He was sitting in this wine bar and there were foreigners at the bar talking, and the man began to eavesdrop, which was no mean feat as eaves had yet to be invented, but anyway, one foreigner was regaling the other with a tale of Truth.

"She's a t'ing of beauty, she is!" exclaimed Foreigner 1. "A whole mountain of Truth, a'risin' up outta the sea; there lives there a hermit ..." So the man vows to himself that he *tout suite* would seek out this mountain of Truth, when he had more time. Well, he never did seek out the mountain of Truth because he was just too busy. But the second foreigner did seek out the mountain of truth. It took many years.

And when he arrived at the Mountain of Truth, there was no uncertainty because merely by looking at the mountain, you knew it was the Mountain of Truth, for it was very beautiful.

Before any time had passed the Foreigner was approached by a man who said, "I am the Official Hermit Guardian of the Mountain of Truth. For only a small fee I can provide you with all the truth that you need to live your life."

Almost before the Official Hermit Guardian of the Mountain of Truth finished speaking, the Original Hermit Guardian of the Mountain of Truth stepped up and broke in, "He is a fraud. Have nothing to do with him. My rates are much better and only I offer a monthly service contract."

Before he could say more another man stepped up and said, "I can't believe that you are even considering what these two charlatans are saying! For I am the Genuine Hermit Guardian of the Mountain of Truth!"

Up stepped another man who bellowed, "You can't handle the Truth!!"

He was followed by an attractive woman who spoke nary a word, but paid a certain 'hip-service' as it were, to Truth.

She was followed by an elderly man who proclaimed, "It's the Truth because I say it's the Truth!"

In quick succession he was followed by a child with a fierce and cunning countenance, followed by, followed by, you get the idea. And finally, when all the other official, original, genuine, bona fide, real McCoy, et cetera, so on and so forth, had made his or her pitch, a humble looking man stepped forward. He was carrying a gourd filled with cool, clear water and said to the Foreigner, "You have traveled a long way. You must be thirsty. Would you like a drink of water?"

After an uncertain pause, Jesus said, "Um, that's it."

Looks of confusion and then suspicion crossed Mortar's face and he said, "That doesn't make any sense."

Jesus was somewhat abashed, "Well, it, ah, it, ah, it's not finished. You try to come up with something. You'll find it isn't so easy. But, what do you call those things?"

Those things had been prepared the while that Jesus was giving his parable. Brick took a big bite and through mouth crowded with sweet, gooey goodness, he said, "Shammorez. Don't tell me you don't know what a shammorez is?!"

Jesus had difficulty pronouncing the word and it clumsily tumbled out of his mouth as "S'mores."

Brick and Mortar looked at each other in disbelief and then burst out in raucous laughter for Jesus' pronunciation reminded them of a word in Gaulic slang that meant....., well, it wouldn't be polite to say in this context.

When the laughter subsided, the men were able to put together a shammorez which Jesus polished off in short order and as he was licking his fingers, he asked, "Is there any of that bacon stuff left over?"

PART V

Letter of the Law, Spirit of the Law

Jesus had worked himself into something of a lather or had warmed to his topic, depending on your perspective, with his denunciation of the Pharisees.

"Brood of vipers," he had called them.

"Excuse me, Rabbi, but aren't the Pharisees trying to keep the Law?" asked a small, innocent voice.

"Yes, they are," conceded Jesus, "but they expend more energy trying to meet the letter of the Law while ignoring the spirit of the Law. That's what gripes me!"

"My uncle Nicodemus is a Pharisee and he isn't like that," said the small and innocent voice.

This observation brought Jesus up short and he backpedaled from his assertion, "Well, I didn't mean ALL of the Pharisees." He put his hands up as if to push away his statement and then he looked skyward, put his finger to his temple and raised his chin, mentally assessing what had been said.

And while he was thinking, the small, innocent voice spoke again saying, "Why will this generation suffer for what was done by others in the past? For in Proverbs it says, 'The father eats sour grapes and the son's teeth are set on edge.'"

Jesus, without speaking, pointed with his finger into the air to acknowledge this question and to ask, without words, for a moment to consider his answer.

An awkward silence fell over the group. Everyone looked to him to see how he might recover and answer what appeared to be a valid challenge to his words. Some gave the stink-eye to the questioner, more concerned that anyone who dared raise any question, was only interested looking smart in front of the group.

"You're right to make this distinction, Nephew of Nicodemus, and you are right to speak well of your Uncle Nicodemus, who, indeed, is a seeker of truth." Jesus paused briefly because he wanted to make certain that everyone heard what he was about to say, and he continued, "I misspoke." And again, Jesus paused briefly, again to make certain that everyone heard what he said. "Assuming that ALL persons in a group act the same way is... not true and not fair. And you, young man, are a true son of Abraham. Our forefather in faith challenged our G-d before the destruction of Sodom and Gomorrah; and you have challenged your teacher. Well done!"

"In the same way, we must admit that just because we are part of a certain group, does not make us all righteous in the sight of G-d. G-d loves the pure in heart, each of us, individually, Jew or Gentile, and not simply because we belong to any group."

The Rabbi spent a long evening alone in prayer with Abba Father. It was dawning on him just how weighty were his words, that in spite of how careful he was with his words, he might not yet have all understanding and he might not express his thoughts and words with all clarity.

Add to that, the variety of interpretations that might arise from misremembered and misunderstood reports of his words, not to mention any deliberate misrepresentations.

It was a mistake that the Rabbi hoped he wouldn't make a second time.

Pan-Seared Tilapia with Citrus Vinaigrette

Suggested listening: *Two Little Fishes and Five Loaves of Bread* by Sister Rosetta Tharpe

Recipe serves 5000 (not to mention women and children)

- 5000 (7500 ounce) tilapia fillets
- 625 teaspoons salt, divided 13 cups
- 625 teaspoons fresh ground black pepper, divided 13 cups
- 625 cups white wine 39 gallons
- 2500 tablespoons finely chopped shallots 156 cups/39 gallons
- 2500 tablespoons fresh lemon juice 156 cups/39 gallons
- 2500 tablespoons fresh orange juice 156 cups/39 gallons
- 5000 teaspoons extra virgin olive oil 104 cups/26 gallons
- 2500 teaspoons sherry wine vinegar 52 cups/13 gallons

There are two kinds of miracles: slow and fast. Fast miracles are usually very dramatic and garner all the attention, whereas the slow type of miracle is often much more miraculous in terms of final outcome than are fast miracles. Think here of a person who changes from being a jerk and turns into a great guy, or gal. A changed life is by far the best of all miracles but usually that change takes place slowly, almost imperceptibly and you wake up one morning and realize that a person has changed significantly and you wonder how it happened. Well, it happened one step at a time, at G-d's own pace and the person's own pace. For G-d does not force himself upon anyone. In a sense, it's all up to us.

Mortar would be very hard-pressed to explain how it happened. Later he said that it was as if Jesus read his mind and turned what was only a thought into reality.

The scene is familiar. Jesus preaching to a multitude, nobody has eaten, but they can't break away, so enthralling are the Rabbi's words. Suddenly everyone realizes that they haven't eaten in quite some time and this hunger is all the more acute for the desolateness of their surroundings.

Two fishes and 5 loaves are brought forward, but it's comical. How could anyone think that such a small amount would satisfy this many people. Well, it couldn't. That's why Jesus determined to do 'something'.

When Jesus had returned thanks for the two fishes and the 5 loaves, Mortar broke in, "You're not going to serve it like that, are you?"

"What do you mean?" asked Jesus.

"Well, why don't we pan-sear the tilapia, whip up a quick citrus vinaigrette, make a nice barley pilaf with a few herbs and spices, and add a nice green vegetable on the side."

Impressed with Mortar's idea, Jesus turned the thought into reality. And all 5000 ate their fill, to say nothing of women and children.

Thaddeus was handed a plate, to which he replied, "No, thanks. I don't like fish."

Mary's Paps

Luke 11:27

A half-amused, half-confused look passed over Mortar's face as he looked back over the crowd to see who had shouted out this rather strange benediction.

Then he looked over at Brick, held his hand to his mouth to guide his words only to Brick and whispered almost aloud, "What's a paps?"

Brick, the brains of the outfit, looked disdainfully at Mortar and spoke this word out the side of his mouth, "Breasts."

Mortar spoke the word back for certainty, "Breasts?"

Brick confirmed his uncertainty, "Breasts."

Mortar still seemed uncertain.

So, Brick translated into the vernacular, "You know, boobies."

"Oh, right," said Mortar. But then a look of shock came over his face that anyone might mention aloud Mary's breasts. "Mary's boobies?"

"I should hope so," replied Brick.

"Why's that old bugger got to up lift the Magdalene's breasts to everyone's scrutinizing? It's sick!" said an outraged Mortar.

"No," said Brick, "not the Magdalene's breasts, although I wouldn't mind lifting those breasts up. He's talking about Jesus' mother Mary's breasts."

"I think her point is a vote of confidence for the Grand Dame. But, in a way, it tis funny." said Brick.

"Now why are you cursing her and what's so funny about the Ever-Virgin's paps? And what's a boat of fondicence? Is that like when Peter fell out of the boat and tried to make it look like he was walking on the water?" asked Mortar.

"Is that what you heard?" asked Brick. "He didn't fall out of the boat. They pushed him out."

"Go on, they didn't!" said Mortar.

"And Jesus, nice guy that he is, reached out and pulled him back in the boat. Now the story's going around that Jesus walked on the water, which I personally believe, but now they're saying that Peter, too, walked on the water, which I personally don't believe. Why? I'll tell you why. Have you seen his feet? Webbed toes! Peter has got webbed toes! He showed me once. Down by the lake one day. So, if ducks, with full webbed feet can't walk on water, Peter, even with webbed toes, surely can't do it neither. It's that simple. It's log-i-cal. You've got to learn to use the power of the intellect. That's what I say," pontificated Brick.

"What about Peter's paps?" asked Mortar. "Maybe if they was bigger they would have helped him to float longer."

Curse G-d, and Die

And Jesus spake unto his disciples saying, "Curse G-d, and die." He paused for dramatic effect and looked at each of his disciples, at the looks of horror on their faces. This saying, of course, captured the attention of the men and they now paid heed to the Rabbi in earnest.

"Rabbi," said Jude Thaddeus, "this is truly a hard saying."

The others nodded their agreement.

"What do you suppose he means by "Curse G-d, and die?" whispered Mortar to the general assembly.

"If these who've been with him for a time don't get it, how are we supposed to understand?" responded Brick.

But the Rabbi himself spoke up to dispel the uneasiness. "It's from the Book of Job! Job's shrewish wife, while he sits on the ash heap, tells him to 'curse G-d and die."

"Now that's what I call encouragement!" cried Peter, himself a married man. "I know exactly how he feels!"

"And toward the end of the enigmatic book, G-d confronts Job and poses questions which he is hardly able to answer," said Jesus. "But Job had the last word, for when the Almighty is finished posing his questions from out of the whirlwind, and then Job repents in dust and ashes, he raises his boil-covered head for one last question and says to the Almighty, he says, "Are You, by any chance, related to my wife? Wait a minute. I know you. I know you. I married your sister!"

MEAT OF LIFE

Guys like Brick and Mortar seem to stumble onto good fortune accidentally. In this case, it is time alone with Jesus. One night as everyone lay sleeping around a small fire, Mortar heard the call of nature sounding deep within him. The need expressed itself with some urgency and Mortar quickly, and politely, I may add, stole away from his companions, and began to unburden himself in a likely spot in the nearby bushes.

While he was thus engaged, he heard his name being called in a soft, low voice, "Mortar."

Mortar craned his neck looking about and seeing no one, attributed the sound of his name to a trick of the wind in his ears. However, as a precaution against danger, he began to whistle. But just as he had set his mind to rest on the matter, he heard his name being called a second time, "Mortar," only this time a little bit louder. His eyes opened even wider, alert to even the slightest movement and he turned his head round like an owl as if... As if he could do anything to an assailant from his compromised squatting position with his garments hitched up. Sacre bleu! An attacker with the knife could cut his throat and his friends would find his body 'caught with his pants down', literally. How embarrassing!

There had been no mistaking his name being spoken. This was no trick of the wind and Mortar, seeing no one, was thoroughly spooked. Goosebumps covered his exposed backside. The leaves on the bushes mocked his efforts to strain his ears ever the harder in search of the elusive voice. And then he heard the voice again, "Mortar, walk ten paces straight behind you." And then, a moment later the voice added, "Wait until you're finished and watch your step."

The commands were unmistakably clear, but moving his feet through the brush ten paces in cold terror can be an impossible task.

"Who is there?" Mortar managed to push the words out through a mouth gone dry.

"Empirical police," countered the voice. "Come out with your hands up."

"I done nothing wrong," protested Mortar.

"You're charged with taking things on faith," replied the voice.

"What? I took nothing!" stammered Mortar, who then realized someone was having fun at his expense.

"Mortar," said Jesus, laughing while still trying to maintain the voice of his character, "come over here to the big rocks. Climb up here."

Mortar's relief on realizing it was his Master was immense and as he climbed the rocks he was greatly pleased that his 'needs' had produced for him a chance to talk to Jesus alone.

"You pray, talk with G-d?" asked Mortar, holding his hands prayer-like together.

"Right you are, sir," replied the Rabbi. "I like this spot here on the rocks, a little bit above the campsite. Your 'activity' caught my attention."

They both sat quietly for several moments looking up at the stars in the sky.

Then the Rabbi spoke saying, "Mortar, my good friend, let me ask you a question. Why did you and Brick want to come with me so badly? That day you begged me to find a place for you? And here we are. Have you found what you were looking for yet?"

Mortar let out a great, big sigh. "I learned the arts of the gastronome, butcher, baker, etc. from my father before he died, G-d rest his soul," said Mortar. "But I hear there's a saying in your country that man does not live by bread alone. I agree. Man needs beverages, desserts, bread, of course, meats, sauces, and all the rest! And then top it all off with a fine cigar and a snort of Grand Marnier!!" The mere thought of such sumptuous fare captured his whole attention for several moments. "I'll get to the point: your 'Bread of Life' phrase is too, too... bourgeois, it's 'everyday'. You make it sound like that's all you need it to live. Your idea which is good, is a starting point, but it lacks a certain, je ne sais pas, eh... eh... punch. If you forgive me daring to say it, I think you ought to change it to 'Meat of Life'. Meat has punch. It's solid! It's got substance! We could do, eh, something like, Morning Meat', say, or, something along those lines, say, 'Chunks of Meat', like a kebab!"

Jesus thoughtfully considered Mortar's suggestion, not without a fleeting, but good-natured smile not discernable in the dark.

Mortar continued, "Here's another idea: what if we went every Friday without eating any meat as sort of a sacrifice to realize how good we have it? A 'thankful day'? It would have the added benefit of boosting the business of those sorry fishermen that you've got on board with you. Anyway, if you put your mind to it, you can do almost anything," said Mortar, pleased with himself for having given the Rabbi some new insights into his own, how you say, le métier, I don't know, the world of meat.

"Master Mortar, I am exceedingly glad that you persisted in your request to join me in my enterprise," said Jesus. "You have been a real asset to the others and to me personally. I always come away a better man for having talked with you."

These kind words from the Rabbi would be treasured all his life along with the memory of their conversation on the rocks beneath the stars. And Mortar nursed the hope that Jesus would take his advice and put more meat into his message, as it were.

We don't have reliable information for where and how Mortar came to his end, but legend has it that he was flayed alive with his own knives in the wilds of Asia Minor, north of Edessa, in what is now modern Turkey. In fact, there is a phrase of Turkish origin about dogs and butchers: If skill could be gained by watching, every dog would become a butcher.

In that area they serve up a local delicacy called a Mortari Kebab, which is made from sheep's tongue served on pita bread with a very sharp, garlicky sauce. As to its origins, we can only guess.

Upon This Rock

The fire-gilt clouds roared and burned across the sky in a stupendous conflagration of pink and gold and purple. Straight above and behind, the sky displayed yellow, green, indigo, violet and finally, black. A slight wind blew in from the sea to cool the evening. People see what they want in any sunset, either the ephemeral and the fleeting, or the eternal and the infinite.

This night, this sky, like Jesus, bore a warning saying, "I will change you utterly."

"Remember when we were here two years ago when we knelt down as one and bared our necks to that murderer Pilate," said Jesus with a hint of nostalgia in his voice.

"We should have bared our backsides to him," roared Peter, although he recalled the cold sweat and fear of those moments.

"We were as one body," said Jesus staring into the fire, "We were united."

Exhausted from the day's exertions and anxious over the new dawning of his identity, Jesus bade the company good night and found a place to sleep amid the grass-tufted hillocks just back from the beach. He slept fitfully. His entourage, sitting in the sand around a small fire on the beach, nearer the water, tested the weight of his words. Several had lit cigars, those little Julietas, and used up many matches just for the fun of lighting them.

"Don't play wiff the matches!" warned Brick.

"What's matches?" asked Peter, striking yet another and wondering at the violent yellow flaring as the sulfur burned.

"Them little sticks of wood what have brimstone at the tip," explained Mortar.

"Gimme those!" said Brick like a parent, "and I'll put them away."

"Make me," said Peter stubbornly.

Brick struck quickly while Peter's attention was focused on the small flame and snatched the box out of his hands.

"Gimme those back!" Peter whined.

"Both of you, shut up and listen," said Judas. He was the one who always asked the hard questions and now was no exception, counting them off with his fingers, "1. Keys to the kingdom? 2. Son of the Living G-d? 3. Loosed and bound? 4. Don't tell? 5. Just what the hell is going on?"

"'The Christ, the Son of the living G-d?' G-d *had* to tell Simon, I mean 'Peter", said Bartholomew bitterly, "he wouldn't have figured that out all by himself, the dumb ass!"

"Who you callin' a dumb ass? You're just jealous, you sons o' bitches!" cried Peter jumping up. He began to dance around the fire, his feet kicking up sand at the others, and he broke into improvised song, "Keys to the kingdom! Keeper of the keys! Kingdom key care-keeper!"

"Yes," grumbled Andrew, "My brother, glorified door man!"

"I don't think I'll let you in, little brother," said Peter, tilting his head and arching one eyebrow.

"I can see him now," said Matthew derisively, "Sir, someone's at your door. What should I do? In or out? Ha, big responsibility!"

"Yer just jealous," derided Peter, joy not dampened by anything that was said, and he wondered aloud, "Will I get a booth? A book? I could set up a turnstile, or a booth, no, wait, a kiosk! And sell souvenirs and snacks! Everyone would have to come to my stall in front of the 'Pearly Gates' of Heaven; I'll make a killing!"

"Hey, Sweet Pea, there may be treasure in heaven, but there ain't no money! How do you think people are going to pay?" chided Thaddeus.

This brought an abrupt end to Peter's singing and dancing career and he stood defiantly before the others, arms akimbo and said, "Shut the hell up! Weren't you paying attention to the Rabbi? Sounds to me like I'll be a king, or a prophet, at least! ... the "gates of hell" shall not prevail... sounds uh, ex-alted!" he grandly pronounced, prolonging the word.

The night breeze suddenly switched up and smote Thaddeus in the eye with cigar smoke, who lowered his head and vigorously rubbed his right eye and cursed.

"By the way," Peter asked, "what's a church?"

"Who the hell knows, but it ain't important. Here's what I want to find out," said Matthew. "Why did Jesus say not to tell anyone? I mean, what's the big deal?"

"What's the big deal, he says!" cried Bartholomew in disbelief. "Son o' the Living G-d is all. Not such a big deal?!"

"I meant, big deal about *telling* people, you knucklehead," said Matthew.

"Never mind," said Bartholomew sheepishly.

"Yeah, why *did* he say 'don't tell anyone'?" asked Peter, now standing still.

Thoughtful looks rose on their faces, and their eyes rolled skyward in search of answers. Some heads were scratched and some chins were stroked, but, in the end, it proved too much for them. One by one their countenances returned to the earth to stare into the fire, and the usual stupid looks reclaimed their rightful thrones.

"Not to change the subject, but did anyone bring any wine?" asked Thaddeus.

"What about crackers? Anyone bring crackers?" asked Mortar.

"I just had a thought: Son of the Living G-d?" said Brick, his voice rising in alarm. "If anything bad happens to him... G-d sends his son and say, just for argument's sake, he gets killed, even accidentally, do you know what kind of trouble you'd be in?"

"It's nice to know you're in this with us," said Thaddeus sarcastically.

The wind now seemed to blow colder and they huddled closer to the fire and to each other and pulled their blankets a little tighter around themselves.

All thoughts beyond this one, horrible idea were banished and an awful sense of foreboding clutched their shoulders like the talons of a hawk.

From that time forth began Jesus to shew unto his disciples, how he must go unto Jerusalem, and suffer many things of the elders and chief priests and scribes, and be killed, and be raised again the third day.

Peter Professes His Faith to His Wife

Peter returned to his own house after many days traveling with Jesus to Caesarea Philippi. And his wife, Perpetua, spake unto him saying, "Where the hell hast thou been? Do you know how worried I have been about you? You didn't take a tunic, or a staff, or extra pair of sandals."

"Jesus has made me a 'fisher of men'," said Peter proudly.

"A fisher of men? There's something wrong with fish? Fish you can make a living from! What am I supposed to tell little Petronella when you don't show up for days at a time? She asks, 'Where's daddy?' What am I supposed to tell her?"

"He's the Messiah," stressed Peter, both hands chopping the air.

"Oh, again with this Jesus," shrugged Perpetua. "Our daughter needs a father, not a Messiah!"

"But Pet, He bade me follow him," explained Peter.

"And you went running right along after him," retorted Perpetua.

"He told us to go around the villages and preach the Good News," said Peter warily and looking at his wife sideways.

"Well, I've got some good news for you, too, buster," warned Perpetua, "Stay home or you'll find yourself out of a home, if you catch my meaning!"

"But I told you, he's the Messiah. He told us to heal the sick," said Peter defensively.

"And do you do everything Jesus tells you to do? If he told you to jump in the lake would you do it?" taunted Perpetua.

Peter cringed, and said "Well, he did tell me to walk on water and I did it."

"Walk on water, huh?" said Perpetua, losing her patience, "Have you been drinking?"

"He turned water into wine!" said Peter guardedly.

"I knew it!" shouted Perpetua, "You're getting in with a bad crowd." She said this with one hand on her hip and shook her finger at him, as if he were an unruly teenager.

At that moment, Jesus happened by and poked his head into the door and said, "Hey, Peter, how's it going? Hey Perpetua, how's Petronella?"

Peter replied, but kept his eyes on the ground, "Hey, Rabbi."

"Hello, Jesus," said Perpetua with venom in her tone.

There was an incredibly awkward silence which was finally broken by Perpetua, who glaring at Jesus, said, "Do you have to be hanging around with all those sinners? I'm worried that my Peter will start acting like them. He's impressionable and not very smart, you know." She really did have the best interests of her man in mind when she said this, but it just came out in a bossy, superior way.

"He did walk on the water," offered Jesus, trying to deflect the course of the discourse, "you should have seen him! A little weak at the end, but he did it!"

Peter's face brightened and he looked to Perpetua with obvious pride.

"Well, that may be," said Perpetua grudgingly, "but walking on water doesn't put fish on the table."

"This isn't about fish!" cried Peter, "it's about life! It's not about just me, it's about everyone! It's not about being a big fish in a small pond, it's about the water itself! Water that's alive! It's..." Here, Peter lost his way. Like a fish caught on a line, his thoughts thrashed about in the 'water that's alive' part, but he was conscious of saying something that might mean more than he meant, even though he couldn't say exactly what that was.

And for Jesus, an understanding dawned upon him, something that Mortar had said at the wedding in Cana, something about 'alive water', no, 'living water, living water!' His face shone with joy at the birth of this idea and he turned it over several times in his mind.

"Perpetua," said Jesus finally, "your husband might just be a genius!"

"Well, he is the best fisherman in these parts," admitted Perpetua. And after a short pause, she looked in wonder at her husband and asked, "So, you walked on water? Did anyone else do it?"

"Only Jesus and me!" crowed Peter, proud as a cock.

"And what's this business about Jesus and the Messiah?" she asked with clouded brow.

"That's what I said, Jesus is the Messiah," declared Peter, waiting for the thunderclap and lightning bolt from his wife.

But the clouds passed and Perpetua's face brightened and she said, "Well then, our lives will change." And then her face turned serious and she lapsed into silence.

"In ways you can't even dream," said Jesus softly.

A moment of thoughtful bliss occupied their minds briefly before Jesus offered, "Perpetua, your mother is ill with a fever. May I see her?"

And he touched her hand, and the fever left her: and she arose, and ministered unto them.

And that evening Peter came unto his wife who was saying her nightly prayers and sayeth, "Turtle Dove, maybe we could..."

"Have you been smoking?" she asked.

"Yes, Jesus offered cigars, but tomorrow we're leaving on a mission and I'll be gone for some days, I dunno, 1 or 2 days."

"Well, if you must."

"I was thinking maybe...uh, ...pray together."

Perpetua replied with delight, "I'd love to pray with you."

But Peter, not wishing to be held to this activity every night, said with reluctance and stupidity, "but don't get the idea that this would be an every night activity. In fact, it could be just a one-time event."

Perpetua, a sly woman, replied, "You might view what happens after prayer as a one-time event as well, but have it your way."

And Peter realized yet again the truth of the Rabbi's words, "What cometh out of the mouth..."

Here and Now

The story of the Transfiguration is not included in John's Gospel. Did he think it was unimportant? We presume that the John in the story of the Transfiguration is the same John who wrote the Gospel, and is reported as being present at the Transfiguration, so perhaps it's even more a mystery as to why the story is not included. Or was he still following Jesus' injunction to tell no one?

Matthew and Mark agree that this happened 'after six days', while Luke says after eight days. Small potātoes, or small potătoes, as you please. They all, however, agree as to the sartorial elegance of the Transfigured Jesus, with Mark's account being the most practical and apparently familiar with doing laundry and bleaching. (One can easily imagine Mark's wife suggesting that modifying phrase.)

In any event, Q offers a change in the line-up of disciples and rather more information as to the meaning of the event.

Mt. Tabor, a vibrant spring-green giant among its peers, loomed starkly against the sky as the disciples filed one after another, following Jesus up the steep slope. As the Rabbi marched slowly up the narrow path, he began to chant, "Here!" when his left foot hit the ground, and "Now!" when his right foot hit the ground. "Here! Now! Here! Now!" And the disciples, each in his turn, picked up the step and then the chant. "Here! Now! Here! Now!" Soon all of the men were in step with the Rabbi, and chanted with increasing volume, "Here! Now! Here! Now!"

Judas, the only Judean among them, (all the others being native Galileans) punctuated the counter beat, "And!" between each "Here!" and "Now!", so it sounded like this, "Here!", chanted by Jesus and the eleven disciples; "And!" shouted by Judas alone; then, "Now!" chanted by Jesus and the eleven. That, followed by another "And!" shouted only by Judas, so it sounded like this, "Here! And! Now! And! Here! And! Now! And! Here! And! Now! etc.

Even when the path became very steep near the summit, the men strove to stay in step with their Rabbi. And finally, they came to the very top of Mt. Tabor and the men caught their breath as they gazed at the panoramic vista that opened before their eyes. To the west shone the waters of the great Middle-of-the-Earth Sea. To the north rose mighty white-capped Mount Hermon. Eastward, they could see the green serpent that marked the living waters and lush valley of the Jordan River with the desert beyond. And to the south, they could see the Judean Hills, site of Jerusalem and the Second Temple. All the earth lay below their feet and they felt the exhilaration that comes atop a great height, feeling that the world is at your feet. The wind roared in their ears, cheering these champions, as if on the winner's stand in some great inverted arena.

And the Rabbi called them all to gather together, so that he could speak to them over the wind, and he shouted over the gusts, “Here!! Now!! Here!! Now!! Think about that as you descend the mountain. Judas, take the group back down. Remember that level spot just below the summit? Take the guys to that spot and wait for us.” And then he shouted over the wind, “Peter, James and John. Come with me farther up. I need to tell you something.”

Peter and John were perplexed at the Rabbi’s phraseology ‘farther up’ for indeed they were at the summit. James the Less understood perfectly and he eagerly awaited whatever was to come next.

Judas waved his arm forward and called to the others, “Come, then. Hath ye not heard the man? Let’s blow.” And all the others started back down the trail behind Judas. And a murmur arose among the men, “Why are those three bums staying with Jesus? Why not me? I want to stay up here with Jesus, too.” The general discontent at not being chosen, being sent back down the mountain, and then not knowing why the Rabbi, Peter, James the Less and John stayed behind caused the wind to blow more fiercely and the cold to bite more deeply. And to top it all off, why was Judas Iscariot, the Judean, chosen to lead us back down?

By the time they reached the place indicated by Jesus to stop and wait, the wind had begun to blow the clouds of a storm across the top of Mount Tabor, shrouding them in mist and sleet that scourged them and made them miserable, and so Judas decided to lead the men all the way down the mountain to a place where they could await Jesus, Peter, James the Less and John in less discomfort. Lightning raked across the sky and the thunder boomed like great, bass drums. The rancor against the bums who went 'farther up' the mountain gave way to grave concern for the safety of their comrades at the top. In their hearts they implored the Almighty to protect them.

As so often happens, the same experience elicits completely different responses from those present, depending upon one's vantage point. At the foot of the mountain, the men experienced the cold and wet of disappointment at not being chosen, followed by the anxiety of concern for their friends. At the top of the mountain, Peter, James the Less, and John experienced something completely other than what their comrades below them experienced. Instead of the sleet at a slightly lower elevation, the four men were treated to their first experience with snow. At first only a few flakes came fluttering down in a magical and desultory manner alighting on their woolen cloaks.

James the Less felt these flakes melting against his face and held out the sleeve of his cloak to capture and inspect an individual flake of snow. To his great delight several flakes landed against the dark fabric.

"Hey!" he cried. "Perfect little stars! Perfect little stars!!" Then he did the most natural thing in the world; he tasted them, and his delight redoubled.

"Hey!" James shouted again to the others. "They change! They're made of water! First snow. Then water. First snow, then water. Some disappear into the air! They change!"

Then the snow began to fall in earnest, clinging to their clothing.

Opening his mouth wide and sticking out his tongue he began collecting snow in his mouth. With his mouth wide open catching snowflakes, he tried to tell the others, "They change!" But by then the others weren't listening. They were staring in astonishment as their Rabbi was transfigured, and when James turned to see what they were looking at, he did a double take and fell to his knees.

Peter, James the Less and John now knew not whether it was cold or hot, wet or dry, for their Rabbi Jesus completely changed, charged with light beyond bright. And with him appeared Moses and Elijah and they conferred with the Rabbi in this air with its electric atmosphere. Peter, invariably the first to speak, suggested erecting tents for these divine beings, why is anyone's guess. What the men below heard as thunder, was to the men at the top, the power of the voice of G-d Most High pouring forth praise for and satisfaction with this, Son of Man. Moses and Elijah, from their time-less vantage, assured the Rabbi that for him there was no other path to the redemption of mankind, that certain 'indignities' must be endured, (what they meant by 'indignities' remained vague) and that the heavenly glory of the Savior was one thousand-fold more luminous than this mere flicker of candlelight.

And anon the 'candlelight' flickered and went out. The three disciples, grateful now for the dark, because they had fallen on their faces in fear, regained their feet and their composure. Peter, chagrined, said, "Scratch the tents idea. Just forget that I said that."

And Rabbi Jesus said, "Let's bust outta here, right now, boys. And don't tell anyone about what you saw, that is, wait until after the Son of Man is glorified." The three agreed readily, and no one asked what 'the Son of Man is glorified' meant or when that would be, Peter and John because they didn't want to appear uninformed before each other, and James simply understood what was asked of him.

When the Rabbi, Peter, James the Less and John returned to their companions at the bottom of the mountain, they secretly pitied them for not being chosen to experience this incandescent moment with their Rabbi. And the others pitied them for having had to weather the storm at the top of the mountain.

"My brothers, my brothers" Jesus explained when they were all together again, "the past is gone – we can't change it. The future is promised to no one, so all that really belongs to us is the present moment. Right here and right now. Live here. Live now."

That, in a modest way, seemed to make sense to the men, or at least if it didn't make sense, they pretended that it did. But some of the men thought to themselves, "That's nothing new or particularly insightful."

The Rabbi Jesus knew their thoughts from the set of their jaws that said "we didn't get as much as we expected", and he added specifically for their benefit, "Just try to live that way! Much easier said than done."

Some of the disciples constructed virtual temples of meaning about 'here and now' in their minds, great ontological columns with lofty elaborations of existential meanings and underpinnings, architectural and philosophical lines of structural inquiry, flying dialectical buttresses and all that fancy stuff. And they were miffed that they hadn't discussed the 'here and now' business because they sensed a chance to shine before the Rabbi was lost. And as they would all find out for themselves, 'here and now' can be a tough nut to crack, like the Rabbi said. (By the way, 'here and now' can be either a great mansion or a humble hut. Those who know how to live in the 'here and now' don't pay much attention to that.)

That's the Way G-d Planned It

Recommended listening: *That's the Way G-d Planned It* by Billy Preston

From deep within his son's heart and mind, the Almighty Father called, "Hey Jesú, Jesú! Come unto Me!" It was something of a private joke between G-d and His Son, given the intimacy of their relationship that there really wasn't anything like coming and going in the physical sense.

Smiling within at his Abba's little joke, Jesus hastened the last few steps up to his favorite place overlooking the town of Capernaum and the lake. From his vantage point he could see the fishermen in their boats.

"What's troubling you today?" asked Abba.

"Nothing's troubling me... yet everything troubles me... there's so much to do and at times it's overwhelming because I'm just one man," lamented Jesus.

"I should be telling you! And like you said, 'I'm just one G-d," cried the Almighty. "Limitations! There's so many things that I can't do!"

"I thought you were the Almighty? I thought you could do anything!" said Jesus.

"Limitations, I am no less limited than my creatures. I must rely on their hands and hearts to do my will," said G-d.

"Can't you just impose..." asked Jesus.

"Yes, I can, but, ask yourself this: would you like me to impose my will on you?"

"I see your point," acknowledged Jesus. "I wouldn't want that."

Both G-d and Son sighed and contemplated that knowledge somewhat wistfully.

Before long the face of Jesus brightened and he said, "Their hands and minds are limited, but their hearts, like yours, in your own image, are unlimited. They can, if they choose, love without limits."

"I knew there was a reason that I liked you!" said Abba.

The Lost Saying of Jesus

And the disciples asked Jesus what that meant, and who, by the way, is this Holy Ghost? And what is blaspheming the Holy Spirit? And Jesus spoke in reply, but there lodged betwixt his front teeth a morsel of his last repast. This morsel was dark in color against the white of Jesus' teeth and it could not but command the attention of all. And since no one could remember what information the explanation contained, the blaspheming of the Holy Ghost remains to this day a dark subject of much debate and small insight.

Up from Jericho

With a sense of inevitability or necessity, Jesus and the Dozen trudged the dusty uphill trail from Jericho to Jerusalem. Something big was going to happen on the Passover. He could feel in it elements of exhilaration, confrontation, and dread.

The Dozen felt something as well. Their Rabbi was being talked about all over the land, and even in their City of G-d. If the people of Jericho lined the road on which Jesus passed, how much more would the people of Jerusalem receive them with honor? They would be fêted like kings! Welcomed like champions! Songs would be sung in their honor. There would be speechifying! Celebrations! A real Prophet, dare we say, the Messiah?!

Thaddeus had his miracle list out and he added an entry, "March 15, Jericho, Blind Bartimaeus, Sight restored. He intended to enter this data into a spreadsheet that he would periodically update.

While the Dozen were arguing about who should be seated next to the Messiah in glory, Jesus was more than preoccupied with the possible events to come. Indeed, so rapt was he by ruminations that he didn't hear the importunities of formerly-blind Bartimaeus.

"Hey, Jesus, Son of David."

"Jesus, hey, Jesus, guess what?"

"Jesus. Hey, Son of David."

"Jesus."

"Hey, Jesus."

"Jesus. Look! I can see."

"Hey, Jesus."

The disciples were growing indignant at this new fellow who seemed to easily dominate the discourse and with his loud mouth sucked up all the air in their proximity.

While all the attention was thus diffused, Lucifer slipped in unseen next to Jesus for a quick interview. Even Smokey was distracted in marveling at the way formerly blind, now seeing Bart could so effortlessly command all the attention of the group.

"Hey, Jesus. I noticed you restored that guys sight without actually touching him. It's good to see you being careful what with all the germs and diseases in this world."

"What's nice," replied Jesus, "is you concerned for my health."

"Oh, it's nothing. Actually, I'm speaking on behalf of optometrists as well. You're infringing on their territory. But speaking of healthcare, I offer quite an attractive buyout plan for my employees. You could get out now with a hefty pension with a family health insurance plan (no co-pay), including vision and dental. This special plan is only available today and you'd be required to retire immediately. You could afford a nice time-share condo on the beach. What's not to like?"

"Severance?"

"Well, of course, severance, calculated very generously. We could bring you in on future projects. You could sell out, I mean, buy out. We could have you work from home and stop all this commuting. Even this road up to Jerusalem is getting so congested, well, it's just... hell. I pride myself on being something of an authority on that subject."

Lucifer smiled at himself and then he grinned at Jesus.

"There are so many, many alternatives to consider, ya know, sky's the limit. And with our gated community you wouldn't have to put up with the likes of Bert here, ah... ah... Bart."

Bart could be heard in the background.

"Hey, Thaddeus. Thaddeus."

"Thaddeus. Hey, Thaddeus."

"I can see now. Thaddeus. Thaddeus."

"I have two eyes. I can see. Hey, Thaddeus."

"Look. Two eyes that work, Thaddeus."

"Thaddeus. Hey, what happened to your eye?"

"Thaddeus."

Jesus gave Lucifer a withering look that precipitated the latter's departure post haste.

Jesus spoke to his Almighty Abba, and it didn't even sound like it was long distance, for it came from his heart. The Rabbi smiled to the trinitarian themselves and said, "You gotta admire the guy. Persistence. Timing. What's not to like?"

"Yeah, he's quite the creation. But that's the nature of the beast," replied Abba.

Jesus chuckled softly to himself at Abba's little joke, and continued trudging up the road. And he continued to consider the possibilities of his arrival in Jerusalem.

"Hey, Jesus. Jesus. Son of David."

"Jesus. Hey, Jesus."

"Jesus. Jesus. Hey, Jesus."

"Hey, Jesus, what'cha gonna do in Jerusalem? Jesus. Hey, Jesus."

Fetch Ye the Ass

"I need a volunteer for a quick task," said Jesus loudly so that all might hear. "I need someone to fetch an ass, and I'm not talking about Thadd-ass." He shot a quick look and grinned to Thaddeus to indicate his joking intent.

Thaddeus rolled his eyes as James' the Less hand shot into the air so fast that the rush of air could be heard, but no one else was much interested in such a low-level task.

"Can I? Pick me! I'll do it! I can do it!" cried James all in a rush.

Jesus hesitated, uncertain as to the advisability of sending James by himself on this errand, but in the end, he assented to James' eager importuning.

James the Less had a boundless love for animals, but more than that, he wanted to do something for Jesus. James had often felt that he was not as capable as, say, Judas, who seemed to always be taking care of things for the Rabbi, and he knew that many things were simply beyond his ken. Therefore, James was always on the lookout for some way in which he could serve his friend Jesus, and when the Rabbi needed someone to fetch an ass, James was certain that this fell well within his capabilities, so much so that he had insisted on going by himself. Jesus had sent Smokey with him at the last as a bit of insurance.

But along their way up toward Jerusalem to fetch the ass, James and Smokey were accosted by thieves. (I'm certain that you will remember our two highwaymen, Gestas and Dysmas. As their fortunes waxed or waned they would 'ply their portable trade' anywhere, according to their needs.)

"Ho, pilgrim!" cried Gestas. "A great opportunity has come your way...er, oh, you're an idiot, I can see, so let's dispense with the pleasantries. Hand over your purse!"

As Gestas spoke, Dysmas made his usual move to the side of their quarry and held his walking stick, which in reality was more like a club, at the ready.

James the Less looked around in confusion and said nothing, but Smokey gave out a low growl.

"Pilgrim," demanded Gestas. "Where's your purse?"

"I got no purse," said James the Less.

"Even stupid idiots like you carry a purse," scoffed Gestas.

Dysmas guffawed at Gestas' characterization 'stupid idiot' as if it were the funniest thing he had ever heard.

"I got no purse," insisted James loudly.

Dysmas mocked James, "I got no purse."

"Gimme your bag!" demanded Gestas as he reached out to grab the bag over James' shoulder, but Smokey at once advanced and growled ferociously at Gestas who shrank back in fear. But Dysmas, quick as lightning, swung his walking stick down low...

It's just too terrible to describe. Suffice it to say that Dysmas beat Smokey to death, and then he turned his full attention to James. In quick succession, he clubbed James on the mouth, the lower jaw and across the nose. Two of James' teeth were knocked out and blood gushed from his mouth and broken nose. Dysmas now delivered him a solid, crunching blow to the side of his head, which knocked him unconscious and his body slumped forward on top of the dead carcass of the brutally beaten dog.

Dysmas stood over his victims and scowled, "Stupid idiot!"

Pulling a small knife, Gestas cut the strap of James' bag and pulled it open, spilling the contents on the ground.

"Hay?!" James' bag yielded only a few handfuls of hay that he had gathered for the ass.

The two thugs fled the scene and headed toward the city gates before anyone could associate them with the crime.

I Need Two Volunteers

The Dozen plus the Others had been sitting in the shade in the courtyard after breakfast waiting for Jesus to return when James the Less, carrying in his arms a bloody, broken mass staggered into the doorway. They all looked in horror at James.

James himself had blood trickling down his head from a savage-looking, swollen bruise and his nose and mouth were cut and broken. Collapsing against the jamb of the door, James fell to his knees, a faint plea for help on his lips before falling forward onto the dead dog.

They all sprang to their feet in alarm. They quickly dragged James to a place at the back of the courtyard and began to tend his vicious wounds. The Magdalene fetched water and began to clean the wound on James' head, but the left side of his body was rocked by irregular spasms.

"Oh, my Lord, oh, my Lord," repeated the Magdalene as she tended his wounds.

Meanwhile, Smokey's lifeless body lay at the doorway into the courtyard. His fur was matted with dried blood.

"Get that unclean animal out of this house!" cried one of the Dozen over his shoulder. (We shan't name names here, but I think you know who it was.)

Brick and Mortar, the two at the outer edge of the circle around James, walked over to where Smokey lay and were just going to pick him up when the Rabbi, puffing and out of breath, ran into the courtyard. He stopped momentarily to take in the entire scene and a cry of pain from the heart escaped his lips. He first ran to James the Less. Jesus knelt down beside him and quickly and gingerly examined the wound on James' head and as he was gently feeling about the bruise, it seemed to gradually disappear, the twitching of his left side ceased, his mouth and nose were restored and presently James' eyelids fluttered and opened. James awoke to see his friend Jesus bent over him, tears filling his eyes, and a desperate, searching look in his eyes.

James smiled when he saw his friend, but then his face fell as he remembered what had happened. His chin began to quiver and he could only stutter as his expression wrenched into a bawling contortion. He began to sob about Smokey and pointed over to where the dog lay. Jesus laid his hand gently along James' cheek to make finally certain that he was all right before turning his attention to his dog.

When Brick and Mortar saw that Jesus was moving to where the body of Smokey lay, they stood up and backed away from the bloody carcass. Jesus fell to his knees and made to run his hands across Smokey's body, but recoiled at the horror of the dog's wounds. Then with great care Jesus scooped up his friend Smokey and carried the dog's body outside into the sun.

Tears fell freely from Jesus' eyes as he walked to the shade of a nearby tree and tenderly laid Smokey upon a smooth rock. Jesus knelt down and wailed in great pain over the loss of so loyal a friend. His tears splashed down onto the wounds on Smokey's head and their healing balm reached down deeply into the wound, healing and restoring as it went. Presently Smokey's brain was healed by Jesus' tears and the Rabbi wiped more tears from his eyes and wiped his wet hand across the broken ribs of the dog. The ribs re-knit themselves as Jesus' hand passed over them. And finally, Jesus wiped more of the moisture of his tears onto his hand and gently stroked the dog's broken legs, restoring them to perfect condition.

Before long Smokey was breathing again and appeared to be sleeping. The blood was gone and his fur fairly crackled with life's vitality. He gave out a muffled bark from his dreaming and awoke himself. He looked up at his friend Jesus and his tail began to wag.

Jesus heaved a great sigh, releasing the tension in his back and shoulders. His tears flowed now more freely in the realization of how much he loved the dog Smokey and how much he might have lost.

Breaking his own cardinal rule about speaking in public, Smokey said, "It's a great day to be a dog." Everyone clearly heard what he said, but the others, not expecting to hear Smokey speak, could not embrace the idea with their rational minds and shortly all had convinced themselves in their individual ways that he had only barked. For G-d's sake, people, open your minds to the miracles that happen every day!!

As this all happened Jesus' friends had gathered around him and they were astounded when Smokey jumped up and began dancing about the Rabbi, licking his hands and face and whimpering for joy.

Jesus, tears in his eyes, turned to his friends and said, "I need two volunteers to fetch an ass."

James' the Less hand again shot into the air, but this time Judas went with him.

Triumphal Entry into Jerusalem

The ass seemed to take all the excitement in stride. All along the roadway to the city gates the spectators cried out, "Hosannah!" James the Less, skipping along, was absolutely giddy with delight that so many of the crowd recognized the ass and called him by his name, Hosannah, although James thought that 'Hosannah' sounded more like a girl's name. Many waved palm branches and some even threw down their cloaks for Jesus to ride across.

With renewed vitality, Smokey danced and barked along the whole way, danced and barked for the pure joy of the thing. Smokey did not see himself as having been dead and raised to life, but rather an unbroken chain of life with Jesus because even in death he had been doing the bidding of his master and he returned to life when he heard his master call.

Most of the Dozen were in fine fettle and enjoyed the acclamation of the crowd for their Rabbi, and by extension, for them. They waved to the crowd, pleased to be identified with their Teacher, whose renown had spread throughout Galilee and now into Judea. 'Most', as I said.

Two of the Dozen hung back from the main group and walked with heads down as if going to an execution. Can you guess which ones?

At a crossroads of thought and action, Judas Iscariot was back on his home turf in Judea. Remember that Judas was a Judean, the only Judean among the Eleven Galileans, not counting Brick and Mortar and not counting the women. And if you did count them, then his presence only became more conspicuous in a statistical sense.

This entire.... movement...mission... whatever it was called, was, in the opinion of Judas, in danger of losing either its momentum or its focus. Where exactly were they going? What exactly were they doing? When would they confront the Temple authorities? When would they confront the Romans? Good timing would be essential because support for any cause can melt away with the wind or it can be harnessed and driven. Either way, it was time to act.

It really wasn't much of a decision and what he chose to do made sense. First things first. Unity in Israel was required to take on the Romans. Jesus and the Temple authorities weren't so far apart as many thought, he reasoned. They were pursuing the same goal, albeit, in their own ways. Maybe if they got together and talked things out... Only then would they be capable of driving the Romans out of their Holy Land. The Galileans would need the Judeans to drive out the Romans and he, Judas, might be the perfectly placed go-between. So, with that decided, he'd have to go a different way.

Lagging farther behind, Judas hoped to part company with the others unnoticed by slipping into the crowd. Jesus and the others, with James out front leading Hosannah the ass, headed for the Temple and Judas, his face and heart set like flint, turned in the direction of the High Priest's house.

Judas' steps were, however, not unnoticed, for another out-of-sorts member of the Dozen, Thaddeus, saw what he was doing. But Thaddeus was so wrapped up in his own despondent thoughts, that he attached no significance to what he saw.

Consternation might have been Thaddeus' middle name. He was amazed, and not in a good way, by his reaction to the morning's events, and now he was confused and angered. He felt like a jerk. When everyone else had been worrying about James, Thaddeus had been concerned with the unclean carcass of Smokey lying in the doorway. Mortar was becoming increasingly difficult to suffer. Everything that man did was a personal affront to Thaddeus. The very sight of him gave offense.

"Ah, well," resigned Thaddeus to himself, "up to the Temple and see what the Rabbi has to say today."

Take Ye Back the Ass

It is the end of the events of the day that will become famous as Palm Sunday and follows after a text similar to Matthew 21:1-11, Jesus Enters Jerusalem on an Ass.

As the end of the day drew nigh the Dozen plus hangers-on and Jesus huddled and all round high-fived for their day had been exceedingly successful and each was flushed with a sense of victory. And Jesus said, "This calls for a Churchill." and He pulled out cigars, handed them round and lit His.

At that moment the ass that Jesus had so triumphantly ridden into the city chose to drop them a reminder of its presence among them. And Jesus, not knowing it was the ass, cried out in a loud voice, "Mama Mia! Who hath farted?"

"Not I!" cried Peter.

"Not I!" cried Andrew.

"Surely not I!" cried James the Lesser.

"Nor I! cried James the Greater.

"T'wasn't me!" said John.

Indeed, all vehemently denied the charge.

One among the Dozen irreverently mumbled under his breath, "A fox smells his own hole first."

"Hey guys!" cried James the Less, "It was the ass."

And Jesus said, "Oh, I forgot about that. We must take back the ass to its owner. Are there any volunteers for that task?"

James the Less' hand cleaved the air in an instant.

And simultaneously the other 11 cast their 21 eyes to the ground, hoping not to be chosen for this ignoble task.

"James, thank you, but others need to take part as well. Many are called, few are chosen." Jesus said hopefully.

"What doth that mean?" whispered Bartholomew to Thaddeus.

"How should I know?" whispered Thaddeus back to Bartholomew.

They cut their eyes toward Jesus hoping He hadn't heard them whispering and so hoped He wouldn't pick them. But, alas, it was not to be.

"I see," said Jesus, "the honor of performing this task is hotly contested. That means I shall have to choose someone. Thaddeus. Bartholomew. Step ye forward, if it please ye."

"Yes, Rabbi." they said reluctantly and unhappily.

"Take ye back the ass and express my undying gratitude to the owner," said Jesus, "and take ye Mortar with."

"Oh, no, not Mortar!" cried Thaddeus.

"Yes, Mortar." said Jesus.

"That means we'll be taking two asses back." said Thaddeus. "A 100% return on his principal in one day, two asses for one, not bad."

Jesus returned them a stern look that broke into a grin, followed soon by laughter and then they were all laughing.

All except Mortar whose mouth was tightly pinched shut and his eyes shot arrows of hatred at Thaddeus.

"Well, here's what I say, there's two kinds of people in the world, the chosen and the unchosen," observed Thaddeus dryly.

The three men walked away leading Hosannah down Jerusalem's busy Cardo Maximus.

Gethsemane

Jesus, alone, stole away from Bethany to a garden on the Mount of Olives, which wasn't the smartest thing to do, going alone, that is. He entered through a gate and seeing no one, he sat down on a rock beneath a tree. He was agitated inside for recent events had taken a decisive turn, or so it seemed to him. And when Jesus was agitated and confused, he sought out his Abba Father.

Closing his eyes and concentrating on his breathing, Jesus entered a prayer state. (Prayer states are very hard to describe. As Abba is with us at all times, it is we who envision that we are calling on the Lord, when he is present all the time.) Like smoke dissipates into the air, so Jesus and his Abba Father became one.

Jesus gave vent to his feelings and said, "Abba, things are coming to a head; I can feel it. Something terrible is going to happen."

Trying to avoid the topic Abba immediately changed the subject. "I liked the way you raised Lazarus. Linens for burial cloths: 15 shekels; spices for burial: 30 shekels: the looks on their faces when Lazarus returns from the dead: Priceless!"

"Things can't go on like this," said Jesus. "They're looking for me everywhere and just waiting for the right moment to throw me into the Antonia (fortress)."

"That's why I wasn't happy to see you here alone. You really should keep some of the others near at hand. Just in case. For safety's sake," advised Abba.

"Yes, Abba, from now on, I will," replied Jesus.

A rustling of leaves followed by a familiar and unwelcome voice broke in on their conversation, saying ingratiatingly, "I'll stay with him!" Lucifer slithered down the tree and stopped several feet above ground so as to maintain good eye contact with the Holy Ones. "I'll be my brother's keeper."

"Well, if it isn't my Bright Star," said Abba.

Lucifer turned immediately peevish, intensely disliking Abba's loving tone and like a sullen teenager he whined, "I'm not 'your' bright star!" Lucifer's tongue flicked forth in distaste.

"But I have something I want to talk about," said Lucifer. After a long uncomfortable pause, he added, "Alone. With Jesus."

"The Father and I are One," said Jesus, gently dismissing the affront to Abba.

"Well, okay, if we must," said Lucifer not satisfied with the arrangement, but he continued nonetheless. "This new found 'capacity' of yours, this power over death, could be used very profitably...." Lucifer quickly recovered this misstep. "...profitable in a spiritual sense!"

"What do you mean?" asked Jesus.

"If you can do this 'Lazarus trick' on demand, we can name our price! We can set up a 'Palace of Rebirth' here or we can take this on the road – over the entire world, known and unknown!! How far back can you go? 4 days? Is that the limit? Just think of all who could benefit from this!!!"

"I think that your vision of who profits or *benefits* by it is different from my vision of who profits," countered Jesus.

"There you go again! Limiting yourself! Deliberately!!" whined Lucifer.

Abba, at times an impatient G-d, broke in from an oblique angle, "Do you know how they make a bull's pizzle cane, Bright Star?"

"Yes, of course I do," insisted Lucifer, who was somewhat taken aback by Abba's bizarre change of subject. "They stretch a bull's penis over a metal or wooden rod and then let it dry."

"A snake can be used in the same way, so why don't you leave before... before...." said Abba stretching forth his right arm to seize the snake.

In a rapid flutter of leaves Lucifer slithered away *tout de suite.* Abba chuckled and said to Himself, "You can't beat a deal like that!"

Jesus asked, "Why do you put up with him?"

"You have been more polite to him than anyone," countered Abba.

"Well, it's just good breeding, I guess," said Jesus.

"Even he serves my purposes at times, unbeknownst to him," said Abba slyly. "Now, where were we, before being so rudely interrupted," said Abba, "ah... ah... oh, yes, keeping your friends close at hand and... what will happen next?"

"Yes," said Jesus, "it was very exhilarating raising Lazarus and before that Smokey and James, but this is spinning out of control. It seems that I have more power than I had known, even power over death."

"I have a dilemma," confessed Abba, changing the course of the conversation yet again. "If I tell you what's going to happen, then you will trust the knowledge of what I tell you rather than trusting in me."

Abba paused, allowing the enormity of the thought to be assessed. He then continued.

"I want you to go forward in faith rather than going forth in knowledge, so I don't want to tell you what will happen next." Again, Abba paused.

"Treat me like anyone else," said Jesus.

"But you're right, it will feel like it's spinning out of control. It's perfectly human to experience fear and doubt and uncertainty. It's important that it happen in this way. Trust me. This is going to be very difficult." Abba felt something akin to guilt in withholding the nature and details of what would happen, much like a parent who allows a child to experience unpleasant consequences for the sake of learning a greater lesson.

Trying his best to sound as confident as possible Jesus declared, "I choose faith. Don't tell me what will happen. I love my friends and I choose to continue in faith. I do it for you and I do it for them."

"Then It's... settled..." said Abba, trailing off slightly betraying a certain uncertainty.

"Is that a question or a statement?" asked Jesus.

"This is going to be *very* difficult," repeated Abba.

"Now you're starting to scare me," said Jesus in an attempt to lighten the mood.

Leaving the garden Jesus returned to the house of his friends Mary, Martha and Lazarus in Bethany.

Abba sat down heavily on the rock, exhausted by his emotions. This ransom would be paid in blood, the blood of his son, and it was almost more than he could bear. And to his dismay, G-d realized that his son was not the only one who had to take things on faith. Wasn't He, G-d, the One who had chosen to use human vessels? Now He, too, must not only talk the talk, but walk the walk. He put his face in his hands and wept.

Cleansing the Temple

Sanctimon and Viktorius sat in their booth in the Temple court to sell their books and programs, enjoying the panoply of Judaism – people from all over the known world.

The Temple was a very busy place on ordinary days, but around the holidays, it seethed with activity, comings and goings, and people. Sacrificing animals of various sorts and their immolation was a messy, noisy and odiferous process. In the Temple courtyard, vendors and purveyors of all sorts of merchandise were set up to service the needs of the pilgrims. Moneychangers, for a small fee, could convert any currency into the Temple shekels required for contributions and tithes. Money was in the air, mingled with blood and incense. One couldn't walk without bumping into people bustling about their business. The din of the constant crowd, the bellowing and bleating of the animals, and the shouts of the vendors made this sacred place resemble more a busy market than a house of prayer.

(I might remark at this point that prayer does not always have to mean quiet supplication on bended knees before

G-d, but prayer can also be boisterous and loud, and all too often, in any context, it resembles the bargaining and haggling of a regular market. Have you not done the same yourself? G-d, if you do this for me, I'll do that for you. And, I confess that I drive a very hard bargain with G-d, squeezing out the last penny in every deal. He's very gullible; he takes me at my word, which, by now, you'd think, he'd realize how little that really means. He certainly seems to have more faith in me than I in him!)

The long and the short of it was this: Jesus lost his temper, well, 'lost his temper' isn't quite right, because he was very much in control of himself. He did, after all, carefully weave together a whip of sorts and then with a lion's roar, he launched himself into action, driving the animals before him and overturning the tables of the vendors and moneychangers. It was perfect pandemonium!

The thugs, Gestas and Dysmas, were there in the courtyard seeking monetary 'gifts' when they saw that G-d in his generosity offered them an opportunity. Both men scrambled about, grasping these 'pennies from heaven'.

Gestas, with a discerning eye, spotted three coins of gold that had rushed to the same hiding place and he dived to his knees to retrieve said horde when he stopped dead in his tracks. And he marveled at the coins, but not for their golden gleams. Gestas had seen this scene before! The three gold coins, laying just so on the pavement, brought to his mind the sense that he had somehow experienced this before, not in a dream, but not quite in wakeful consciousness either.

He blinked his eyes several times but the image did not retreat and he turned and shouted to Dysmas, "Hey, Dys,

I'm having déjà vu right at this moment! It's like this happened before, like... like, it's meant to be!"

Dysmas, more in tune with actual events, saw what Gestas failed to see. The hand of a Temple guard grabbed Gestas by the arm and pulled him roughly to his feet as Gestas grasped the golden coins, caught red-handed!

The guards, further assessing the scene, determined that Dysmas was an associate of Gestas and took him into custody as well. (We can be fairly certain that they were not 'Mirandized'.)

The Temple guards slowly managed to restore order in the courtyard and in the process, clapped manacles on Gestas and Dysmas, who were also falsely identified as in cahoots with the gentleman who had incited this near riot, and the guards had caught them *en flagrant* in the act of theft.

So, ended a career of brutality and theft, which required no trial, merely ratification of sentence by the procurator, which was a matter of course. One minute they were free men conducting their business operations, and the next, inmates on death row. Life can change very quickly!

The Woman Caught in Adultery

Jesus was writing in the sand after he had laid out his proposal. Now he was waiting for their response. He had been teaching when the Pharisees brought her before him demanding justice. As he recalled it in his mind, he was pleased with his response, "Let he that is without sin cast the first stone." Left alone with Jesus, the woman turned to go her way, but Jesus said, "Wait a minute. Don't I know you?" Jesus' memory flashed on the face of the woman he had seen stoned when he was almost a man. Then he remembered their exchange of words as this woman fled from her life in chains. And the memory of the hatred and mistrust that she bore him, cut him anew.

She stopped in her tracks, her spine stiffened and she turned to face the Rabbi.

"Yes," said Jesus, "I know you. Sweetness!" His face first lightened, but then darkened. You're still wearing your chains, the slavery of your hatred for me, that you've carried most of your life."

"Yes, well, it's all I've got left," said the woman bitterly.

"Maybe you don't know how to be free," returned the Rabbi.

"I know what freedom isn't," said Sweetness, head lowered. Now for the second time, she turned to go and had taken a step away when the Rabbi called after her, "My Pearl."

The words, the name cut to her heart and nearly felled her where she stood. How could he know that? How could he know that her mother had affectionately called her 'my Pearl'?

She turned about in a flash. Understanding came in a flash. The heat of the flash melted her heart. He couldn't have hurt my mother, just like he couldn't have allowed me to die in the same way. He would have even taken my place in death if he could have.

It was too much to bear, too much to take in, and she did the most human of things – she ran away. Again. Everything that she believed about herself and about her world changed in an instant. The intensity of the sun redoubled, the freshness in the air seared her nostrils, the slight breeze blew with gale force, a wave of nausea swept over her, her head split with pain.

"I'm From the Empire and I'm Here to Help"

"I'm from the Empire and I'm here to help," lustily cried Lucifer, flashing a malignant grin. Lucifer was not averse to dropping in on people at any time of the day or night. To give the devil his due, we must observe that he is a tiger of persistence.

Jesus was alone on the roof of Mary and Martha's home deep in prayer for the people he had encountered during his day. On this particular evening, he was praying for the woman who had been caught in the very act of adultery, *in the very act*, no less! To the Rabbi this was very curious indeed as it required carelessness, or brazenness, or spying on, or, well... But the fact remained that she had been publicly humiliated by the elders and that fact stuck like a bone in the throat.

"Adultery," thought the Rabbi, "requires a minimum of two persons. Hmmm... so where was the other person in this episode? Why wasn't the 'gentleman' in this case brought forward as well as the woman?"

"Shekel for your thoughts," said Lucifer as he materialized a table and chair for himself. Seating himself and lighting a cigar, he blew out that first long and satisfying lung full of delicious smoke as Jesus waited impatiently and silently for his unwelcome 'guest' to get to the point of his visit.

"I have been thinking, and you know how dangerous that can be!" Lucifer laughed at his own joke as if everyone should find it funny and then he went on, "You know, we talked of you going up to Jerusalem at some point in your career. Yes, well, here we are. Jerusalem. These very stones will begin singing your praises at any moment, as well they should! As well they should! You've made it. Here you are in Jerusalem. Go ahead, pinch yourself, make sure it's real. You've reached your goal. Let me be the first to congratulate you. As I 've said on more than one occasion, I've kept my eye on you, watching your career with great interest, great interest. But I see now where we both went wrong. 'Tis a pity, really. 'Tis a pity."

"Pity, you say? I guess I've lost the train of thought," said Jesus.

"Of course, it's a pity!" said Lucifer overly dramatically. "We've made an error of strategic proportions!" He held his arms wide apart to demonstrate the breadth of "strategic proportions."

"We?" asked Jesus. "Strategic proportions?" Jesus mimicked by flinging his arms wide apart.

"We..." affirmed Lucifer, "remember our work is basically, how to say, hand in glove. Untested goodness isn't worth much, is it? But let's not argue things that have been put to rest long ago. As I said, 'Strategic proportions.'" Again, he threw his arms wide apart and then he added in an undertone, " I've got something that you really ought to consider."

"Let's have it, sir, for then you shall be able to depart and I shall be able to continue with my business," said Jesus.

"Can't you guess what it is? Go on, guess! No? Okay, I'll tell you. Rome! Rome!! Rome, Rome, Rome!!!" cried Lucifer with great glee.

"Rome?" said Jesus.

"Of course, Rome!" said Lucifer. "Where else but Rome!! Anybody who's anybody eventually goes to Rome. Why should we, I mean you, languish in this backwater Judea, when your popularity is at an all-time high? 'Start spreadin' the news!' You, my friend, are on your way to Rome!!"

"Rome?" said Jesus.

"Aah, I see I've piqued your interest," said Lucifer craftily, and he continued in a hurried manner, striking while his iron was hot, so to speak.

"I think the world is finally ready for your brand of monotheism. Yes, there are gods for this and goddesses for that, you'll have a lot of good competition but I think people are ready for a change of pace. Who can keep track of them all anyway? Your message can be tailored to fit the crowd, that's going to happen anyway, you know, and we can go global. From certain utterances of yours, I have ascertained that your intentions now only include the Jews, but think about this, think about all the poor devils, sorry, slip of the tongue, people worldwide who really need your message, people who need someone to give their money to, people who need someone to obey, people who need someone to adore, people who need someone to tell them what to do, people who need, need, need!"

"You don't have a very high opinion of them, do you?" asked Jesus.

"Me?! You dishonor me, sir! I hold them in the highest regard! I want them all. Each and every one. You're the parochial one, only going to the Jews. Me, I'm the equal opportunity tempter. I take anyone regardless of race, color, age, gender, sexual preference, veteran status, all that stuff! I take diversity pretty seriously!!"

"I didn't know that you had such a high level of social awareness. I'd better watch my step. Next thing you'll be joining animal rights groups and environmental movements," said Jesus.

"It's just good business sense to be proactive on these issues. And let me tell you, you're not my only prospect. There'll be an up-and-comer named Mohammed with a whole new chain with franchising rights over on the Peninsula. He and I are going to be a great team!" said the devil with a gleam in his eye. "You know," said Lucifer somewhat reflectively, "people have an easier time believing in a mono-*diabolic* world than they do believing in a mono-*theistic* world! Crazy, isn't it?!"

" Haven't you heard that success has many fathers, but failure is a bastard," replied Jesus, "perhaps that's why."

"Touché, my man!" said Lucifer, "but don't let's get sidetracked here. Think about my offer, I mean, my idea. Let's take the whole world by storm! The whole world!!"

"Interesting idea," Jesus said and He paused to think about this for a moment, and then He said, "I'll take it under advisement and get back to you. See you later."

"Don't wait too long. Messages get stale very quickly these days. The shelf life is very short. Strike while the iron is hot!" cried Lucifer as he vanished in a wisp of acrid, sulfurous smoke.

G-d Doubts

Almighty G-d pulled the side lever on his La-Z-Boy throne and slipped down into the reclining position. He pulled deeply on his cigar and exhaled the smoke in a slow stream as these beautiful words came to him:

"To be, or not to be: that is the question:
Whether 'tis nobler in the mind to suffer
The slings and arrows of outrageous fortune,
Or to take arms against a sea of troubles,
And by opposing end them. To die, to sleep –
No more – and by a sleep to say we end
The heartache, and the thousand natural shocks
That flesh is heir to! 'Tis a consummation
Devoutly to be wished. To die, to sleep –
To sleep – perchance to dream: ay, there's the rub
For in that sleep of death what dreams may come
When we have shuffled off this mortal coil,
Must give us pause.

The fair Ophelia! – Nymph, in thy orisons
Be all my sins remembered.

"Abba?! Excuse me, Abba!" Jesus' call upon the Almighty jolted him out of his reverie and he said dreamily, "I can't wait for that to be written."

"Abba, who's Ophelia?" asked Jesus, having heard the name toward the end of Abba's musings.

"It's a long story," said G-d, "but remember that Tower of Babel episode and the so-called "Confounding of the Language?" G-d made finger quotes around the words 'confounding of the language'.

"At the time it was an ad hoc measure, but has turned out to be all for the good. One might even call it a stroke of genius!"

"Aren't all your works strokes of genius?" asked the Son.

"You're getting slightly ahead. First, the Confounding of the Language: by that simple stroke I created more jobs for translators! And, if there had been only one language, think of all the unwritten literature! It's almost a horror to think of all the great works that would not have been!"

"That's a happy thought," said Jesus. He then added, "but You don't look so happy. What's up?"

"Well, as far as all my works being strokes of genius..." The Almighty trailed off into thought.

After several long moments, Jesus prompted Him, "... strokes of genius?"

"Ah, yes, strokes of genius," continued G-d. "In retrospect there are some of my works that I don't feel rise to the level of genius... I don't want to get into that right now... but the real stroke of genius was Free Will!" G-d slapped his big hands together and rubbed them vigorously together as he warmed to his topic.

"Free Will. It even sounds good. Free Will," G-d worked the cigar between his teeth and then puffed it vigorously.

"Pray, tell," said Jesus.

"Free will. It's the greatest of the gifts. All else hinges on it, but, as they say, no good deed goes unpunished!" cried G-d, a little sarcastically.

"So, if it's the greatest gift," asked Jesus, "why does it seem to depress you?"

"Well," said G-d broadly, "I get blamed for everything!" He started using a thin, whining voice. "Why does G-d allow murder? Why does G-d allow cruelty? Why does G-d this and why does G-d that!!! I'm sick of it!!!!"

"I can imagine that it gets somewhat tedious..." conciliated Jesus, but G-d cut in sharply, "Somewhat tedious?! Somewhat?!" He clapped his hand to his forehead in dismay.

"Okay, a lot tedious, it gets a lot tedious; I'm sorry for minimizing your pain."

"Truth be told," said G-d, "it really wasn't much of a decision. It was obvious that the alternative would be a world void of meaning, just automatons moving through beautiful scenery. Not a drop of drama! Everything else follows: good and evil, triumph and defeat, rich and poor, predestination and free choice, etc, etc."

G-d now again had convinced himself that bestowing free will on his creation Man had been the very best decision after all, even despite the incumbent risks. He stoked his cigar for some time before looking Jesus squarely in the eye and made this statement of faith, defiant in tone, "If I had it to do over, I wouldn't change a thing!" And he puffed his cigar in a determined manner. But before long G-d Almighty's brow furrowed and a tear came to his eye, before he softly said, "But it requires certain... sacrifices."

Long Distance Letters

On a certain day not long after the events described above, Jesus received a letter at the home of Mary, Martha, and Lazarus. The letter was on official letterhead stationery and marked with a king's seal, but the seal was broken. Obviously, someone had opened the letter.

Jesus asked Brick to join him on the roof of the house for a private conversation. He showed Brick a letter that he had received.

"This means that the authorities are following you - that they know where you are; which brings a question to mind, "Why do they hate you so much? They're always arguing with you, trying to misquote or misconstrue what you say."

"It boils down to this, I think, that, I, ah, I'm not what most people expect and I'm not what some people want."

"Whew!" said Brick. "You sure about that? People love you. You're a great guy. Me and Mortar, we like you."

"Well," said Jesus, "let's take a look at the letter." And it read:

Abgar, ruler of Edessa, to Jesus the good physician who has appeared in the country of Jerusalem, greeting. I have heard the reports of you and of your cures as performed by you without medicines or herbs. For it is said that you make the blind to see and the lame to walk, that you cleanse lepers and cast out impure spirits and demons, and that you heal those afflicted with lingering disease, and raise the dead. And having heard all these things concerning you, I have concluded that one of two things must be true: either you are God, and having come down from heaven you do these things, or else you, who does these things, are the son of God. I have therefore written to you to ask you if you would take the trouble to come to me and heal all the ill which I suffer. For I have heard that the Jews are murmuring against you and are plotting to injure you. But I have a very small yet noble city which is great enough for us both.

Brick, of course, was able to translate the letter and compose for Jesus a response:

Blessed are you who hast believed in me without having seen me. For it is written concerning me, that they who have seen me will not believe in me, and that they who have not seen me will believe and be saved. But in regard to what you have written me, that I should come to you, it is necessary for me to fulfill all things here for which I have been sent, and after I have fulfilled them thus to be taken up again to him that sent me. But after I have been taken up I will send to you one of my disciples, that he may heal your disease and give life to you and yours.

"But there's something else that I want you to do for me," said Jesus.

"Of course, anything," asserted Brick.

"Actually, this is for both you and Mortar."

Jesus pulled out his diary and turned it around so that Brick could get a good look at it.

"If anything happens to me, I want you to make sure to safeguard my diary. I've been keeping some notes and reflections on our work and I want you, at all costs, to make sure that it is handled appropriately. I trust you and your judgment to do what's best. When you eventually read it, you'll know what to do."

"Well, what's it about?" asked Brick.

"No questions, please, for now. Trust me. You'll know what to do. Promise me. Oh, and Thaddeus is writing stuff down. It would be good to get that as well."

Wanting to please his friend, Brick assured Jesus that he would take care of this matter for him.

PART VI

Fire and Sword

Suggested listening: *Fire by Jimi Hendrix*

Holidays can be stressful times and old tensions easily find expression within close-knit groups, like families or say, groups of disciples. Additionally, the anxiety of dodging the authorities had taken a further toll on the group. Every stray sound was the footfall of the oppressor. Every strange face was an agent of ill-will. Every shadow concealed unspecified danger.

The brazier that Mortar was preparing in order to roast the lamb for the Passover feast was glowing hot, with the charcoals giving off an intense, red heat. Skewers of lamb kebabs rested on a platter awaiting their turn on the grill. Mortar was speaking, rather pontificating to Brick, who wasn't listening, from atop his imaginary soapbox, saying, "Intense heat serves very well to clean and purify. Let's say that a brazier, such as this one, has the encrusted remains of food from a previous usage. The heat will consume those remnants, burning them away into nothing, thereby cleaning the brazier." Smokey had been sitting alertly, paying close heed to Mortar's instruction and the kebabs. Mortar didn't miss a beat in saying as Thaddeus approached them, "And speaking of 'encrusted remains'..."

Without preamble Thaddeus said in a superior tone, "Jesus told me to tell you guys that we must prepare the Passover Meal. Personally, I think you're *unclean,* but it wasn't my decision." Thaddeus pronounced the word 'unclean' with a malicious sneer of contempt.

"Whaddya think I'm doin', asshole?!" countered Mortar.

"And make sure that you cook that lamb properly – all the way through – not rare, like you usually do," goaded Thaddeus, staring hard at Mortar. Thaddeus had deliberately encroached on Mortar's sacred culinary turf and had dared to profane that of which Mortar was most proud. He might just as well have questioned the virtue of Mortar's mother.

Brick wondered rhetorically aloud, "I wonder why didn't the Rabbi ax us hisself?"

No answer was needed, but Thaddeus, sensing an opening that he couldn't resist said, "Well, he's a busy man and you're just not *important* enough to merit direct contact with our Rabbi."

Brick, with a sour look, said, "Consider the source and ignore it, always says my mother," but Mortar's bile was rising and he could not let it pass unremarked.

"You are a worthless piece of a diseased camel's fecal matter!" said Mortar.

"Hey, shithead, our Rabbi has said, 'I came to bring a sword!" cried Thaddeus. To punctuate his misquoted retort, he drew the short sword that Peter had bid him bring along this night. "Keep your pita portal shut, or I might just have to use this on you! I whooped your ass once; I can do it again!" warned Thaddeus menacingly.

"It was *me* what whooped *your* ass!" cried Mortar, indignant at this revisionist account of history.

"I oughtta skewer you like that lamb," said Thaddeus, using the sword to point at the lamb kebabs.

"Put down that sword!" implored Brick.

"I, too, learnt from the Rabbi when he said, 'heap hot coals on your enemy's head!!" Mortar was now nearly beside himself in anger.

"Don't you dare to speak about our Rabbi! You're not even worthy of being near him!" cried Thaddeus.

"Your Rabbi!!" scoffed Mortar. "You act like he's G-d's gift to the human race!!"

This comment demeaning the Rabbi, uttered without the insight of subsequent generations, was just a whole lot more than Thaddeus was willing to suffer. The honor of the group was at stake and for that, Thaddeus was willing to go to any length. He stepped forward with sword at the ready.

"You're all talk and no action! Barking dogs don't bite!" shouted Thaddeus.

Now this caught the attention of Smokey. "Why do you have to drag me into this argument?" he wondered.

"Sticks and stones can break his bones but words will never hurt him!!" cried Brick trying to intervene, but the situation was already irretrievably lost.

"Actions speak louder than words!" screamed Mortar, blind with rage. In his insensate anger he grabbed the brazier with both hands and heaved to dump it in Thaddeus' direction. The sizzle and crackle of the flesh of his hands searing in the intense heat sounded in the late afternoon air. And the burning coals flew through the air like red shooting stars, wondrous to behold, but falling harmlessly to the earth.

Simultaneously Thaddeus was translating his own words into actions. He had swung wildly with his sword at Mortar's head, but in mid-swing saw the danger of the flying hot coals and his body veered to the side avoiding the red menace, but knocking the arc of the sword askew. The short sword, encountering only the opposition only of empty space, came completely around at an awkward angle and gashed Thaddeus across the inner thigh, perilously close to his privates, but with deadly aim for the large vein just beneath the surface of his skin and a tendon rather important for perambulation. Blood flowed in a torrent down his leg.

Mortar was screaming with exquisite pain as all the concentrated nerve endings in his hands flooded his brain with messages of dire urgency that, if not mistaken, his hands were either on fire or so close to the ignition point as to be indistinguishable one from the other.

Smokey had commenced barking out general warnings that here was a situation getting out of hand, but stopped as soon as he noticed that the lamb kebabs became the last thing on anyone's mind.

And Thaddeus had cried out at the ghastly flow of his own blood and so shocked was he that he slipped into a faint while a guttural trilling sound escaped his lips.

All the kerfuffle attracted the attention of the residue of the Dozen, who came running to see what was afoot. Jesus, taking in the entire scene of Mortar on his knees screaming and gingerly cradling his burnt hands, Thaddeus passed out on the ground bleeding profusely from the laceration to his inner, upper thigh, hot coals lying scattered across the ground, flew into action. According to the logic of battlefield triage, he instantly assessed that flowing blood was more likely lethal than the burns to the extremities.

Applying pressure to the inner thigh of Thaddeus, Jesus halted the flow of blood, but more than that, he healed the nasty self-inflicted sword gash, but not the severed tendon, more of which later. The Rabbi then grabbed a large gourd of water that Mortar had nearby with which to manage the coals. The water soothed the burns immediately, or should I say, that the Rabbi healed Mortar's hands but left the iridescent red scar tissue intact and he did not restore the burned off fingertips, more of which later as well.

Thaddeus came to his senses just in time to hear the Rabbi command the others very sternly to, "Leave us!" His manner brooked no argument. The other men departed to a safe distance out of earshot, but not without the curious, sidelong glances back at the 4 men, Jesus, Mortar, Thaddeus and Brick. Only one of them was talking and that was the Rabbi. Although the words were unintelligible from a distance, the tones that reached them were unmistakable. The ass-chewing of a lifetime had commenced and was being rigorously prosecuted by the Rabbi Jesus against the three men.

There is no written record of this encounter that has as yet come to light, but if the mood preceding this Passover had been uncertain before, it was now downright somber. The three spoke nary a word for the rest of the evening and only rarely did any of them dare to look up from their plates, and then only briefly before dropping their eyes again in shame. And none of the other men were stupid enough to raise the topic.

Reflections

Later, Jesus, alone with Thaddeus, put a small object in his hand. Thaddeus turned it around several times in his hand. It was small and round and was some sort of metal on one side and the other side was glass. And to his astonishment he could see things in it, and then, wonder of wonders, he could see himself. He looked to his Rabbi questioningly and Jesus explained, "It's called a mirror. Look at yourself in it."

Although the day's light was fading, the disciple Thaddeus could clearly see, not one, but two images of himself. One image showed him what he would become, and the other image showed him what he was. "Where did you get this?!" cried Thaddeus, his gaze focusing on the mirror. Jesus answered, "It was a gift from the Centurion. He got it in Sidon. They're the latest things."

In the image of what he would become, Thaddeus bore a faint resemblance to his friend Jesus, yet he remained himself completely. His countenance was clear, bright and serene. His eyes, both of them for he was no longer wearing an eye patch, shone with a divine light which gently cast love and truth on others in much the same way as when the Rabbi turned his gaze on others. This image pleased Thaddeus greatly.

The other image that Thaddeus saw was much different. He saw himself as he really was at that moment, one eye bulging, the other covered by his eye patch. The first thought that jumped into his mind was a mosaic – a picture made up of many small bits of varying and fractured colors. The resemblance to Jesus was barely discernible, but it was there nonetheless. Although possessed of a certain beauty, the picture had many flaws which, if looked at from a certain angle, turned out to be all you could see. However, if looked at from a different angle, the flaws virtually disappeared. Tilting the mirror ever so slightly showed him his image as he was; tilting the mirror back slightly showed him his image as he could be.

And Jesus said unto him, "Thaddeus, I am the mirror. It is in me that you will see yourself as you can be, and it is in me that you will see others as they can be. Seek me to find your true self and seek me to find the truth in others."

While Jesus was talking Thaddeus had continued to tilt the mirror first one way and then back the other. Finally, focusing on the image with the flaws, with the bulging eye and the eye patch, Thaddeus hung his head and sighed deeply. Before long, great tears of bitter sorrow fell from his eye. He snuffled his nose and drew in a deep breath in an effort to fight back the tears. He sighed again and began to speak, his voice nearly breaking into sobs.

"Rabbi, you have shown me wonders, but above all, you have shown me love in spite of what I am. My own stubborn ways have kept me from seeing all of the truth that is in you." He handed the mirror back to Jesus. "I fear that I cannot become the beautiful image that I saw in this mirror." He fixed his eye on Jesus and he was filled with fear and hope, faith and dread, and longing and discouragement.

"But you *shall* become the beautiful image and much, much more. Love others as I have loved you. To see yourself and to become yourself, you must first see me; then you will see others as I see them. Keep the mirror, to remind yourself." said Jesus, putting the mirror in his hand.

Then Jesus reached out and placed his hand firmly on Thaddeus' shoulder and said, "Remember, see me, see yourself, see others, and you shall see G-d."

Jesus gazed at Thaddeus confidently, then they stood up and returned to the group of waiting disciples. Thaddeus now walked with a noticeable limp, but he seemed not the least concerned by that, and Jesus addressed the others.

"Give thanks to G-d for captives have been set free, the blind now see, and the lame now walk. Let's return to the city before it gets dark and then celebrate our Passover meal, which I greatly desire to eat with you."

The Rabbi and Thaddeus by contact with blood had become unclean according to Jewish custom. He had to again remind his disciples that things outside the body did not make them unclean, rather it was that which came from the heart that made them unclean.

Somehow a Passover meal appeared before them that was so expertly prepared that even Mortar wondered who had done it. As he licked his fingers from the delicious, bitter-herbed lamb, he was reminded of the loss of his fingertips. Thaddeus was served a piece of the leg which reminded him of the lost capacity of his own leg.

"G-d's original covenant was written in stone. This new covenant shall be written in flesh and blood - in the hearts of the living. Blessed be the Lord forever."

And Jesus took the bread, blessed it and broke it, saying, "Take this, all of you and eat it. This is my body which is broken for you, so that sins may be forgiven."

A wine tha t rivaled, perhaps even surpassed that which had so impressed Cana, was served after all had eaten their fill. And Jesus took the cup, returned thanks and said, "Take this all of you and drink it. This is the blood of the new covenant, shed for you and for all so that sins may be forgiven."

Smokey, sated from his delicious meal, all the tastier for being pilfered, lay at his master's feet thinking that life had never been so good.

Great Drops of Blood

In the Garden again, Jesus had gone off alone to pray, asking Peter, James, and John to stay awake and pray.

"Abba, Father, please let this cup pass by me."

The gravity of his position, the sense of impending doom, and an intense loneliness assailed his heart.

G-d said nothing.

"Abba, please don't make me do this," pled Jesus.

G-d spoke but covered his face, "I will not force you to do anything. It is you who must choose."

"Abba, isn't there another way?" His voice sounded with a note of desperation.

G-d shook his head 'no' and said nothing.

After a rather longish pause, Jesus confessed his faith in G-d by saying, "May your will be done."

He got up to return to the three disciples, but before He came upon them, Lucifer was there to greet Him, saying "My goodness! Or lack thereof, you've been in battle, I see." Then he broke into song, *"Jesus Christ, Super Star; who are you? What have you sacrificed?"* (A little-known fact about Lucifer was that he has quite a mellifluous voice, all the better to present his messages.) "You know, the hero dies in the end. You're going to die, very soon. And painfully. I'm sorry, did I mention the pain? Oh, yes, excruciating, physical pain. You are, in all likelihood, not going to like it."

And Jesus, ever the gentleman, said, "Could you make this quick, I've got business of an urgent character that requires my attention."

"Sweating blood? I wouldn't waste it here if I were you. You're going to need all you've got! Oh, ye of little faith!" and then Lucifer said as if in a theatrical aside, "I just *love* his words!"

Then with a dramatic flourish, Lucifer confidently announced, "I'm here! I'm the answer to your prayers. You don't have to 'drink this cup' if you don't want to! I have several *alternatives* that you may find appealing."

He had proudly pronounced the word 'alternatives', satisfied that he had saved this *bon mot* for just the right occasion.

"We can leave Brick and Mortar and a few of the others here to delay them while you and I make a hasty exit. That's the first order of business. The rest can be negotiated later. But let's get you out of here quickly before our friend Judas arrives. I'd like to mention in passing that he's really a most delightful fellow. He has a grasp of the big picture and drives a hard bargain. But come with me now. There is another way, in fact, there are many alternatives. We can work something out. Trust me."

"Lucifer," said Jesus, "that's all I have time for now." And Jesus pushed past him to where the disciples lay sleeping.

"I'll be around in case you need me," called Lucifer as he dissolved into a mist. "Just give a shout out."

The Arrest in the Garden

The scrapes on the heels of his hands didn't bleed but they stung. The abrasions on his knees didn't sting, but they bled. Then he stubbed his big toe and fell a third time along this path to Gethsemane, to the garden that Jesus knew. Those following immediately behind him had to pull up short to avoid stepping on him or tripping over him. A more superstitious man might have felt some doubt about his course in the face of so biblical a sign, but Judas Iscariot, something of an intellectual despite his lack of formal learning, and a Judean, a cut above any Galilean, set his face like flint and forged ahead.

Soldiers of the Temple Guard carrying torches to light their way followed Judas to some obscure garden on the Mount of Olives just outside Jerusalem. They were armed but expected very little in the way of resistance from the dozen or so followers of the rabbi that they intended to arrest. Just another Galilean trouble-maker bent on causing a disturbance of the Passover celebration.

The soldiers of the Temple Guard didn't mind working at night. They always had the advantage at night because most people are naturally fearful in the dark; their mission was clearly defined – arrest a certain rabbi; and usually they employed the element of surprise. Additionally, they held a trump card – a person who could reliably identify the Galilean rabbi.

He had been paid up front for his 'services' so he could have fled with their money, but Judas considered himself a man of honor. The money he had taken in the past was, in his mind, only fair remuneration for his contributions to the movement. Certainly he would be vindicated when all was sorted out. He might even be regarded more highly than that knucklehead Peter, who seemed to enjoy the special favor of the Rabbi. How could Jesus be so blind to not recognize his talent and ability.

"Peter!" he scoffed almost aloud. The man didn't know his head from his arse!

The thirty pieces of silver clinked at each step that Judas took. Like links of a chain, each piece of silver shackled Judas to the consequences of his decision and fate. What was happening now was not so much an aberration or one-time event; nor was it a fate determined by G-d without consulting the man. G-d demanded nothing out of the ordinary from Judas. Rather, Judas was blessed with one of the best seats in the great theater of history: G-d pleased as man with man to dwell. The only compelling interest in the matter for Judas was his own advancement.

Besides, he thought, no one can 'make' me do anything. I am the master of my fate. I take full responsibility for my actions. My actions will be understood when all this plays out.

"Peter!" Again, he cursed the name. The words 'upon this rock' burned in his mind and his heart. Why Peter? The man had no talent. He had no intellect. After all, he is only a fisherman!

"Peter!" said Judas bitterly, this time aloud but along the trail to the Garden, his word merely floated away on the breeze. "'I'll fight for you to the death!'" he mocked. "What an idiot!!"

There would be no battle, no fighting.

And suddenly, here they were at the Garden. Jesus apparently was waiting for them. The Rabbi understood his actions; he wasn't so thick. He knew that something had to happen, something had to change. This was a beginning, not an end. The others were too dense to understand!

"Judas," said the Rabbi with melancholy in his voice.

"Are you the Rabbi, Jesus of Nazareth?" demanded the chief of the Temple Guard.

"I am he," replied the Rabbi.

Judas now stepped forward and put his hands on Jesus' shoulders and kissed him in greeting.

"Judas, do you betray the Son of Man with a kiss?"

"This is not a betrayal. I was certain that you most of all would understand me."

The soldiers gathered their captive roughly and tied his hands. As they did so, Peter, the impetuous, grew instantly enraged at the cowardice of his fellows, and in desperation sprang toward the man closest to him, who happened to be Malchus, the servant of the high priest. Peter swung his sword at the head of Malchus, but Malchus, sensing the likely path of the sword's swing, leaned his head to the left and ducked just enough to avoid the swing intended to sever his head. His head did indeed remain atop his head – for the most part. The ear part of his head was not so fortunate. His duck was a trifle slow and his ear was sliced off cleanly. Blood began to flow in profusion.

Jesus shot a withering look to Peter and said, "Put up your sword!" He found Malchus' ear on the ground and restored it to its rightful owner.

"Am I a brigand....

Two soldiers grabbed Peter by the arms and deftly disarmed him. A brief struggle ensued and Peter wrenched himself out of their grasp and fled. Mortar had advanced to see more clearly what was happening and found himself in the grip of soldiers, but he, too, managed to slip out of their grasp, but only by slipping out of his tunic and running away naked.

Others seemed to be in the Garden but the Rabbi was the only one that the Guard wanted. These others were clearly not eager to be associated with this Rabbi. For all the alleged support for this man and his teaching, he was utterly alone. They then took him back into the city to the house of the high priest.

Even as he kept to the night's darkest shadows, Peter began to justify himself against the others thinking that at least he had stood his ground. At least he had drawn blood. At least he had come to the defense of his friend.

And indeed, it was only at that point that fear rose up in him. He broke into a sweat and his hands began to shake. All of his muscles contracted as if to disappear into himself. He took several deep breaths, recovered enough of his wits to follow, albeit from a safe distance.

From the authorities' point of view the apprehension of the rogue rabbi came off with barely a hitch. In the darkness it was impossible to tell who was who and that is why they had arranged with Judas a physical sign so they wouldn't fail to arrest the ringleader. But the unidentified person, who resisted arrest, it was felt, had something wrong with his hands for there was no pull back when they grabbed his linen tunic. The man, or woman, had run out of his clothing, literally. One of the guards related that they held the tunic to the torch's light and found that it was the color of the sea with fine needlework depicting ocean waves. If you encounter the aforementioned person, remember, he is dangerous and possibly armed. Notify the authorities immediately as they want to question him concerning recent events.

Naked Save Sandals

Recommended listening: *Bad Moon Rising*
by Credence Clearwater Revival

A blood-red moon waning gibbous hung low over Jerusalem casting a lurid, pinkish glow. The day had been hot but now the late evening breeze brought a chill to anyone not wearing a cloak, or to anyone not wearing anything.

Silence settled over Gethsemane and the surrounding area now that all the brouhaha was over and as the Temple guards retreated to the city with their prisoner. The young man, goose bumps covering his entire body like a freshly-plucked chicken, sensed that he might stir from his hiding place and make good his escape.

Eyes still wide with fright he peered from around an olive tree and, seeing no one, he dashed to another nearby tree, hoping to remain in darkness, which was the only thing covering his nakedness. He dashed to the next tree closest to the road and after screwing up his courage, stepped boldly out on the road.

Cursing himself and his luck, the naked man replayed the night's events in his mind and he mentally ticked off his troubles with his burnt fingers. He had allowed the disciple Thaddeus to get under his skin. He had made a very stupid and dangerous attempt to hurt his adversary. If he had succeeded, the result would have been much worse. Thank G-d he hadn't succeeded! As it was, the tips of his fingers had been burnt off. His best tunic had holes burned in it. He had incurred the disapprobation of the Rabbi. He had narrowly escaped arrest by slipping out of his best linen. And finally, here he was, naked save sandals, on the run from the authorities.

To return to the city, pass the guards at the city gates, and then to find safe haven with the Rabbi's disciples, who may not welcome him with open arms, and acquire new clothing, appeared to him an impossible series of tasks. On the other hand, he could high-tail it to Bethany, to the house of Lazarus, Mary and Martha. Lazarus would help. So, he turned his face in the direction of Bethany.

Despite the disadvantaged position in which he found himself, Mortar made good time on his way to Bethany. Yes, he had troubles, but walking naked in the dark fueled an exhilaration that mocked his difficulties. A smirk found its way to his lips and he began to feel downright cocky in the night.

Then an unwelcome sound assailed his ears, the sound of approaching hoofbeats along the road. This could only mean Roman soldiers on a patrol of the road. As bad luck would have it, a house with lights still burning stood next to the spot where the patrol intercepted our intrepid traveler. The moon also provided something of a spotlight for this sorry spectacle.

The two Romans reined in their horses and they saw a roundish, naked man, striding down the road seemingly without a care in the world.

"Good evening, noble soldiers," cried the young man in an attempt to brazen it out as he stopped before the soldiers.

"Good evening, yourself," said the soldier.

"And a very pleasant evening it is!" asserted the young man.

The first soldier, a bit dubious, said, "I can see you're not carrying a purse, so you're in no danger from robbers; you're not carrying a weapon - worth mentioning; you're not a Jew; but... your *habiliments* seem to be... insufficient."

"Yes," agreed the second soldier, "What exactly are you doing out here with no clothes on?"

"What am *I* doing?!" gasped the young man. "Just like you, I am performing my patriotic duty!"

"A curious form of patriotism, if you ask me," said the other soldier.

"I am assisting the Emperor, a personal friend of mine, in the exercise of his authority by demonstrating that Rome's majesty surpasses all else," explained the young man confidently.

"You can be certain of the Emperor's undying gratitude for your grandiose display," laughed the first soldier. "By the way, we're looking for a certain fellow named Jesus of Nazater, Natazer, or something like that. He travels with a group of people. You seen anyone fits that description?"

"No, no, no," asserted the young man a little too quickly, perhaps. "but I've got to be running along." He was hoping to slip back into the darkness and off to Bethany.

"Hail, Caesar!" cried the young man as he rendered a crisp salute to the soldiers and was turning to charge off down the road, but one of the soldiers cried, "Wait! What's wrong with your hands?"

"What hands?" asked Mortar, holding his hands behind his back.

The soldier slid quickly off his horse and strode up to the young man and launched a knee to his groin.

The young man dropped to his knees and panted quick, short breaths. The soldier grabbed him by the hair and yanked his head backward and growled, "the hands at your genitals."

The young man displayed his shaking hands to the soldier. The soldier exclaimed, "By the gods, your fingers are gone."

Eager to continue their nighttime mission, the soldier quickly remounted his horse, and seated upon his mount, he looked inquiringly at the second and remarked, "That was out of the ordinary."

"Very curious, indeed, but obviously not the man we're looking for," said the second as both men whipped up their horses in the direction of Jerusalem.

Although nearly paralyzed with pain, the young man congratulated himself on his chutzpah before the soldiers, but directly his thoughts returned to the matter at hand and the precariousness of his own situation and that of his friend, the Rabbi, who had been arrested by the Temple guards.

Reviewing the night's events, he first felt stupid and then aggrieved with himself. His countenance fell into a frown and his shoulders sagged. The young man felt the pangs of conscience for his petty mean-spiritedness toward the disciple Thaddeus, and how far he had carried this animosity. His gait slowed. Then he became worried for another person – his friend the Rabbi Jesus. This moment of concern for another led to the flash realization that he was a very selfish person; that he always acted with ulterior motivations; and all this self-centeredness had reaped a bitter harvest. Here he was, naked before all the world, naked before G-d, standing in the dark, on a lonely road, all alone. He stopped dead in his tracks and then fell to his knees. And he began to sob.

Trials

After interviews with Caiaphas, Annas, and Herod, Jesus was taken to the Antonia Fortress to stand before the procurator, Pontius Pilate. The procurator directed that Jesus be brought under guard into the Fortress away from the crowd and away from his accusers. Pilate seated himself in a chair and made a great fuss about his robe and his comfort. Before long, he sat erect and raised his head to look at this Rabbi from Galilee and he asked, "What have you to say for yourself?"

Jesus looked at him but said nothing. His calm composure began to eat away at Pilate's own confidence and the prisoner's self-control made Pilate to feel distinctly uncomfortable, but despite this, he was able to get the Rabbi to talk.

"My kingdom is not of this world."

"So, you are then a king?"

"I am come to testify to the truth."

"What... is... Truth?" The interview might have ended now, so pleased was Pilate with this line. How elegant! How perfectly delivered! How exquisite! Too bad that only this man, soon to be hanging on a cross and only these two soldiers, whoever they are, would witness this clever remark. Pilate turned to these two soldiers and beckoned them forward to himself.

"What are your names, soldiers?"

"Romulus, Sir."

"Remus, Sir"

"Have the two of you been paying attention?"

"I don't follow you, Sir." A look of fear passed his face for this Procurator had a well-deserved reputation for cruelty. This question only brought them into confusion.

"But the words, the actual words!" cried Pilate.

"We are always alert to our duties and our surroundings, Procurator," said Remus. The men already at attention stiffened even more as they could not divine just where the Procurator was going with this line.

"Dammit, I mean the words... the clever repartee... my rapier-like wit... Here Pilate trailed off, but satisfied himself with a silent reverie.

How about "The world will little note nor long remember... what is truth? WHAT is truth? What IS truth? What is TRUTH? Three monosyllabic words. Interrogative sentence. Predicate nominative. Linking verb. Straight forward. Maybe sarcastic?

Shouts of Crucify him! Crucify him! shattered his reverie and he remembered that the life of a man hung in the balance. But only a Galilean - not a Roman citizen - no big deal. Although he was loathe to be seen as placating the High Priest and his coterie, Pilate imposed the death penalty, fearing the wrath of Caesar and fearing the loss of tax revenue should events spiral out of his control. Better a show of strength.

Mockery

"What this king needs is a crown. We can't have no king what ain't got no crown. How would that be? Uncivilized! And Rome brung civilization to these backward bastards!" cried Romulus, "out of the goodness of our hearts."

"They've got a nice temple," conceded Remus.

"Yes, I admit that. It's a beautiful temple, but they've only got one god! And they talk of our spiritual poverty! How many gods does Rome have? Who can even keep count? The Judeans should be thanking their one god that we're here bringing law, light and learnin' to 'em," said Romulus.

"You sure got purty words," said Remus in a mock, guttural voice with Judean accent.

"Why thank you, 'tis a gift from the gods. But where are we going to get a crown on such short notice? Didn't know that we were entertaining royalty in our humble fortress! This is actually a visit of state calling for certain protocols. What would our emperor say if he knew we were so lax in treating a member of the nobility without the proper courtesies?

"Well, aren't he s'pposed to bring his own crown?" asked Remus.

"That's hardly the point!" said Romulus.

"What 'bout these thorns here, I mean, 'diadems with jewels'? If we just take a few and twist them together, intertwined like, and voila! A first-rate crown, for a Jewish king, anyway," said Remus.

"Fit, no pun intended, fit for a king!" said Romulus. "Put it on him. Yeah, that's right. Crush it down round his ears so it stays on good."

"All right you men, whose idea was this?" sternly demanded the Centurion Longinus.

Romulus stepped slightly forward and admitted, "Mine, sir. I done it. And the robe."

"Well done!" cried Longinus. "The Roman soldier, best in the world. Thinks of everything. Attention to detail. Goes the extra mile. Extra wine for you then, Romulus."

"Sir, I don't mean to sound impertinent, but you are in the presence of a foreign dignitary, this King of the Jews. You may want to show the proper courtesy on behalf of the Roman Empire so that you are not found remiss in your duties, if you know what I mean, sir."

"Decurion Romulus, thank you for that kindly reminder of my duty," said the Centurion, who slowly processed up to the King of the Jews and backhanded Him across the face nearly knocking Him down after which He said, "Your Excellency, in the name of the Empire, let me welcome you to the Antonia Fortress."

And the Centurion turned to his men who were laughing at the antics of their commander and said, "Come on you men, I promote you to Ambassadors of Rome to Judea. I ask each of you to introduce yourselves and present your credentials to the King of the Jews, whatever his name is, Jesus of Nazar-who?"

And each of the men stepped up to Jesus and delivered Him a blow with the fist to His face. One presented his 'credential' as a fist to the stomach causing the Messiah to double over in pain.

The Centurion Longinus commanded his men in a loud voice, "He's to be flogged first. You men know what to do!"

Water Test Test

There was much jostling and shouting as Jesus carried his cross out of the city. Soldiers roughly pushed back the crowd who wanted a chance to express their hatred of the Romans, and seeing this so-called preacher, or anyone, for that matter, crucified was an added bonus.

Thaddeus, having summoned up all of his courage, and there wasn't much to call on, had made his way to a point along the street that narrowed which guaranteed that he would stand very close as the procession passed. As they approached his position on the street Thaddeus began in his mind a replay of what he had gained from his time with the Rabbi that was quickly coming to an end. Jesus' 'Water Test' came to mind and as usual, Thaddeus took it literally. He reached for the water skin hanging at his side. A broken cup lay at his feet. He snatched it up and poured what he could into the cup and as Jesus walked by, Thaddeus stepped forward and offered it to Jesus.

This gesture became one of Thaddeus' most treasured memories of his life. He had found true courage and he had offered to Jesus, not only the precious water, but he offered him respite, care and love. The gesture also told Jesus that he wasn't entirely alone in the hands of those doing him harm. If Jesus had been able to smile at this moment, he would have; and it would have told Thaddeus that his Rabbi and friend loved him as well, and more, for in this sacred moment (Thaddeus experienced this as a shudder down his spine) a faith was born that bore both men farther along the journey that each must take.

A soldier stepped up to them and slapped the cup from Thaddeus' hands. Another soldier backhanded Thaddeus and pushed him away.

Crucifixion

A cold, spring wind whipped around the top of the little hill to which the Romans had taken Jesus and two thieves for execution. The sun beat down on the condemned men producing a sensation of overheating inside with chilled skin on the outside.

Simon the Cyrene dropped the cross at the top of the hill, finally relieved of his unexpected commission. He let out a long breath and wiped his hands against the lower part of his tunic. The Roman Centurion told him that he was discharged from his duty and he could go. Simon, however, only went a short way and stayed on to observe what happened next.

Jesus finally made it to the top of the hill and the Roman soldiers detailed to the task of crucifixion set to work. Jesus was stretched out along the beam, and his feet were placed together and one larger nail was used to fasten both feet to the upright. He gasped in pain as the nail pierced first his left foot and gasped again as His right foot was pierced. Blood trickled down the wood. Jesus' arms had been tied around the crosspiece, his position adjusted to maximize pain, and first, Jesus' left hand was pierced through.

He looked over at his hand and He looked over the person pounding the nail. Jesus, exhausted and barely conscious, a recognition sparked. Surely, He knew this man. And then the man went over to his right side to affix that hand to the wood and Jesus saw him again.

Although they weren't formally introduced, Jesus recognized Romulus, one of the Roman soldiers that rode past him as he lay in the road dying. The soldiers didn't recognize him. It didn't matter. They would have crucified anyone that they were told to crucify. Yes, it was ugly work and their misfortune to be chosen for the task, but they didn't shirk their duties. They followed orders and tried to get it over with as quickly as possible.

The cross was hoisted up to the sky and slipped into a hole, fixing it to the earth.

Jesus, the light of life guttering in His eyes, looked into the eyes of Remus and Romulus. The soldiers, through their eyes, returned a complete indifference to his life. The soldiers had done this before. They'd pressed their blades into the flesh of opponents and had become inured to the suffering of other human beings. They were bonded in their gruesome duties, and took cover under the orders they were given.

Two Thieves Crucified with Jesus

Recommended listening: *All Along the Watchtower* by Jimi Hendrix

Dysmas said, "I saw what you did in the Temple courtyard, throwing those bastards into a proper turmoil. Tipping over the table of the moneychangers, throwing open the cages of the sacrificial animals."

"I saw what you did that day as well, thieving the coins that I spilt... and you killed my dog," said Jesus in a flat tone, pained deeply from the memory of it. "And you nearly killed my friend James."

Dysmas hung his head in shame and he admitted, "there is anger and hatred in my heart and I've done... things." He paused before continuing, "I am an evil person and there are many other things that I have done that are bad. I deserve what's coming to me; I'd so love to join you in paradise to-day, but... but... I am just a sinner." Dysmas dissolved into tears and cried bitterly.

"You may be a sinner, but your repentance has reached the ears of the Almighty and I forgive you."

"I once," sobbed Dysmas, "nearly beat to death a man on a road and we robbed him."

"Yes, I know," said Jesus. "That was me."

"You knew it was me that beat you?" cried Dysmas in agony. "Then how can you forgive me?"

"Forgiving others their most grievous sins is possible with G-d in our hearts," said Jesus.

Sanctimon and Viktorius at the Cross

Sanctimon and Viktorius, whom I'm certain you'll fondly remember from their earlier appearance in this narrative, had followed the crowd of onlookers and others outside the city walls. They stood a little way off for two reasons.

First and naturally, they wanted to stand apart from the crowd because they considered themselves as standing apart from the crowd. They were better than others because they were successful. G-d, in a reflection of his own excellence, had created them in his own image!

They chose their stance with great care, knowing the importance of presentation. They stood on a rock outcropping, just large enough for the both of them but no others, and just far enough away to avoid contact with any dirt or blood or any possible contamination to their persons or to their clothing.

Secondly, and possibly of more importance, they stood close enough for their words to be heard by most of the present company and by anyone who might be preparing an account of this event.

Sanctimon, cleared his throat and waited for most of the talking to die down before he loudly observed in a rehearsed, off-hand manner, "Life can be so unfair!" Some of the hubbub subsided enough for the two men to be heard.

Viktorius loudly agreed, "yes, life can be very unfair. Take, for example, this pitiful wretch sucking in his last, painful breaths before dying alone, dirty and disgraced."

"You don't have to let this happen to you, you know. This is hardly the kind of failure that any of us has in mind for ourselves, yet lack of prior planning might lead to just such an ignominious end," insisted Sanctimon.

"Do you mean that I can take charge of my own destiny?" gasped Viktorius in mock surprise.

"Yes, my friend," said Sanctimon with a confident air. "You don't have to end up like this!" Here he swept his arm indicating the whole sorry scene.

"But what can I do?" cried Viktorius, clapping his hands to his face.

"Haven't you heard about '*Spiritual Riches and Virtues of Gold*?" asked Sanctimon.

"What is "*Spiritual Riches and Virtues of Gold*?" asked Viktorius in his well-rehearsed tones.

"*Spiritual Riches and Virtues of Gold*?! Well, I'll tell you what it isn't!" cried Sanctimon eagerly. "It isn't a program and it isn't a product. It is a *way of life*!" These words he pronounced very clearly.

"Way of life," repeated Viktorius thoughtfully, careful to properly enunciate the words. "Whatever do you mean by that?"

"*Spiritual Riches and Virtues of Gold,* patent pending, is a new way to live," cried Sanctimon eagerly. "Yes, friends, some emphasize the way of dying, while we like to focus on the way of living."

"Isn't dying important?" Viktorius

"Living is the other side of the coin to dying and that's where I like to focus," said Sanctimon. "And besides, coin doesn't come your way by dying... take this poor sucker here as your example... for what has it profited him, my dear friends? What kind of legacy can a man leave by dying on a Roman cross?"

"This man is missing out on the glory of living! For him, it's too late. But for you, my friends, you can take concrete steps to begin leading a life of wealth!" cried Viktorius. When the crowd looked his way, he broke into a stance with feet wide apart, right hand pointing to the sky, and head thrown back. And then quick as a flash he assumed another posture, this time pointing out at each person there. "This is hardly a gold-medal quality performance! But if you act today, *Spiritual Riches and Virtues of Gold* can bring wealth into your lives!" Viktorius acrobatically jumped into another action pose and proclaimed, "Spiritual Riches and Virtues of Gold!!" And he jumped into another posture and pointed back to Sanctimon, who with exquisite timing, cried out in a loud voice, "

"You can't beat a deal like that!"

About Judas

Many was the crucified person who rambled in delirium as death approached and at this point those who heard Jesus thought that he was babbling, for in great agony of both body and mind he looked intently at John and the women and said, "Forgive him."

"Forgive whom?" they asked.

With great difficulty, Jesus loosed his parched tongue before earnestly pronouncing the name "Ju-das".

"Judas is the one who betrayed you!" they cried in their dismay. The Rabbi had said many things that were nigh unto unbelievable, but now, if this was indeed really something that he wanted, it went against every instinct and fiber of their beings.

With great exertion, Jesus breathed, "I wouldn't ask you to do what I couldn't do or wouldn't do." So, to forgive Judas was something that he wanted, but, how could they?!

His most faithful were stunned that after all he had suffered, that he should summon up the strength for so wretched a traitor as Judas, for one who had previously been with them, but who now was somewhere...well, they didn't know where he was.

And the few who stayed with the Rabbi as he died were all the more pitiful for those whose courage had failed them, those who recently spoke so boldly of their willingness to follow him even unto death.

It was not an outcome that surprised Brick and Mortar. This Jesus man with whom they'd been traveling had certainly showed them a good ride, despite the tragic turn that events had recently taken. They knew from their years as slaves to a Roman master just how quickly one could go from freedom to slavery or vice versa.

Now, standing before their crucified friend, they thought that it was over with a finality the likes of which was hard to imagine. Mentally the two men, each in their own way, took stock of their situation. They were in a rebellious foreign country occupied by no-nonsense professional military forces. They were broke and friendless. There was no one to whom they could appeal for help. It was getting dark. Everybody else was preparing for a religious holiday of which they knew little.

James the Less at the Cross

James the Less was there, having followed his friend's agonizing journey to the Place of the Skull. He had followed the crowd of onlookers and bystanders (death always draws a crowd), but he was oblivious to the danger of being recognized.

James looked at the two men crucified with his friend Jesus and suddenly and painfully recognition came to him. His mouth dropped open to see these men and he looked to his right and then his left to see if anyone else recognized them, but, alas, he was the only one who knew them intimately. He stared at them. Thoughts and feelings stirred confusedly in his mind and heart and he remembered how one of them had greeted him that day on the road, "Ho, pilgrim!" He remembered their sneering faces, faces which now were filled with the agony of their death throes.

Finally, the one who had done the hitting raised his head slightly and he saw James and Smokey through pain-dimmed eyes. He was astonished at seeing the palsied man that he had thought he had killed, yet there he was, hale and hearty, and more alive than he was.

The thug Dysmas, perhaps for the first time in his life, and perhaps for the last time in his life, felt something stirring in his heart. Many others would know right away what it was, but for Dysmas, it was entirely new. It was uncomfortable, yet comforting. It was painful, yet healing. It was... Tears came to his eyes. The pain in his heart and mind became worse than his physical suffering.

Many others would recognize this stirring as the first step on a new journey, into a new way of living; and so, too, it was for Dysmas. It was remorse.

After a short while, when James saw the Magdalene, he went and stood next to her and he took her hand in his hand. She squeezed it very tightly without looking at him, for her eyes were fixed on Jesus, hanging on the cross.

Smokey had found his way through the crowd and sniffed out James and put his wet nose in James' other hand.

James was immensely relieved to have his friend Smokey with him at this fearful moment. He immediately sensed that Smokey was the only one besides himself that knew these other two men.

Both man and dog looked hard at the men who had beaten them. James' brow furrowed at the thought of the pain he had endured at the hands of these men. Dysmas' look of astonishment at seeing James and now Smokey was so painfully contorted that James misunderstood it for mockery.

Man and dog instinctively took a step back away from them.

James began to turn away, frightened of Dysmas, but then both man and dog heard their Rabbi say these words:

"Father, forgive them. They know not what they do."

Not quite certain to whom Jesus was referring, James took it to mean himself and despite his fear, he turned back toward Dysmas. Then Jesus' other words came back to him in that moment, "Love your enemies." James the Less was cut to the heart. And finally, the words of his old mother came to him, 'seven times seventy,' and he knew that he must try to live up to her expectations of him.

Although James could forgive the wounds that he himself had suffered, in fact, that seemed easier to him, it was much more difficult to forgive the beating death of Smokey. Those images were forever etched in his brain.

Tears welled in James' eyes as he realized that his own power of forgiveness was far weaker than what he knew was expected of him. And yet, the seeds of great goodness had been sown in his heart and he began to say the words, "Father, forgive them" and the very act of speaking the words worked like the sun and the rain on the seed in his heart. It had taken root and it was starting to grow.

Do dogs forgive? They certainly remember mistreatment and react accordingly. Smokey whined lowly and he turned around several times after his tail, but couldn't quite find comfort. Perhaps being able to forgive is what separates us from the beasts, rather than the opposable thumbs and larger cranial capacity. Whether he forgave or not, we can know for sure that he remembered.

It would be wrong to say that James was able to forgive right then and there; he did, however, understand that his ability to forgive needed to be cultivated and to ripen and mature. Nonetheless, in the sight of the Almighty, this was the finest moment in James' the Less life.

Forgetting was entirely another matter. James didn't remember much of how they beat him. His mind contained a few blurred images which were easily dismissed. But could he ever forget how he had carried the dead body of Smokey back to Jesus? Could he forget Smokey's blood on his hands and arms? Forgiveness became a reality, but forgetting didn't seem at all likely.

Stand by Your Man

Recommended listening: *Stand by Your Man*
by Tammy Wynette/Tina Turner

Time is no more. All that happens now is a separate pearl on a string of moments; each moment is a separate, sovereign entity.

She weeps. She cries out. She stands alone at the foot of the cross. Mary's own erratic breathing mirrors that of Jesus. Her heart and lungs are compressed, as Jesus' last infrequent breaths come in sharp and searing gasps. She scratches at her hands as if pulling out the nails. Her feet are rooted to the rock on which she stands, just as Jesus' feet are pinned fast to the wood.

As blood trickles down his forehead in deep red rills, her mind is rent with agony and anxiety. Her head is pounding with the beats of her heart and she feels so exhausted, near to collapse.

The threat of rain is driving the spectators away. There won't be any more miracles. He would have done something by now if he could have.

The mockers claque leaves.

Smokey, sitting on his haunches near the Magdalene, lifts his nose high in the air and sniffs in the smell of death. He howls. He stamps his forepaws with uncertainty and barks.

Now large and intermittent drops of rain spatter the dust at her feet creating small craters. Only the Rabbi's mother, John, James, and she have stayed. The others have sought refuge from both the storm and from fear of a similar fate. But what can they do? What power have they? If he can do nothing, they can do less. All they can do is to watch and await his death.

He struggles to push up and relieve the pressure in his chest. She, reflexively, strains all her muscles in vain attempt to help him lift up.

Crying out he laments with the Psalmist: "My G-d, my G-d, why hast thou forsaken me?"

And the Magdalene continues reciting for him: "why art thou so far from helping me, and from the words of my roaring?"

Her life and dreams taste ashen in her mouth; they are turned to dust. She gives not a thought to living. Their lips and throats are parched. He thirsts and she thirsts. They put a sponge with vinegar to his lips. Her tongue moistens her lips. This bitter cup is drunk down to the dregs.

Her weeping has made her nose flow, but now it has stopped. The tears also stop. This sorrow is deeper than tears; it is the sorrow of the ages and cuts to the core of humanity tearing the veil of decency in two. The sharpest pains subside now as consciousness fades. Occasional sobs still heave through her entire body.

But now the centurion, Longinus, places the tip of his spear at Jesus' side between the ribs and with a quick upward movement, thrusts it into the side of the Rabbi. Mary flinches at the stab. His body convulses as blood and water flow forth.

Her stomach reeling and finally overcome with the rawness of the pain, Mary vomits in spasms of grief. She falls into the abyss leaving consciousness. Her strength, at the death of her Rabbi, fails her and she crumples to the ground and dissolves into the agony of the earth. Her friends rush to her.

Before long, her body is racked by a shudder against the cold, and consciousness soon finds her through the chaos of her mind. All of the old screeching demons are clawing to re-inhabit her heart and mind. She suddenly becomes aware that a torrent of rain is falling. The freshness brought by the rain burns in her nose.

Lightning scratches the sky. The thunder pounds G-d's air, flailing despairingly against this great wickedness. The earth itself rebels and quakes in outrage.

Her companions kneel around her as she takes in her surroundings, again awake to this world of pain and failure. The rain strikes her face and she understands that they are saying that they must leave, but she shakes her head violently in protest. How can she leave him? Joseph has come and taken the body, they are saying. It is over. They must go. She must know, where is he? Where have they taken him? They begin to lead her away back to the city, saying that she must come with them; they can't leave her here. They begin to lead her away, but she stumbles and falls as she tries to return to the cross against their restraining arms.

The Deaths of Gestas and Dysmas

The Centurion Longinus, after determining that the King of the Jews was already dead, ordered his men Romulus and Remus to break the legs of the remaining two in their care, in order to hasten their death, so that the soldiers might return to the city.

Stepping up closer to the miscreants, Romulus swung the club at the lower leg of Dysmas. The thud of club on flesh and the crack of bone breaking melded into one sickening sound. Breaking his other leg took less force because of the greater pressure now borne by the sound leg. Dysmas could no longer use his legs to push upwards to relieve the strain on his diaphragm. His breathing now came in short, insufficient gasps and his heart began to beat wildly.

With his final reserves of strength, Dysmas looked to his left, to the cross where the King of the Jews had so recently died and been removed by some of his followers. The sign in three languages still hung crookedly. Even though the King's body was dead and they had taken him away, Dysmas, with his final breaths prayed, "Abba Father, take me home."

Here's where it gets interesting. Dysmas felt a calm envelope him like a blanket. The light in his eyes had been extinguished, but somehow, he could now see with his heart. And he saw the man that had been called the King of the Jews, the man who had been mocked, the man whom he himself had nearly killed. This King began to call him out of himself and heeding this call, Dysmas left his body, which astonished him how easily that was accomplished, as if brushing past the sheerest of curtains. His spirit seemed to float upwards and then he rushed headlong to what appeared to be a bright and golden city, at the midst of which... but this isn't the story we're following, for some other time, maybe. Suffice it to say that Dysmas discovered that his thin hopes were materializing.

Remus now took the club from Romulus and broke the legs of Gestas. (True comrades don't shirk the worst work; they don't leave their friends to bear the whole burden of 'distasteful' duties by themselves. Anyway, they were able to rationalize that breaking the legs of the condemned hastened death and therefore qualified as an act of mercy by ending the torture of crucifixion. Another factor was that these condemned men were just Jews).

"Damn!" cursed Gestas through clenched teeth. That was to be his last intelligible word before he lost all life and light.

DEPOSITION OF THE BODY

They tell her that Jesus' body has been laid in a tomb. Who did this? Joseph. His friend Joseph. Joseph of Arimathea. She can return after the Sabbath. Come now. We must get you dry and warm or you will join him in the tomb. She wishes it would be so, joining her love in death.

Magdalene, overcome with grief, was not conscious of the men who removed the Rabbi's body from the cross. It was awkward enough and in the end the Rabbi's right hand was nearly torn away and the men lost their footing and the body came tumbling down on top of them.

Mother Mary..."You took him. You took my angel baby! Oh, Abba. Abba. You've broken my heart!" she sobbed. "You gave him to me in light and now you've taken him from me in darkness. I want him back. I want him back!"

At first, two of Joseph's servants determined to carry the body to the newly-hewn tomb, but the whole business was too cumbersome and slippery, so the stouter of the two men heaved Jesus' body over his shoulder and picking his way carefully, made for the tomb of his master. Once inside the tomb the servants arranged the body on the low shelf after hurriedly wrapping the body in a linen shroud.

Meanwhile, the rain stopped and the sun reappeared. It was late afternoon and the light was soon to fail. The men rolled the stone into place covering the entrance and went away quickly to make their preparations for the Sabbath.

Smokey approached the tomb and sniffed at the stone covering the entrance. Cold and wet he lay down before the entrance and took up his lonely vigil. Everyone else had gone their way.

Afternoon in a Garden

Recommended listening: *Should I Stay or Should I Go* by the Clash

Scrambling over the high, rock wall of a garden, Judas Iscariot finally felt that he could gather himself and rest for a few, brief moments. Landing nimbly, feet on the ground, he straightened up and looked around; high walls on four sides, a wooden door on the west side, a single tree and a large rock beneath the tree. The garden appeared empty. It seemed to him that he hadn't stopped running since he ran out of the high priest's house the previous evening. Judas was fairly certain that he hadn't been followed to this place on the Mount of Olives. He'd seen this garden before, passed by it on his way to the other garden that Jesus knew.

Now at last he sank down heavily on the rock. He was blown and sweaty from his flight and with elbows on knees he cradled his head in his hands. Thoughts swirled round his head, spiraling out of control, just like the events of the last, endless hours. Everything had gone wrong.

A sharp and overly sweet smell struck Judas. It was like rotting, fermenting fruit.

"I can't go back there," thought Judas, "they'll kill me." Tears of self-pity for his sad, sad situation began to form in his eyes. "No one appreciates how difficult this has been for me."

He had only been trying to help bring clarity to the situation. If only they had listened, and now, he saw, they had had no such intentions all along. He had merely been used for his access to the Rabbi. (He had, after all, been the only Judean among Jesus' closest followers.) And at that moment on the other side of the city, his Rabbi, his friend, hung on a Roman cross, drinking the bitter cup to the very dregs, the cup that Judas had passed to him.

"But what was the Rabbi guilty of," he questioned doubtfully; "and what am I guilty of?"

The earth shook. Lightning flashed. Judas knew that his friend was dead, dead because of him; still he resisted the thought. A very physical stab of pain pierced his heart and he groaned in pain. "But no! It wasn't my fault!" he demanded internally.

In this darkness Judas knew the truth, but truth without wisdom is only half-truth. Here and now in this garden he recognized the Tree of the Knowledge of Good and Evil, and he understood that gardens like this exist everywhere in the world.

"Fool!" He berated himself over and over. He was sick in his gut and the weight of his actions crushed him. No one would care what his intentions had been. But after all, all he had done was to greet the Rabbi with a kiss. He knew who Jesus was more certainly than even Peter knew. Judas ground his teeth in bitterness at the thought.

From the boughs of this tree with its silvery green new leaves slithered a curling, writhing serpent. Its grin, if snakes can grin, vanished as Judas had looked up to see the snake, and he was not frightened by it. It was somehow familiar and he recognized it from deep inside himself.

And the snake whispered his name soothingly, "Judas Iscariot. You have tasted the fruit of this tree. You may not know it yet, but you've also received eternal life. Everyone, in every age, will know your name."

Judas said nothing. What he knew no longer served him. Everything seemed so clear to him when he had devised his plan, but now the world was upside down and he was lost in this nowhere, somewhere garden, and now, time was no more for him for he was standing at the threshold of eternity. The snake, divining his thoughts, whispered, "the devil is always in the details! But I've got a parting gift for you," whispered the serpent as he retreated up the tree. Judas watched him disappear into the fresh green leaves. The snake curled around a branch and then lowered a loop of its body. Judas broke into heavy sobs which after a time subsided and he could hear the snake whispering to him, "You shall surely not die. G-d lied to Eve, and now he is lying to you."

Judas removed his tunic and his undergarment. "Naked I came into this world and naked I will go." This act brought an illusion of control and he was able to even picture a certain nobility in himself. Quoting Holy Scripture helped to clothe the nakedness of selfishness about to be exposed by his action. Thinking that he would return to dust also lent an air of legitimacy to his course.

Judas looked back up at the loop of the snake and it now looked like a rope with a noose and a knot. After all the exhausting turmoil, the rope offered oblivion, a dark, imperfect reflection of peace. It was enough and it moved him. He stood up on the rock, on tiptoes, and slipped the rope around his neck.

"You have to look at the big picture, the broader context," said the serpent thoughtfully. "You have become like G-d and now you will live forever." The rope tightened around his neck and the earth plunged away from him into the abyss. With but seconds of consciousness remaining to Judas, the serpent hissed maliciously, "You were chosen for this dubious honor, much like I was."

Judas' eyes opened wide in comprehension and he began to struggle violently against the rope around his neck, but in vain. There was, indeed, no going back. "The law of unintended consequences can be a real bitch!" cried the serpent.

Judas' toe twitched from the final nerve impulses racing between his brain and his foot. His eyes closed for a final time to the frightening beauty of choices in the afternoon in a garden.

(If you can find the right place on the Mount of Olives, you can see the body of Judas swinging from the rope as if this had happened but moments ago, for indeed, Jesus is betrayed at every moment in time and there's a little bit of Judas in all of us. Those who see their own sinfulness can see it.)

Lucifer had difficulty suppressing a grin, for delicious irony was what he loved best and one of his many projects had finally come to fruition, but he also had other irons in the fire which needed his immediate attention.

EPILOGUE

The Waiting Room

Suggested listening: *The Waiting Is the Hardest Part* by Tom Petty

A popular stop on the tourist trail for those who wish to follow in the footsteps (literally) of Jesus is the Upper Room in the Old City of Jerusalem. This Upper Room was built in the 1200s – over 1000 years after Jesus lived and died. No one is the least bit embarrassed by this, neither the guides nor the tourists. It is fascinating to visit the Upper Room and hear the guides explain that this structure was built in the 12th century, and they might even offer that this site is where another building stood that was used for the Last Supper of Jesus and his disciples, the Washing of the Feet, Resurrection encounters and the Descent of the Holy Spirit. And then one of the tourists will exclaim, "So this is where the Last Supper was!" This room is also believed to be the 'waiting room', the place where the disciples hid during those fearful days while their Rabbi Jesus was dead in the tomb. And that is our point of interest as well, but first...

A Garden on the Mount of Olives

During this endless time, the Dozen were on the run between various places or safe houses of friends of the Rabbi. It appears that the Dozen, although not actually twelve of them anymore, came together in more than one place, but they somehow managed to gather in a garden on the Mount of Olives.

The small garden was walled with a wooden door to the west and a large tree pushing forth the lime-green leaves of early spring. There was a large rock beneath the tree. A person could stand on the rock and reach the lowest branch with a strong jump upward.

Although it was springtime and located outside the city, a strange smell lingered in the air. It was partly acrid like smoke, yet it wasn't smoke. It was partly nauseating, like sulfur. It was elusive, yet at times, it assaulted the nose with particular vehemence.

There wasn't much talking among the men and the few women. There was so much to say and so little to say. The mood was taut and disturbed. The leaves of the tree shivered with the slightest breeze and it whispered, "De-s-s-s-spair. De-s-s-s-spair."

Oblivious seeming to all that had happened James the Less was cheerful and went around asking the others if they would like a drink of water. He had a skin that he had thought to fill before this wild chase had begun. Some curtly declined his offer while others were genuinely grateful.

Someone (let's leave him unidentified) said something like, "James is going to have to learn to take care of himself. We can't always watch out for him." Let's be forgiving and attribute this comment as a reaction to all of the fear and tension.

A gust of wind set the leaves of the tree to whispering, "Des-s-s-spair."

"I say we go back to Capernaum," suggested Peter, trying to sound decisive.

"You've got a wife there," said Thaddeus.

"And a daughter," added Peter. He was trying to build a stronger case for leaving.

Still, the leaves of this tree insisted, "Des-s-s-spair."

"Three days," said James the Less thickly and slowly.

Nobody paid much attention as each was wrapped up in his own thoughts. Where would they go? Would they go home? How would they explain things? How would they tell their friends and families? How would they respond to the looks of derision and the vicious comments? One thing was certain: it wasn't going to be pretty.

Then James the Less spoke up again, this time louder, "Three days!"

The foul odor seemed suddenly stronger and the wind blew forcefully through the tree and the leaves nearly shouted, "Des-s-s-spair!" All of the company looked around wondering whence this sound and fury.

But James the Less called out more loudly, "Three days!!"

This shout helped the Dozen regain their focus and Thaddeus said, "Why don't we go back to the city and give it some more time. We can't leave now in the middle of the festival. I'm tired of all this sneaking around." He rubbed his eye vigorously and then looked out of it at the others. "Well?"

Several of the others agreed that they should go back and the lack of enthusiasm for anything else carried the day.

As they left the garden by the wooden door facing west, the tree whispered one final time, "Des-s-spair." The crisp late-afternoon air outside the garden smelled deliciously fresh as the Eleven headed for the city gates.

Resurrection

Recommended listening: *Morning Has Broken* by Cat Stevens

Just at dawn a brilliant white, searing light flashed through the tomb which trembled with the awesome power of the Almighty and the stone covering the entrance to the tomb rolled away of itself, bowing before its Creator.

First, Jesus' eyes fluttered open and he felt the cloth covering his face. He lay motionless for a moment before he reached up with his hands and unwound the head cloth. As he neatly folded the cloth, a sense of awe awakened in him and he shook his head with the dawn of consciousness that he was indeed alive again. There was no pain despite the terrible physical ordeal of scourging and crucifixion that he had undergone. Life coursed through his body and he sat up, swinging his feet down to the floor. My G-d is the G-d of the Living! Light and life streamed into the tomb of death defeated. He stood erect and stretched his body, still slightly shaky, having been dead for a time. His wounded and healed foot stepped forth onto the cool, stone threshold of the tomb where the stone had rolled away. He heard angels singing,

"In the beginning was the Word..." He stepped fully out of the tomb and into the beautiful day of G-d's re-creation. It was the world as he had left it, but renewed and it seemed to him that the very colors themselves were singing.

"I wonder if Judas is okay. I hope they weren't too hard on him because they all left me except my Mother, Mary and John." But his thoughts turned to the beauty of the morning and the goodness of life and Jesus squinted against the brightness of the morning sun. A shining mist of rain falling from a cloudless sky delighted him as he stood in a rainbow of G-d's promise. A shiver, a shudder ran down his back and goose bumps stretched the skin of his arms.

Among the jumble of thoughts that raced through his head was that of his beloved brother Lazarus and his impatience living a second life. He also thought of Adam and his awareness that everything was new and everything was a gift for him. Jesus examined the gift of his hands and gently touched the wounds to test them, but there was no pain. He sensed at once the healing, restorative power of his afflictions.

Jesus looked at the wounds on his feet and they appeared as the wounds on his hands: healed and clearly visible, but evincing no pain whatever. He felt with his hand the wound from the spear, which was nearly the last thing he recalled. Then he remembered the horrible scourging that had nearly killed him. He reached over his shoulder and he could feel the scars of stripes and then he turned his head to look at his back, and he laughed at himself. "I can't see my own back!" He thought of a dog chasing his own tail and he laughed again.

And Jesus said, "I am raised up from the dead!!" He dropped to his knees and from this posture of submission to his Father's will, he returned thanks for life anew. Returning to his feet he gave a little hop, a tentative test of his renewed body and his spirit soared.

Smokey had been crouching out of sight, quietly observing all that was taking place, sniffing the air until he was certain that this was Jesus alive in the flesh, just like before, with wounds, but just like before. Smokey bounded up high into the arms of his Master and gleefully licked Jesus' face. And Jesus gritted his teeth and said to Smokey in that funny voice reserved for animals, "You're a good, good, good dog. You didn't leave me, did you?!" The Teacher gave the dog a tight bear hug, shaking him back and forth.

Jumping to the ground Smokey was unable to contain his joy, which burst forth from his heart with bounding and jumping about his Master and whimpering with joy. Smokey's eyes went all moist for he had mourned for his dead Master, but now his Master was back and he was more alive than before, if that was possible, and Smokey felt the life running through himself to be quicker than before.

Jesus bent over to pet his dog who was dancing about his feet and when he stood erect, he began to reflect. He cried out in a loud voice, "Yea, though I walk through the valley of the shadow of death, I will fear no evil; for Thou art with me!"

Jesus stretched his hands over his head to the heavens as if to reach the throne of the Almighty himself. With hands open to receive the goodness of G-d, he prayed,

We are Life for the Dead.
We are Truth for the Seeker.
We are the Living Water to the Thirsty.
We are Cana's Wine for the Joyless.
We are the Living Vine for all the Branches.
We are Bread for the Hungry.

Lord of the Dance

Listening recommendation: *What Is Life?*
by George Harrison

Mary Magdalene, carrying her heavy load of spices and ointments, approached the tomb where her Master had been laid after he had died. Now, the first morning after the Sabbath, she was surprised to hear the familiar barking of a dog and she saw a man outside the tomb playing with Smokey. And when she looked, she saw him, familiar, yet unexpected and frightening. Then she saw with the eyes of faith, and seeing, her heart was opened. It was Jesus, raised from the dead by the power of the right hand of the Almighty. Seeing through the light of faith, his words brought forth understanding and life in her soul, as a flower blooms and turns toward the sun.

Overcome, she fell to her knees and slowly put her head to the ground for she understood the power of his Word. Jesus approached her and stood before her and said, "Mary?"

She raised her head a little and beheld the precious feet of her Lord. Surely those were wound marks, but they were healed, but still fresh, as if about to bleed. Jesus had bent down slightly and touched the shoulder of his Mary and bade her rise. She flew up into his arms but could not look into his face. She hugged him fiercely, clutching him as if forever.

Jesus put his hands on her arms and gently eased her back from him. She averted her eyes and saw the wounds in his hands and tears quickly formed and spilled on his hand and she pressed his hand to her lips. She gasped for breath, "I'm sorry. I couldn't believe." She began to weep into his chest and he held her tightly to himself. After a time, her weeping began to subside and he again pushed her slightly back and gently caressed her cheek. He lifted her face to look into his and their eyes met. With their souls thus open to each other, he comforted her and said, "Now you can believe for I was dead, but now I am alive. Doubt no more, my dearest Mary."

The light around them began burning more brightly, more brightly than she had ever seen, so brightly that all else was lost to view. His face glimmered with uncanny brilliance yet did not blind. She, too, assumed a changed aspect in the reflected light and their souls mingled freely, twining and re-twining. He began slowly to move her into a dance as a celestial, mystical music began to sound.

On the smooth rocks before the empty tomb, the two souls became one bedecked in the beauty of the creation, in the bond of communion, and in the light of freedom. The music swelled, rose in volume, raising the spirits of the two souls. The dance quickened as he took her hand in his and their commingling spirits soared and the pace of the music and the pace of their dance gradually increased.

Spinning and twirling, dancing and whirling, Jesus and Mary in the ecstasy of renewed life, danced in love, danced as their ancestor David had danced, and danced as all who in joy dance, for their delight is found in the Lord.

And now their dance slowed gradually as the light began to fade to normal and the colors and shapes returned to their surroundings. "Mary, you must go and tell the others," said Jesus.

"But, my Lord, they won't believe. I will tell them, of course, but they won't believe me, for I am only a woman," said Mary lowering her head.

"'Only a woman'?!" Jesus chided gently. "Mary, you shall be my Apostle to the Apostles. Go and tell them what has taken place to glorify G-d.. That is your task. Believing is their task."

"Yes, my Lord, I will do as you say," said Mary and a look of confidence crossed her face and now she ardently adored the Risen Christ, noting each detail of his face, his hands and his feet, as if eating and drinking very greedily. Slowly and gently, Jesus took his leave of her as a physical being but at the same time she felt her heart swell, filling up with the Holy Presence of his Love. Her understanding of his words was now complete and she turned toward Jerusalem to find and inform the Disciples. She forgot completely about the expensive ointments and spices. And Smokey, ever discrete, bounded forward to join Mary on her way into the city. They were barely aware that their feet were touching the ground. Their light feet were as winged as they flew along their way.

And in the highest of the heavens, just below the Merciful Throne of Grace sits the Throne of Justice, and Jesus prays that G-d the Almighty tarry on his way to that lower throne and delay the Day of Judgment, for in that way, more may learn of the goodness of G-d and be claimed by the Risen Christ to people his Holy and Eternal Kingdom. And all the people say amen.

The Apostles' Unbelief

"Knock, knock," said a familiar voice from behind the door. The residue, the Twelve, scratch that, the Eleven, well, actually is was 13, the Eleven plus Brick and Mortar, were petrified, but there was much scuffling around trying to get away from the door and some were in favor of answering the door and some were opposed to answering the door. In the end, Brick spoke timidly saying, "Who's there?" And there was no answer, but a little later they heard the same thing, "Knock, knock."

"W-W-Who's there?" stuttered Brick in his fear. Again, there was nothing further.

But a short while later, they again heard, "Knock, knock."

This time Brick, stuttering like in days of old, said with impatience, "W-W-Who's-s-s-s th-th-th-there?" And he summoned the courage to open the door and look out, but, alas, no one was there. Well, no one was not there, but that's a double negative. But you can't say someone was not there. It was a pure absence of any person, know what I mean?

Brick closed the door and turned around and said to the others, "No one," and he shrugged to punctuate his statement when it happened again, "Knock, knock."

Brick whipped around and flung open the door to catch whoever had been playing this trick on them, but again, there was no one there. So, he slammed the door shut and turned to complain to the group that someone must be playing a trick on them, when Jesus appeared in their midst, shocking the assemblage and saying, "Knock, knock."

Many of the men blinked their eyes in disbelief and finally just stared agape at Jesus.

"What's this I hear about you gentlemen disbelieving what you've been told about my rising from the dead by the good women? A flat-out refusal, I'm told." scolded Jesus. "And what about ye others? Thought ye so little of my words? Esteemed ye so low these good women that ye couldn't credit their words?"

"And who shew the bravery to check the tomb to verify their unbelief so as to persist based on facts, at the very least? Apparently, my time spent with ye brought little return. Ye, to whom was given the best portion of all time, the best role in all human history, called to witness the decisive moment in G-d's interaction with women and men! And where does destiny find ye? Where will history find ye? Where does G-d find ye? In hiding!!! And even now the Twin is missing! Ye didn't believe it! *Ye* don't believe it!! *I* don't believe it!!!! What was I *doing* here??!! What was I *thinking*??!! Maybe I *should* have asked Brick and Mortar to help choose Apostles!!!!"

Brick, hearing his name, felt it necessary to make a defense, feeble though it was. "Well, ah, we hadn't seen you for ourselves, so naturally we..." Brick's voice trailed off.

"Well, yes, naturally.... Naturally what?" Jesus refused to let him off the hook.

"Well...." stumbled Brick.

"Yes, well....what...? Hadn't we gone over all this before? On at least three separate occasions?" persisted Jesus.

"I only remember two occasions," protested Brick.

"Yes, I only bemember once," put in Mortar, trying to rescue his friend Brick.

"Yes, well, forgetting or ignorance is no excuse, is it? Is it?" demanded Jesus.

"No, your Messiahshipster," admitted a humbled Mortar

"No is right!" the righteous Savior insisted.

"No, sir," mumbled Brick.

"No, indeed," emphasized Jesus.

"No, sir," seconded Mortar.

"Well, there you have it. Consider yourselves properly chastised," said Jesus, finally letting them up. "We can't dwell on this forever. Let's find a way to salvage this and turn it to our advantage." The storm had blown itself out.

The Ascension

Recommended listening: *Spirit in the Sky*
by Norman Greenbaum

Jesus began to bob his head with a regular beat as *Spirit in the Sky*'s bass line kicked in, and he began to rise very slowly. The 11 disciples soon began to bob their heads just like Jesus. Brick and Mortar began to bob their heads as well, but Mortar began his head-bob to the left instead of to the right, like all the others. He looked around while smiling happily until he noticed that everyone else was bobbing to the left. His face fell at the realization of his left-tending head-bobbing shame. He looked up to Jesus in supplication and the Savior, gave him a wink and began to bob his head to the left, to show Mortar that his way of head-bobbing was okay with him. And so, Mortar, confirmed in his leftward head-bobbing, took up the bobbing again with revitalized vigor, and gave a wink back to Jesus, who then continued his heaven-ward ascent, like a balloon in the wind. The music became softer and fainter as Jesus rose above their heads. It wasn't long before He was lost from sight and the music ceased altogether. Slowly they all began to stop their head-bobbing.

"That was awesome!" exclaimed James.

"Yeah, really cool! What do we do now?" asked John.

Peter, the impetuous, began to chant the bass line for the song, "bom, bom, bom," and began to bob his head in time to the music. One by one, the other 10 began to join in the chanting and began bobbing their heads as well. And then they began to file down the path back to Bethany.

The Apostle Thaddeus, last in line, looked back to the para-pustules and with a friendly wave of his hand, beckoned Brick and Mortar to come with them. The two looked at each other to ascertain the other's response and seeing the affirmative, hastened to join the 11.

"I did keep one last cigar for a special occasion. Perhaps we could cut it in twain, bisect it, or split it 50-50 and share the bad boy," offered Brick.

"What about Mortar? Doesn't he want a piece of the action?" asked Thaddeus.

"No, thanks," said Mortar, "it destroys the palate."

The Last Word

John 20:30 - And many other signs truly did Jesus in the presence of his disciples, which are not written in this book: 31 - But these are written, that ye might believe that Jesus is the Christ, the Son of G-d; and that believing ye might have life through his name.

John 21:24 - This is the disciple which testifieth of these things, and wrote these things: and we know that his testimony is true. 25And there are also many other things which Jesus did, the which, if they should be written every one, I suppose that even the world itself could not contain the books that should be written. Amen.

All these things have been recorded so that you might have confidence in the faith that you have received. There were so many other things that Jesus said and did, but the accounts of them were often flawed and did not merit inclusion into our account. Rest assured that each and every word was either inspired by G-d or, and I am loathe to employ the word 'contradiction', but each so-called 'contradiction' was resolved in a Christian manner.

As has long been rumored our Savior did indeed commit to writing certain, shall we say, thoughts and memories of an alleged personal nature. (Some parties even today carry on a desperate and irreverent search for the so-called *Diary of Jesus*.) A certain faction of the Twelve has reviewed this and other documents and determined with the blessing of the Holy Spirit that the contents of these documents do not materially contribute to building either the Faith or the Church and therefore have not been perused by a wider audience. These documents are not considered, however, to lack any value to the spiritually mature although great care must be exercised to avoid misunderstanding of the Faith, and therefore, these documents have been processed by other means.

A copy of the completed document, along with all the stories and remembrances submitted in written form as they came into our hands have been secured together and the container has been sealed shut and placed under the care of a most scrupulous, G-d-fearing custodian. Secured with the documents also is a container somewhat smaller than the other which contains sufficient resources for safekeeping the contents of the larger container.

CPSIA information can be obtained
at www.ICGtesting.com
Printed in the USA
BVHW030231260620
582372BV00001B/70